"VERTIGO-A-GO-GO" (ISSUE #2):
Sonic meets the madcap
Horizontal and Vertical
during an unplanned trip
to The Unknown Zone!

"THE BOMB BUGS ME" (ISSUE #3):
It's an intriguing series of subterfuges
and dastardly disguises...
and a surprise ending, too!

"RABBOT DEPLOYMENT" (ISSUE #3):
The first comic book
appearance of Bunnie Rabbot!

"LIZARD OF ODD" (ISSUE #4):
The first comic story to feature Super Sonic...
and just in time, as the deadly
Universalamander threatens everything in sight!

"TAILS' LITTLE TALE" (ISSUE #4):
The first Tails solo story!

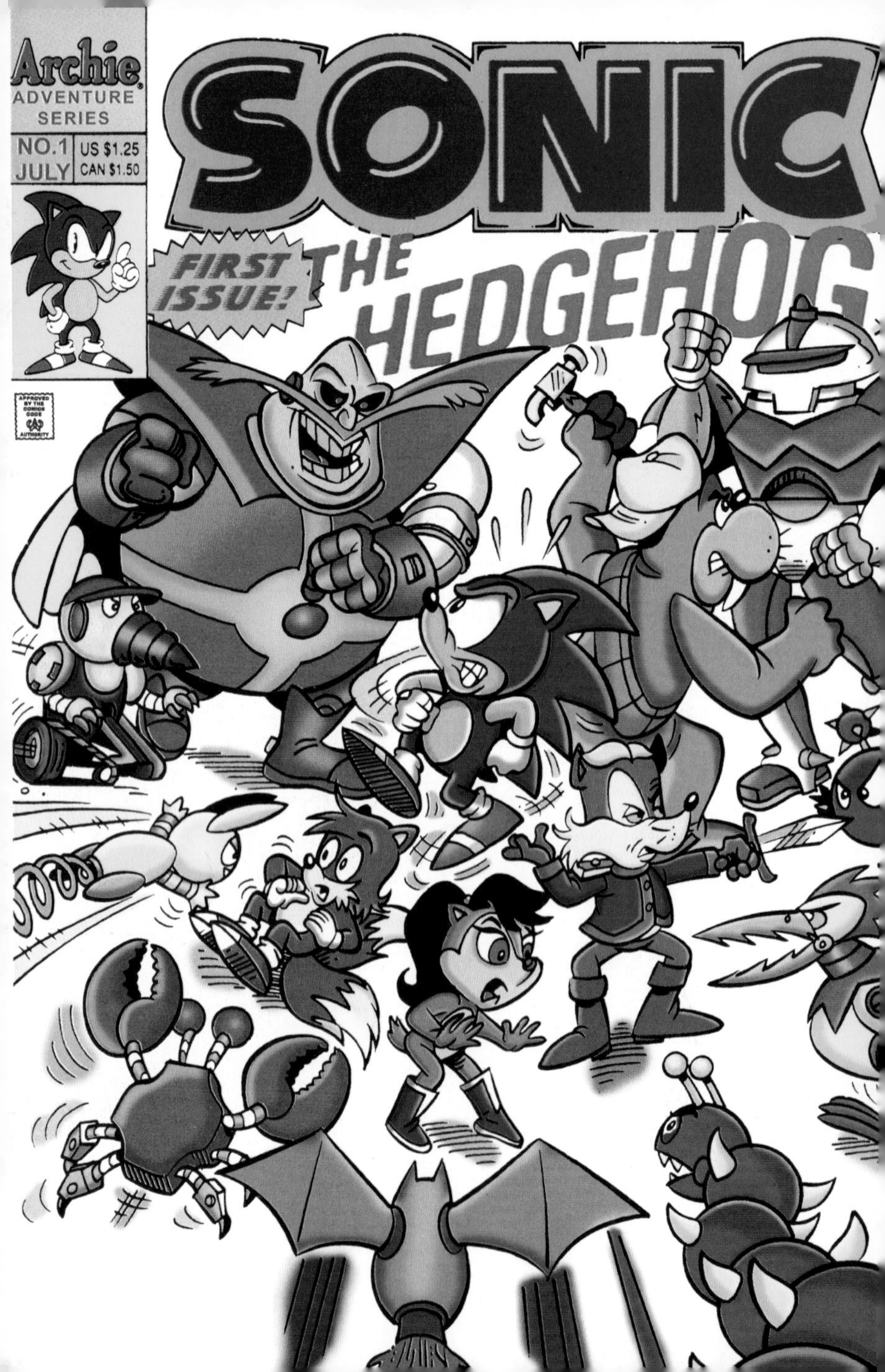

Archie
ADVENTURE SERIES
NO.1
JULY
US $1.25
CAN $1.50
SONIC
THE HEDGEHOG
FIRST ISSUE!
APPROVED BY THE COMICS CODE AUTHORITY

ARCHIE COMIC PUBLICATIONS, INC.

chairman and co-publisher
MICHAEL I. SILBERKLEIT

president and co-publisher
RICHARD H. GOLDWATER

vp/managing editor
VICTOR GORELICK

vp/director of circulation
FRED MAUSSER

editor
MIKE PELLERITO

art director
JOE PEP

covers
PATRICK SPAZIANTE
www.archiecomics.com

www.sega.com

SONIC THE HEDGEHOG ARCHIVES, Volume 1. 2006 Second Printing March 2008. Printed in Canada. Published by Archie Comic Publications, Inc., 325 Fayette Avenue, Mamaroneck, NY 10543-2318. Richard H. Goldwater, President and Co-Publisher, Michael I. Silberkleit, Chairman and Co-Publisher. Sega is registered in the U.S. Patent and Trademark Office. SEGA, Sonic The Hedgehog, and all related characters and indicia are either registered trademarks or trademarks of SEGA CORPORATION © 1991-2008. SEGA CORPORATION and SONICTEAM, LTD./SEGA CORPORATION © 2001-2008. All Rights Reserved. The product is manufactured under license from Sega of America, Inc., 650 Townsend St., Ste. 650, San Francisco, CA 94103 www.sega.com. Any similarities between characters, names, persons, and/or institutions in this book and any living, dead or fictional characters, names, persons, and/or institutions are not intended and if they exist, are purely coincidental. Nothing may be reprinted in whole or part without written permission from Archie Comic Publications, Inc. ISBN-13: 978-1-879794-20-7   ISBN-10: 1-879794-20-9

TABLE OF CONTENTS

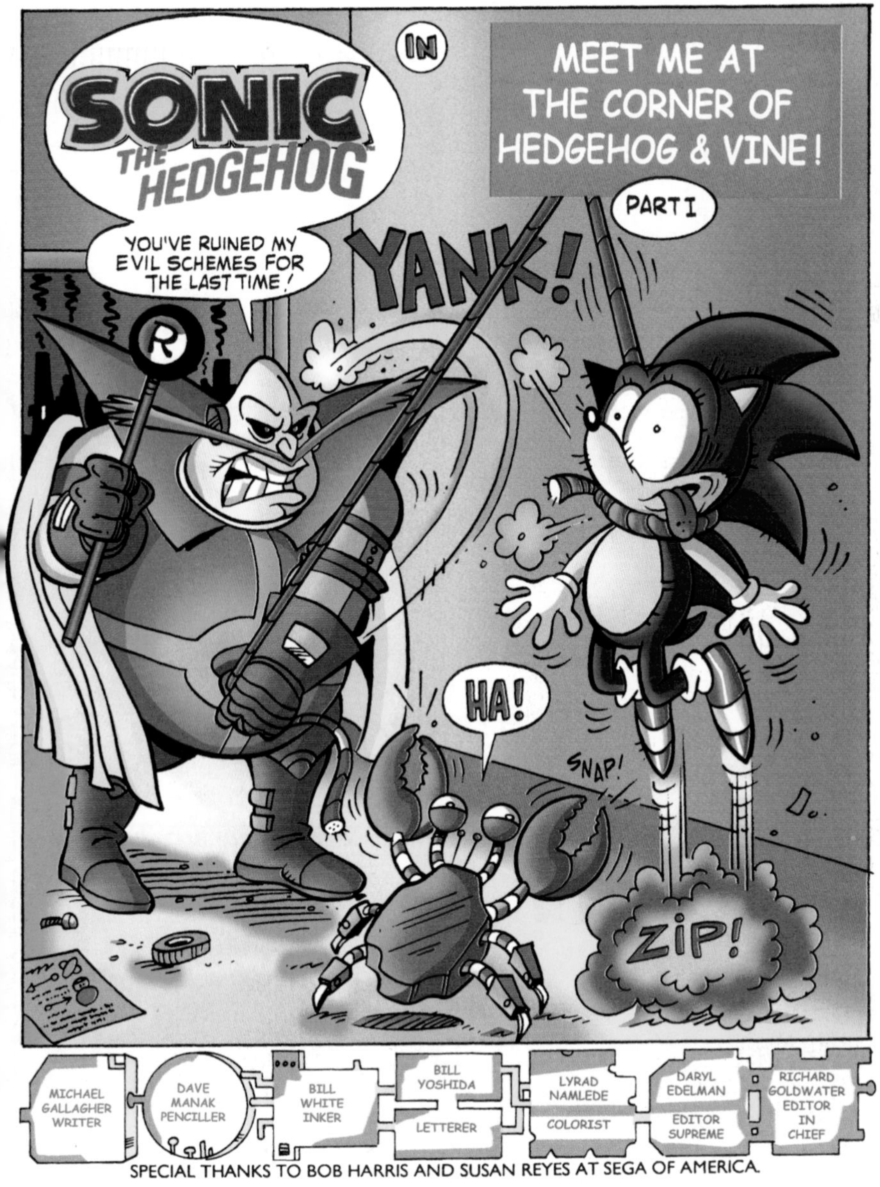
SONIC THE HEDGEHOG
IN
MEET ME AT THE CORNER OF HEDGEHOG & VINE!
PART I
YOU'VE RUINED MY EVIL SCHEMES FOR THE LAST TIME!
YANK!
HA!
SNAP!
ZIP!

MICHAEL GALLAGHER WRITER
DAVE MANAK PENCILLER
BILL WHITE INKER
BILL YOSHIDA LETTERER
LYRAD NAMLEDE COLORIST
DARYL EDELMAN EDITOR SUPREME
RICHARD GOLDWATER EDITOR IN CHIEF

SPECIAL THANKS TO BOB HARRIS AND SUSAN REYES AT SEGA OF AMERICA.

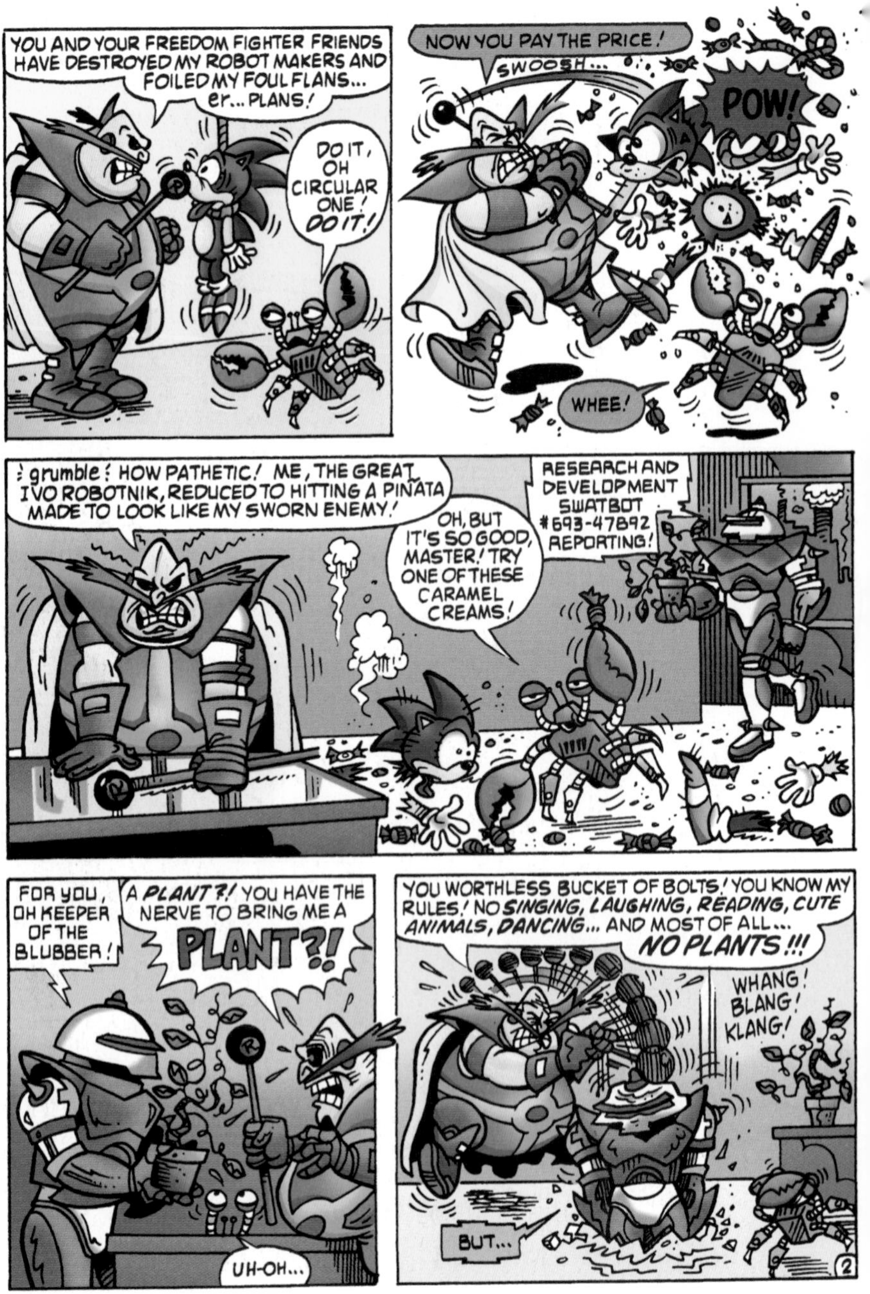

YOU AND YOUR FREEDOM FIGHTER FRIENDS HAVE DESTROYED MY ROBOT MAKERS AND FOILED MY FOUL FLANS... er... PLANS!
DO IT, OH CIRCULAR ONE! DO IT!
NOW YOU PAY THE PRICE!
SWOOSH...
POW!
WHEE!
grumble! HOW PATHETIC! ME, THE GREAT IVO ROBOTNIK, REDUCED TO HITTING A PIÑATA MADE TO LOOK LIKE MY SWORN ENEMY!
OH, BUT IT'S SO GOOD, MASTER! TRY ONE OF THESE CARAMEL CREAMS!
RESEARCH AND DEVELOPMENT SWATBOT #693-47892 REPORTING!
FOR YOU, OH KEEPER OF THE BLUBBER!
A PLANT?! YOU HAVE THE NERVE TO BRING ME A PLANT?!
UH-OH...
YOU WORTHLESS BUCKET OF BOLTS! YOU KNOW MY RULES! NO SINGING, LAUGHING, READING, CUTE ANIMALS, DANCING... AND MOST OF ALL... NO PLANTS!!!
WHANG! BLANG! KLANG!
BUT...

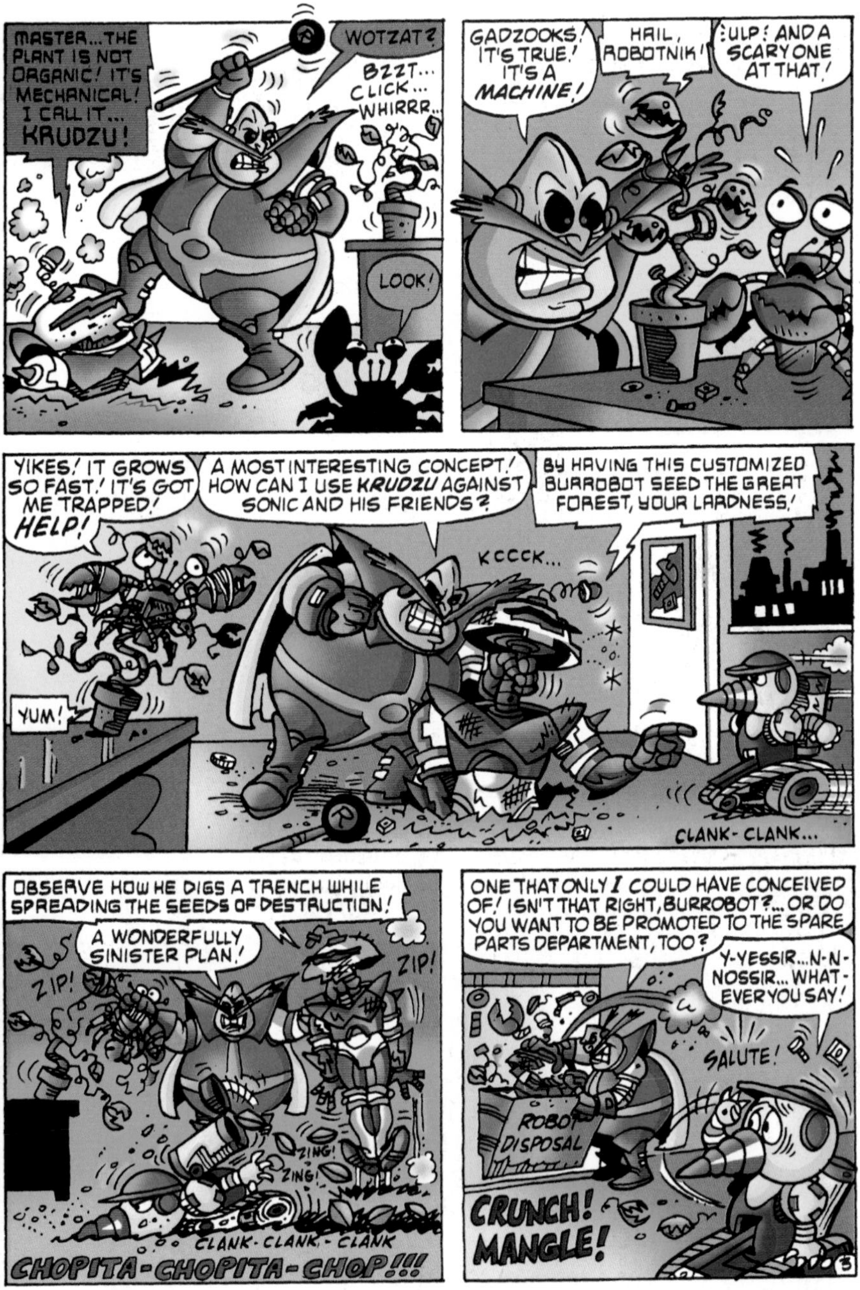
MASTER... THE PLANT IS NOT ORGANIC! IT'S MECHANICAL! I CALL IT... KRUDZU!
WOTZAT?
BZZT... CLICK... WHIRRR...
LOOK!
GADZOOKS! IT'S TRUE! IT'S A MACHINE!
HAIL, ROBOTNIK!
ULP! AND A SCARY ONE AT THAT!
YIKES! IT GROWS SO FAST! IT'S GOT ME TRAPPED! HELP!
A MOST INTERESTING CONCEPT! HOW CAN I USE KRUDZU AGAINST SONIC AND HIS FRIENDS?
BY HAVING THIS CUSTOMIZED BURROBOT SEED THE GREAT FOREST, YOUR LARDNESS!
KCCCK...
YUM!
CLANK-CLANK...
OBSERVE HOW HE DIGS A TRENCH WHILE SPREADING THE SEEDS OF DESTRUCTION!
A WONDERFULLY SINISTER PLAN!
ZIP!
ZIP!
ZING!
ZING!
CLANK-CLANK-CLANK
CHOPITA-CHOPITA-CHOP!!!
ONE THAT ONLY I COULD HAVE CONCEIVED OF! ISN'T THAT RIGHT, BURROBOT?... OR DO YOU WANT TO BE PROMOTED TO THE SPARE PARTS DEPARTMENT, TOO?
Y-YESSIR... N-N-NOSSIR... WHATEVER YOU SAY!
SALUTE!
ROBOT DISPOSAL
CRUNCH! MANGLE!

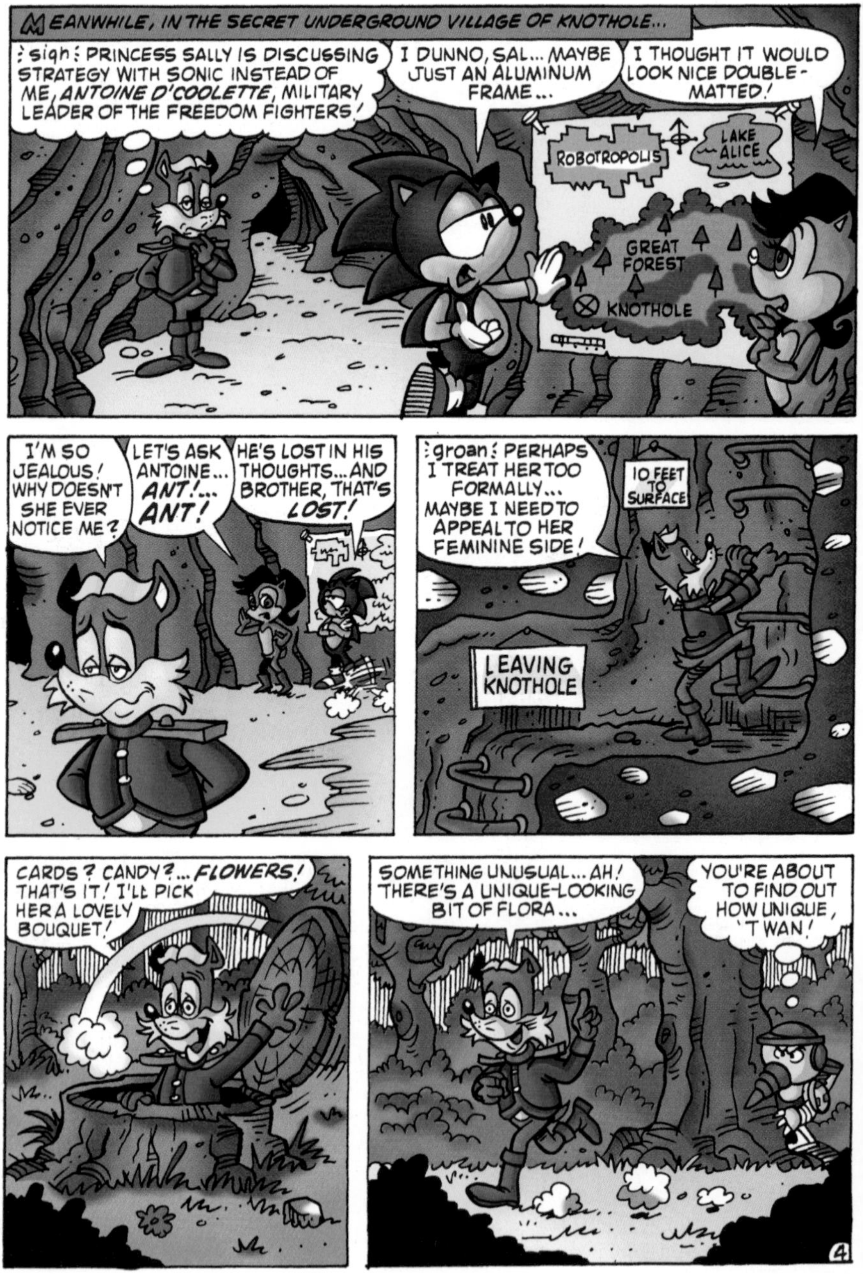
MEANWHILE, IN THE SECRET UNDERGROUND VILLAGE OF KNOTHOLE...
:sigh: PRINCESS SALLY IS DISCUSSING STRATEGY WITH SONIC INSTEAD OF ME, ANTOINE D'COOLETTE, MILITARY LEADER OF THE FREEDOM FIGHTERS!
I DUNNO, SAL... MAYBE JUST AN ALUMINUM FRAME...
I THOUGHT IT WOULD LOOK NICE DOUBLE-MATTED!
ROBOTROPOLIS
LAKE ALICE
GREAT FOREST
KNOTHOLE
I'M SO JEALOUS! WHY DOESN'T SHE EVER NOTICE ME?
LET'S ASK ANTOINE... ANT!... ANT!
HE'S LOST IN HIS THOUGHTS... AND BROTHER, THAT'S LOST!
:groan: PERHAPS I TREAT HER TOO FORMALLY... MAYBE I NEED TO APPEAL TO HER FEMININE SIDE!
10 FEET TO SURFACE
LEAVING KNOTHOLE
CARDS? CANDY?... FLOWERS! THAT'S IT! I'LL PICK HER A LOVELY BOUQUET!
SOMETHING UNUSUAL... AH! THERE'S A UNIQUE-LOOKING BIT OF FLORA...
YOU'RE ABOUT TO FIND OUT HOW UNIQUE, 'TWAN!
4

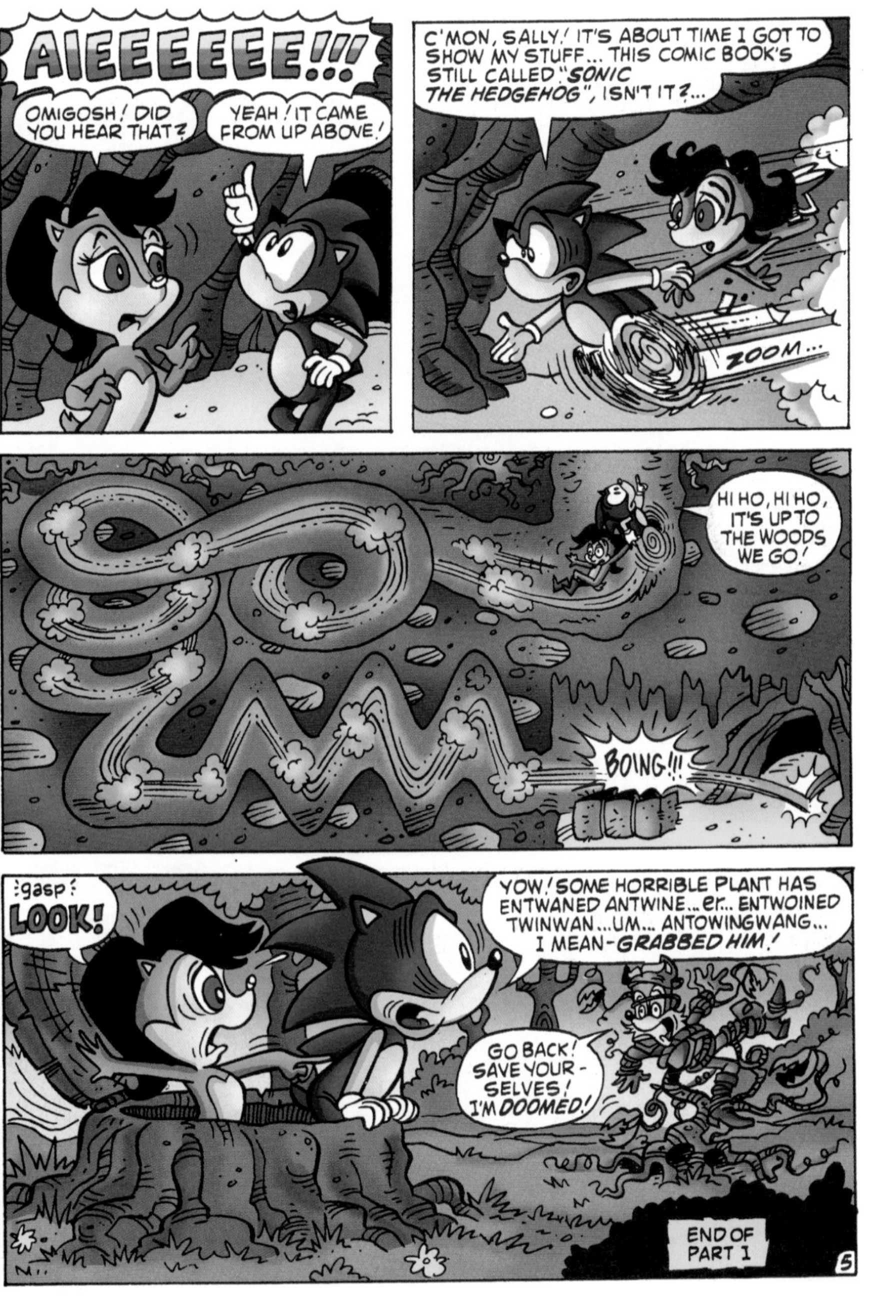

AIEEEEEEE!!!...
OMIGOSH! DID YOU HEAR THAT?
YEAH! IT CAME FROM UP ABOVE!
C'MON, SALLY! IT'S ABOUT TIME I GOT TO SHOW MY STUFF... THIS COMIC BOOK'S STILL CALLED "SONIC THE HEDGEHOG", ISN'T IT?...
ZOOM...
HI HO, HI HO, IT'S UP TO THE WOODS WE GO!
BOING!!!
:gasp: LOOK!
YOW! SOME HORRIBLE PLANT HAS ENTWANED ANTWINE... er... ENTWOINED TWINWAN... UM... ANTOWINGWANG... I MEAN-GRABBED HIM!
GO BACK! SAVE YOUR-SELVES! I'M DOOMED!
END OF PART I

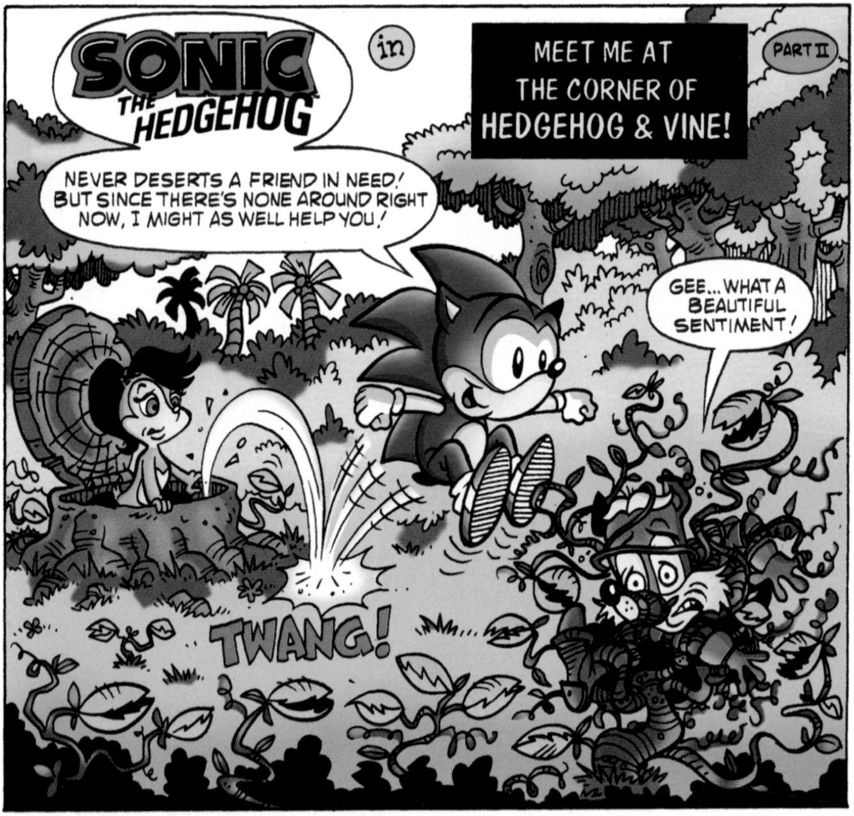
SONIC THE HEDGEHOG
in
MEET ME AT THE CORNER OF HEDGEHOG & VINE!
PART II
NEVER DESERTS A FRIEND IN NEED! BUT SINCE THERE'S NONE AROUND RIGHT NOW, I MIGHT AS WELL HELP YOU!
GEE... WHAT A BEAUTIFUL SENTIMENT!
TWANG!

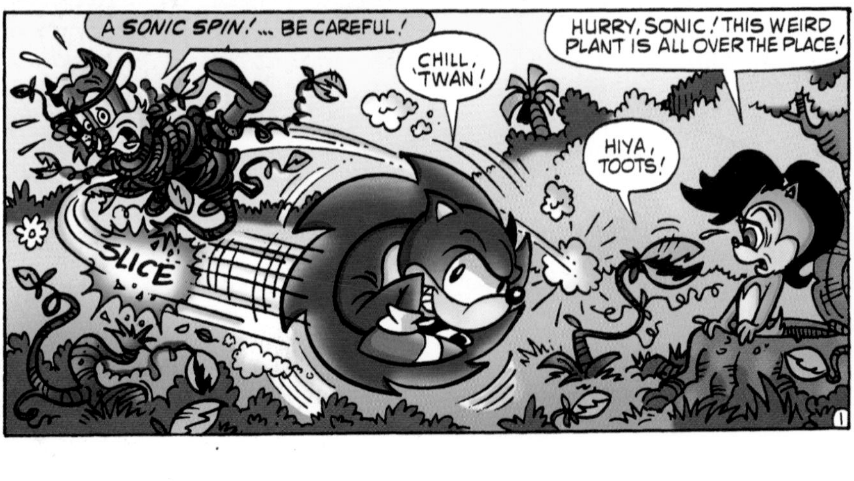
A SONIC SPIN!... BE CAREFUL!
CHILL, 'TWAN!
HURRY, SONIC! THIS WEIRD PLANT IS ALL OVER THE PLACE!
HIYA, TOOTS!
SLICE

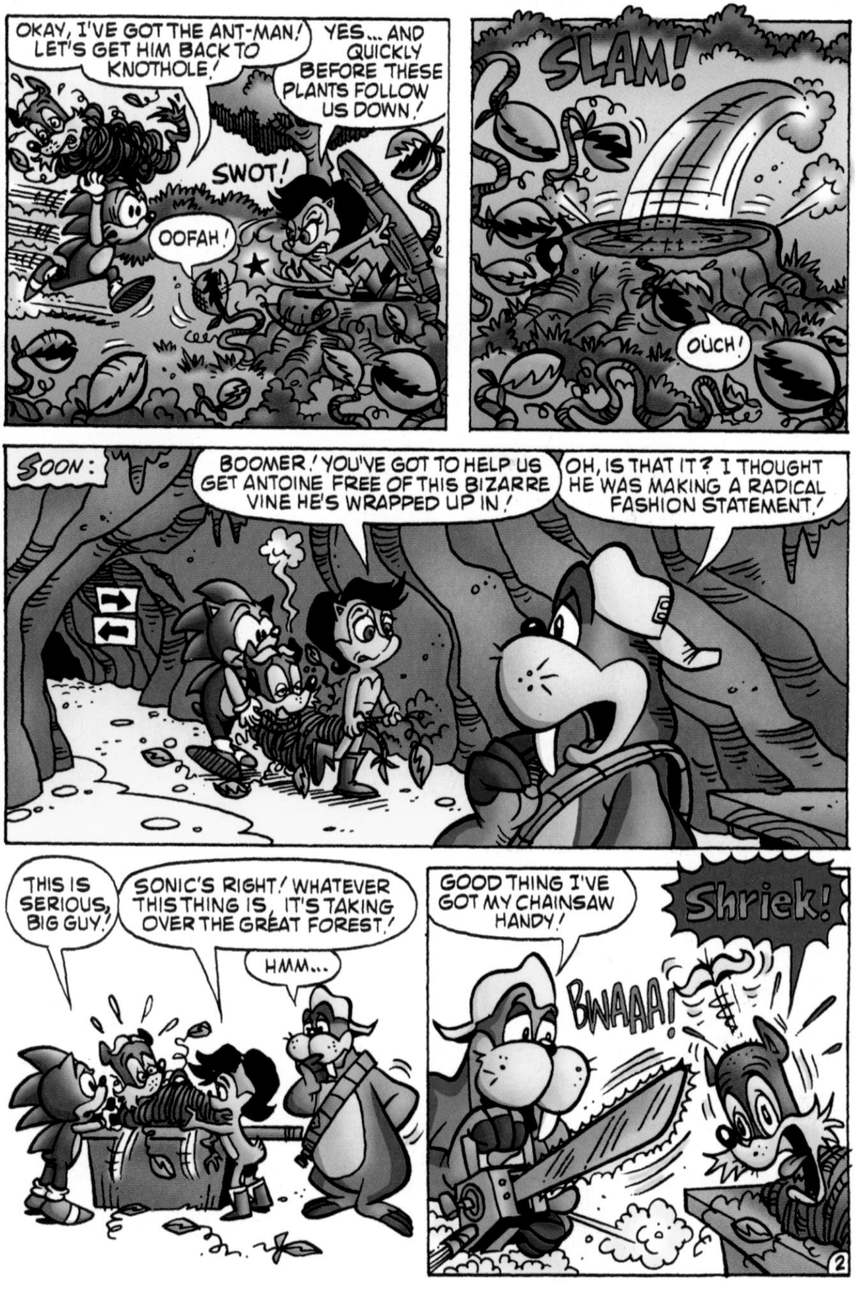
OKAY, I'VE GOT THE ANT-MAN! LET'S GET HIM BACK TO KNOTHOLE!
YES... AND QUICKLY BEFORE THESE PLANTS FOLLOW US DOWN!
SWOT!
OOFAH!
SLAM!
OUCH!
SOON:
BOOMER! YOU'VE GOT TO HELP US GET ANTOINE FREE OF THIS BIZARRE VINE HE'S WRAPPED UP IN!
OH, IS THAT IT? I THOUGHT HE WAS MAKING A RADICAL FASHION STATEMENT!
THIS IS SERIOUS, BIG GUY!
SONIC'S RIGHT! WHATEVER THIS THING IS, IT'S TAKING OVER THE GREAT FOREST!
HMM...
GOOD THING I'VE GOT MY CHAINSAW HANDY!
Shriek!
BWAAA!

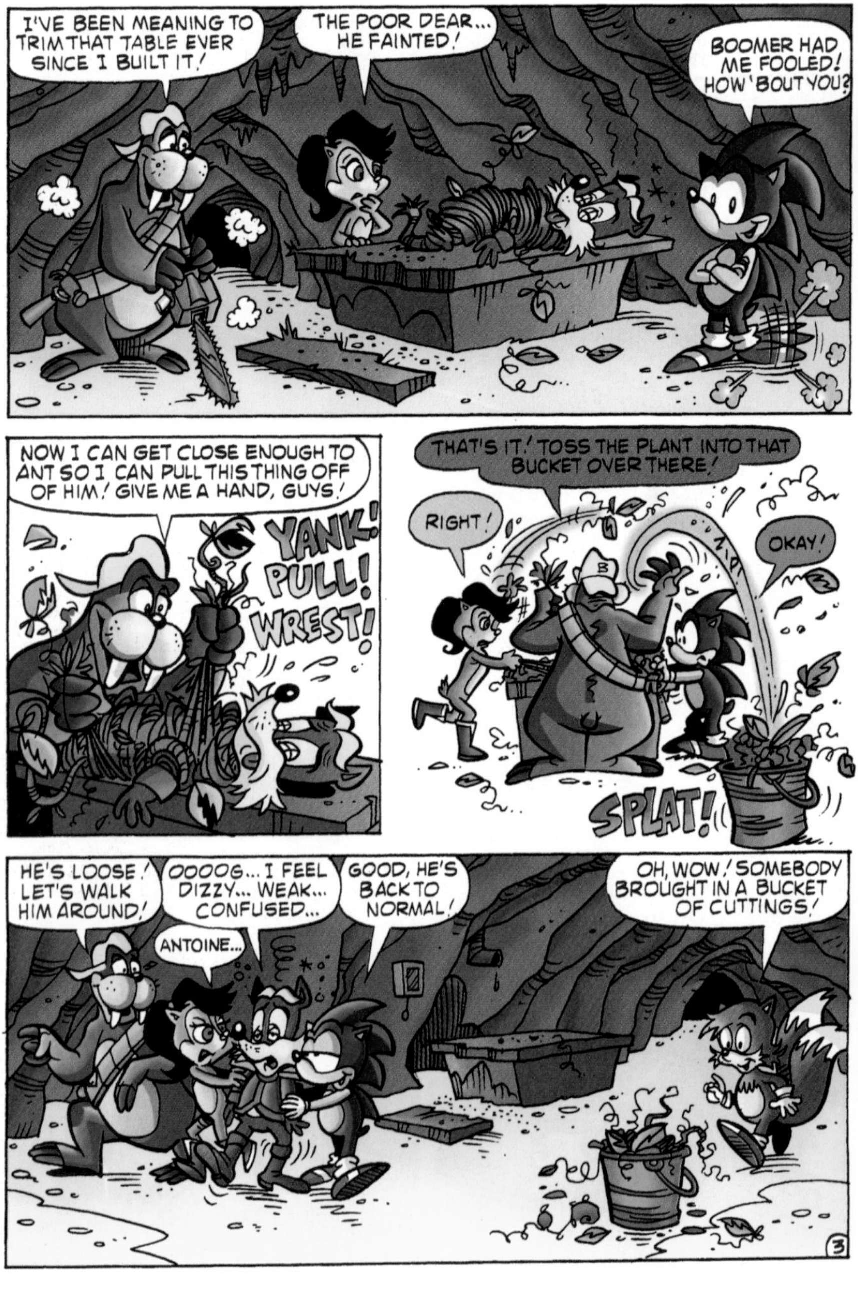
I'VE BEEN MEANING TO TRIM THAT TABLE EVER SINCE I BUILT IT!
THE POOR DEAR... HE FAINTED!
BOOMER HAD ME FOOLED! HOW 'BOUT YOU?
NOW I CAN GET CLOSE ENOUGH TO ANT SO I CAN PULL THIS THING OFF OF HIM! GIVE ME A HAND, GUYS!
YANK! PULL! WREST!
THAT'S IT! TOSS THE PLANT INTO THAT BUCKET OVER THERE!
RIGHT!
OKAY!
SPLAT!
HE'S LOOSE! LET'S WALK HIM AROUND!
OOOOG... I FEEL DIZZY... WEAK... CONFUSED...
ANTOINE...
GOOD, HE'S BACK TO NORMAL!
OH, WOW! SOMEBODY BROUGHT IN A BUCKET OF CUTTINGS!

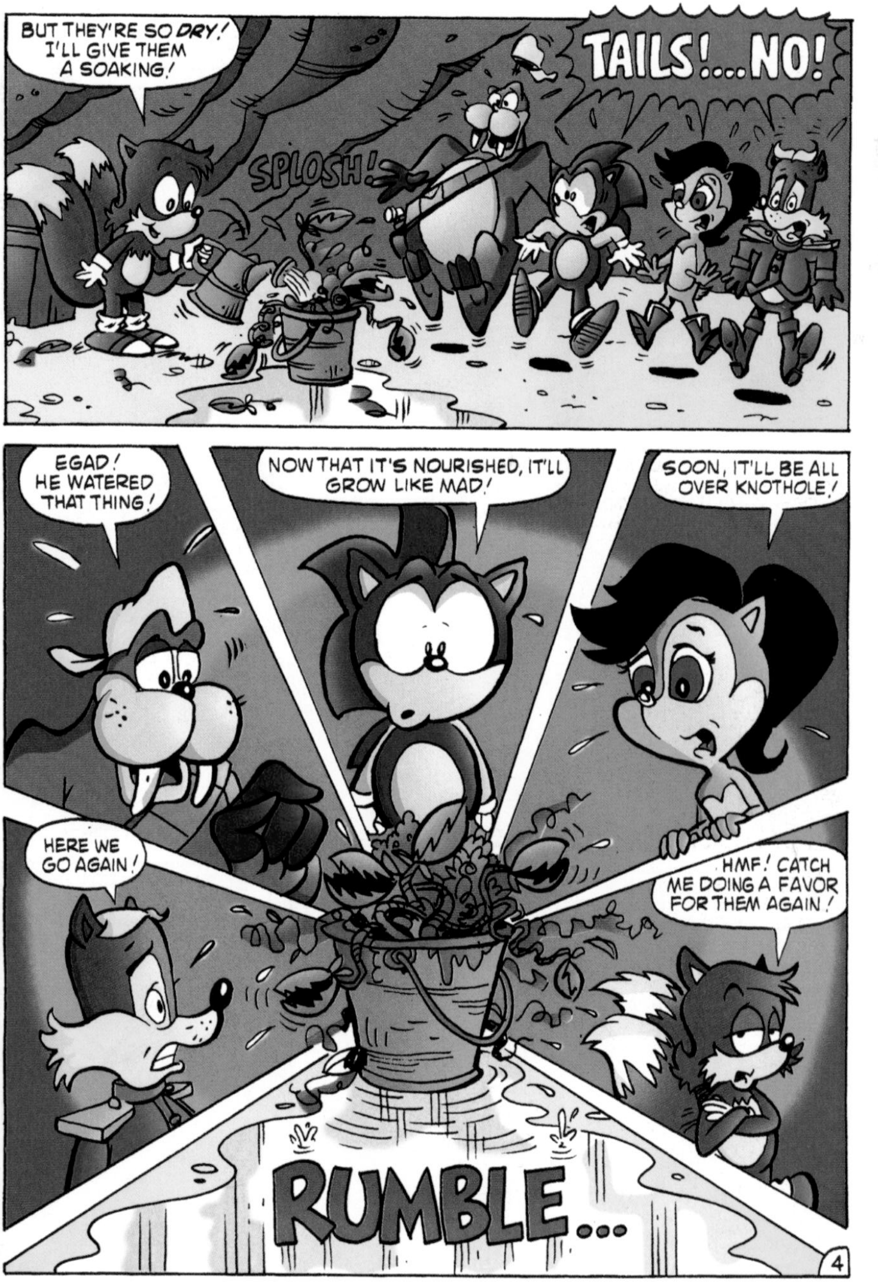

BUT THEY'RE SO DRY! I'LL GIVE THEM A SOAKING!
TAILS!...NO!
SPLOSH!
EGAD! HE WATERED THAT THING!
NOW THAT IT'S NOURISHED, IT'LL GROW LIKE MAD!
SOON, IT'LL BE ALL OVER KNOTHOLE!
HERE WE GO AGAIN!
HMF! CATCH ME DOING A FAVOR FOR THEM AGAIN!
RUMBLE...

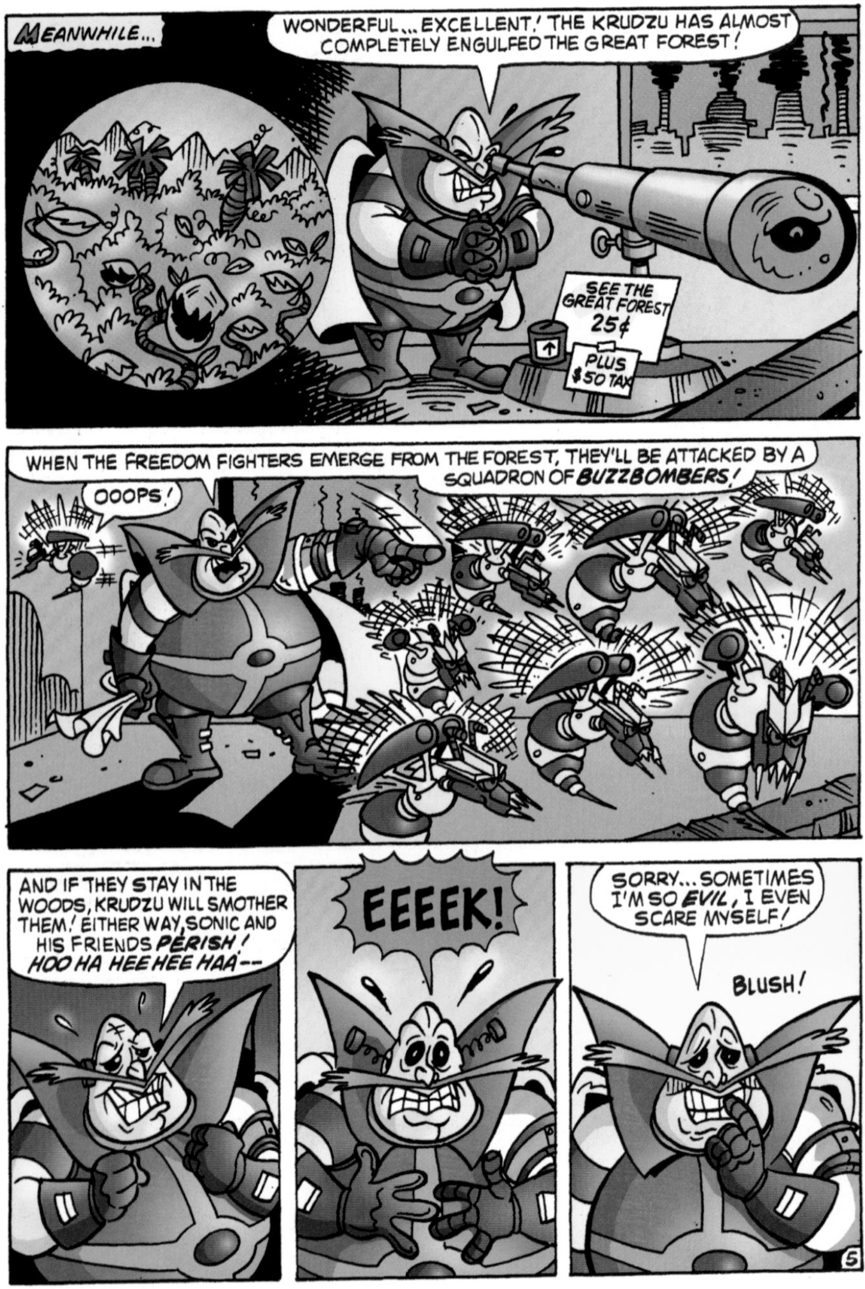
MEANWHILE...
WONDERFUL... EXCELLENT! THE KRUDZU HAS ALMOST COMPLETELY ENGULFED THE GREAT FOREST!
SEE THE GREAT FOREST 25¢
PLUS $.50 TAX
WHEN THE FREEDOM FIGHTERS EMERGE FROM THE FOREST, THEY'LL BE ATTACKED BY A SQUADRON OF BUZZBOMBERS!
OOOPS!
AND IF THEY STAY IN THE WOODS, KRUDZU WILL SMOTHER THEM! EITHER WAY, SONIC AND HIS FRIENDS PERISH! HOO HA HEE HEE HAA--
EEEEK!
SORRY... SOMETIMES I'M SO EVIL, I EVEN SCARE MYSELF!
BLUSH!
5

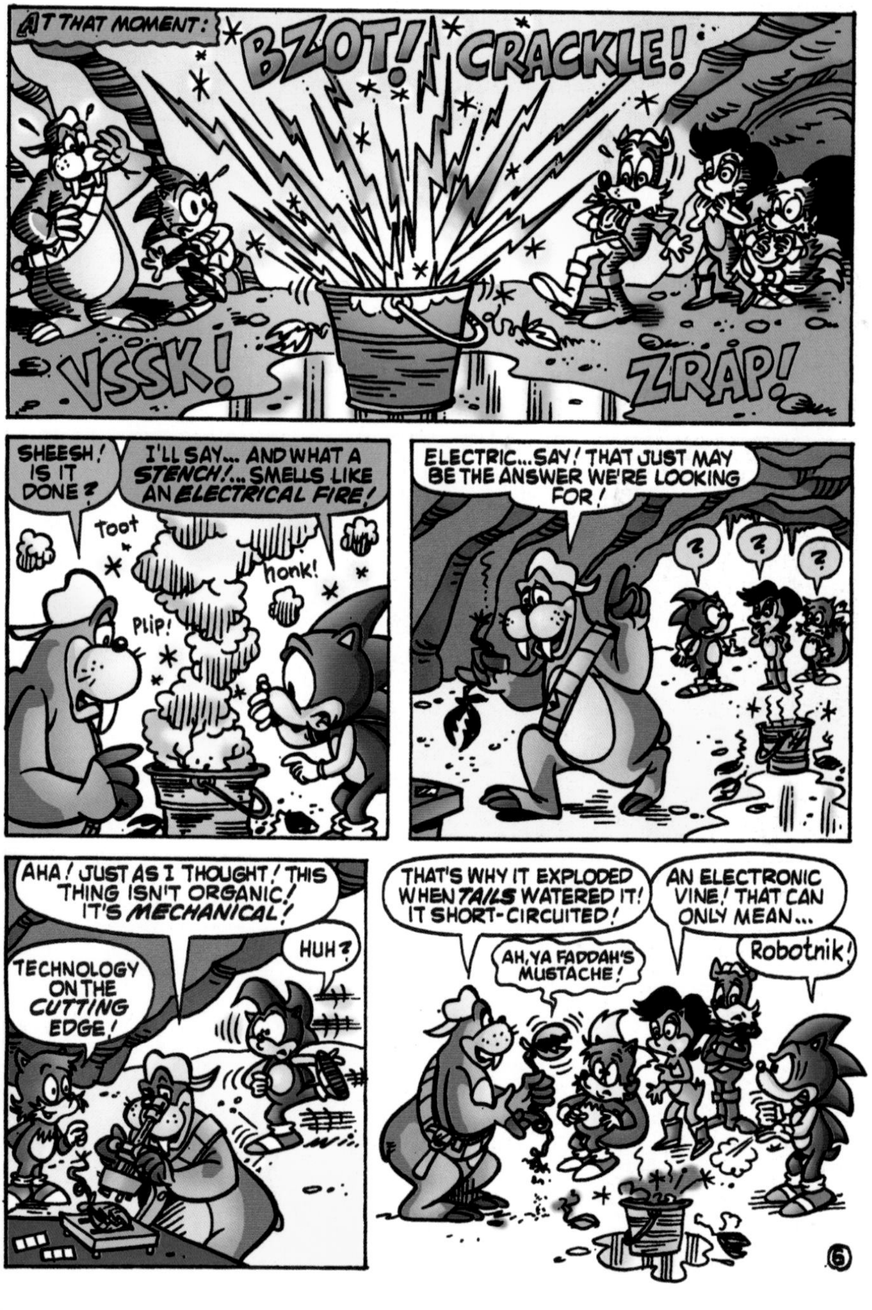
AT THAT MOMENT:
BZOT!
CRACKLE!
VSSK!
ZRAP!
SHEESH! IS IT DONE?
I'LL SAY... AND WHAT A STENCH!... SMELLS LIKE AN ELECTRICAL FIRE!
Toot
honk!
PLIP!
ELECTRIC...SAY! THAT JUST MAY BE THE ANSWER WE'RE LOOKING FOR!
AHA! JUST AS I THOUGHT! THIS THING ISN'T ORGANIC! IT'S MECHANICAL!
HUH?
TECHNOLOGY ON THE CUTTING EDGE!
THAT'S WHY IT EXPLODED WHEN TAILS WATERED IT! IT SHORT-CIRCUITED!
AH, YA FADDAH'S MUSTACHE!
AN ELECTRONIC VINE! THAT CAN ONLY MEAN...
Robotnik!

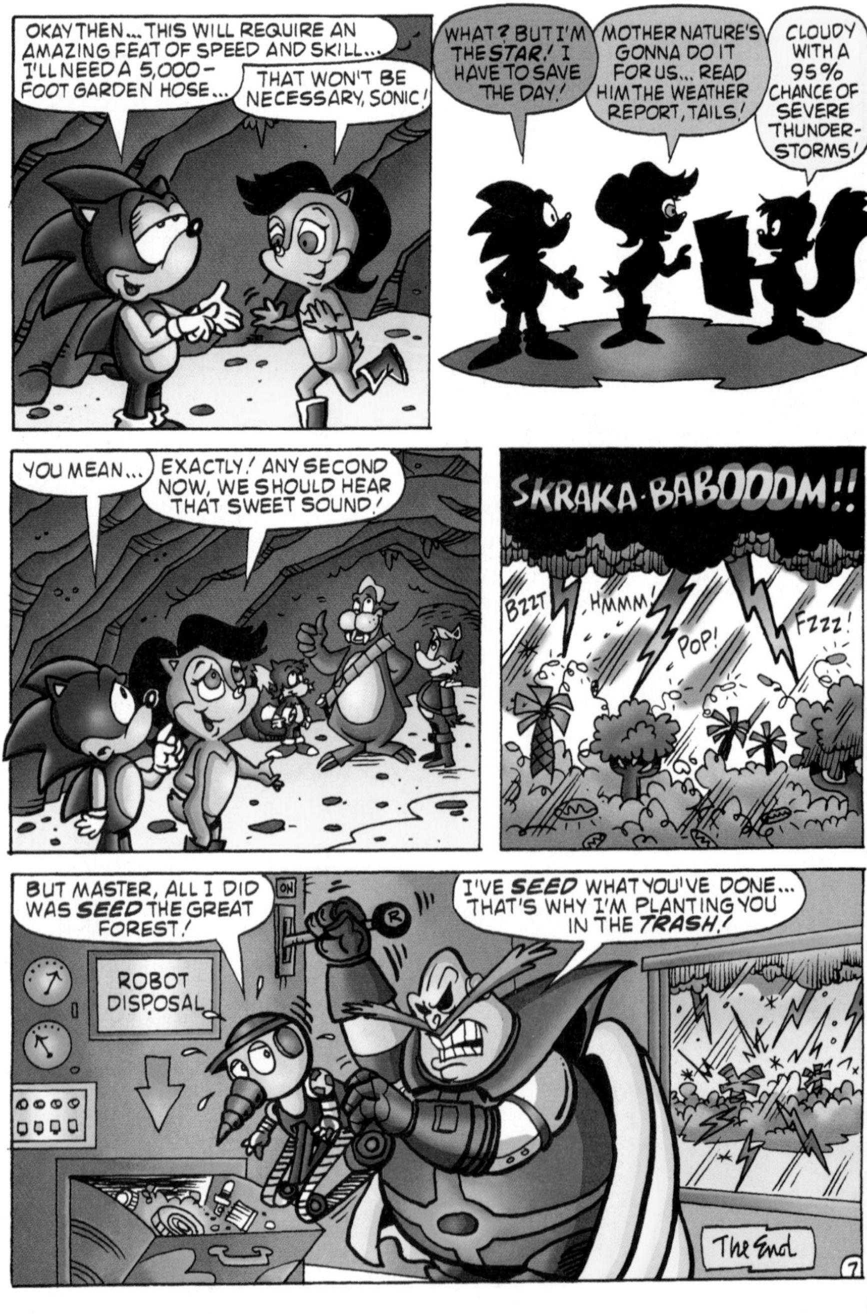
OKAY THEN... THIS WILL REQUIRE AN AMAZING FEAT OF SPEED AND SKILL... I'LL NEED A 5,000-FOOT GARDEN HOSE...
THAT WON'T BE NECESSARY, SONIC!
WHAT? BUT I'M THE STAR! I HAVE TO SAVE THE DAY!
MOTHER NATURE'S GONNA DO IT FOR US... READ HIM THE WEATHER REPORT, TAILS!
CLOUDY WITH A 95% CHANCE OF SEVERE THUNDER-STORMS!
YOU MEAN...
EXACTLY! ANY SECOND NOW, WE SHOULD HEAR THAT SWEET SOUND!
SKRAKA-BABOOOM!!
BZZT
HMMM!
POP!
FZZZ!
BUT MASTER, ALL I DID WAS SEED THE GREAT FOREST!
ON
ROBOT DISPOSAL
I'VE SEED WHAT YOU'VE DONE... THAT'S WHY I'M PLANTING YOU IN THE TRASH!
The End

SONIC THE HEDGEHOG BUMPER STICKERS

CLIP AND TAPE TO YOUR FAMILY VEHICLE!

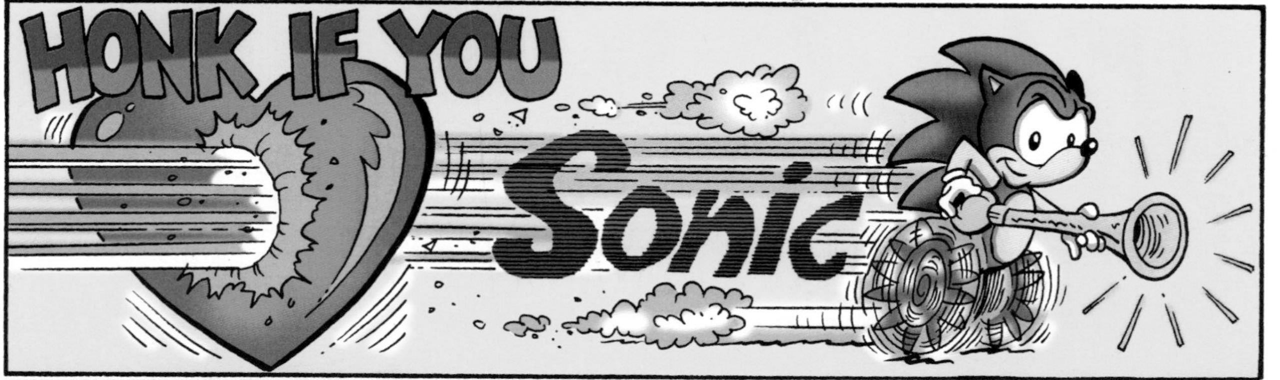
HONK IF YOU
♥
SONIC

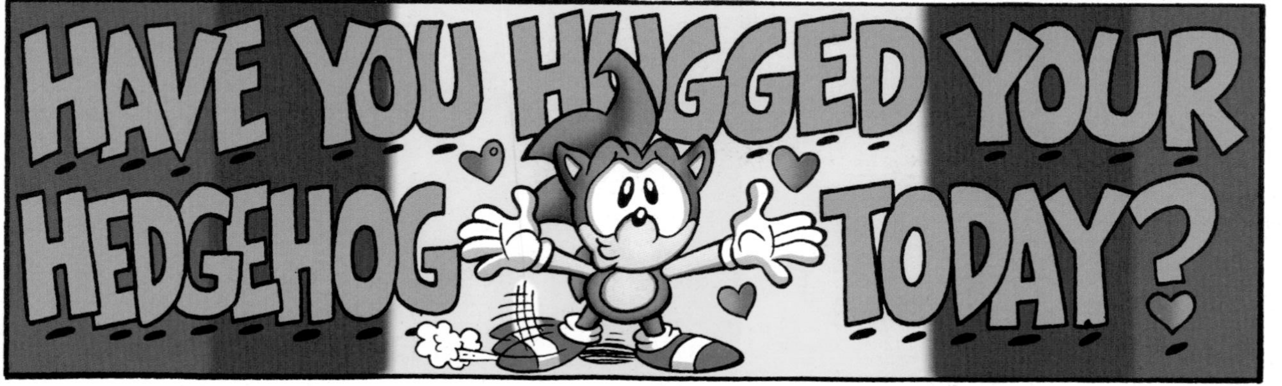
HAVE YOU HUGGED YOUR
HEDGEHOG TODAY?

I'D RATHER BE PLAYING
SONIC THE HEDGEHOG

IF YOU CAN READ THIS..
YOU SHOULD BE READING
SONIC THE HEDGEHOG COMICS!

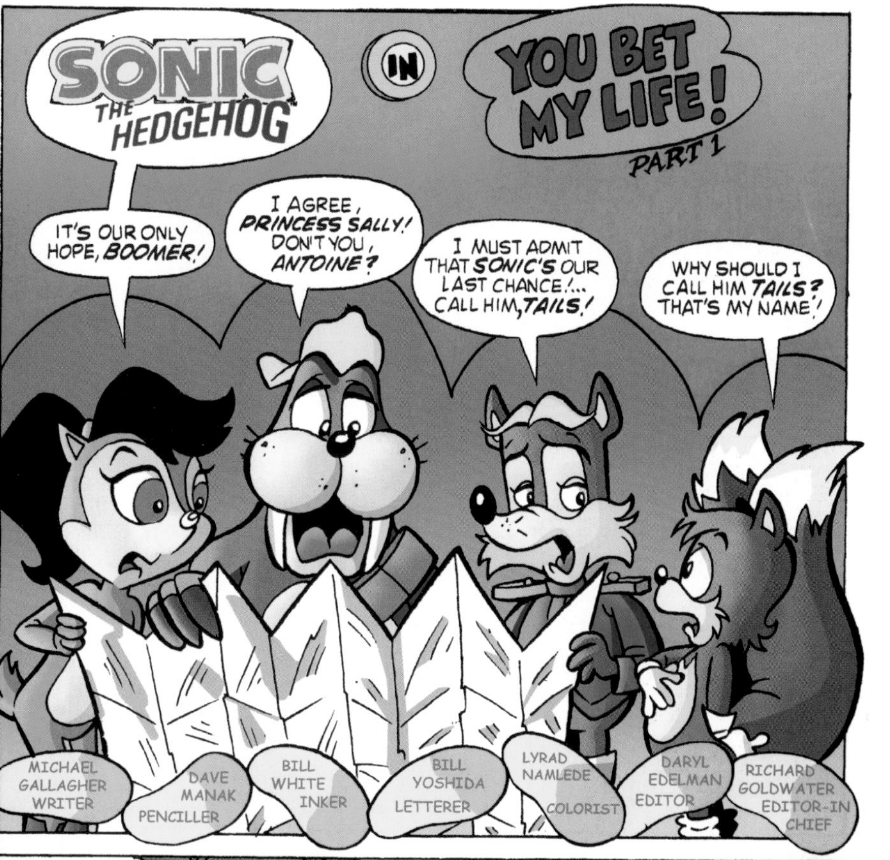
SONIC THE HEDGEHOG
IN
YOU BET MY LIFE!
PART 1
IT'S OUR ONLY HOPE, BOOMER!
I AGREE, PRINCESS SALLY! DON'T YOU, ANTOINE?
I MUST ADMIT THAT SONIC'S OUR LAST CHANCE!... CALL HIM, TAILS!
WHY SHOULD I CALL HIM TAILS? THAT'S MY NAME!
MICHAEL GALLAGHER WRITER
DAVE MANAK PENCILLER
BILL WHITE INKER
BILL YOSHIDA LETTERER
LYRAD NAMLEDE COLORIST
DARYL EDELMAN EDITOR
RICHARD GOLDWATER EDITOR-IN CHIEF

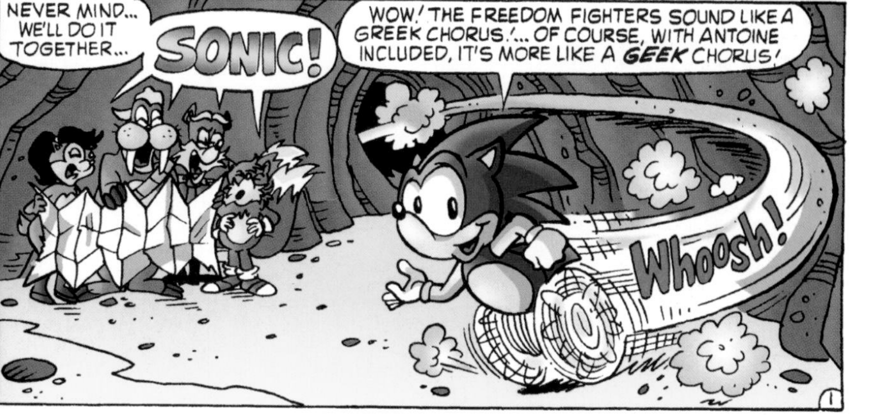
NEVER MIND... WE'LL DO IT TOGETHER...
SONIC!
WOW! THE FREEDOM FIGHTERS SOUND LIKE A GREEK CHORUS!... OF COURSE, WITH ANTOINE INCLUDED, IT'S MORE LIKE A GEEK CHORUS!
Whoosh!

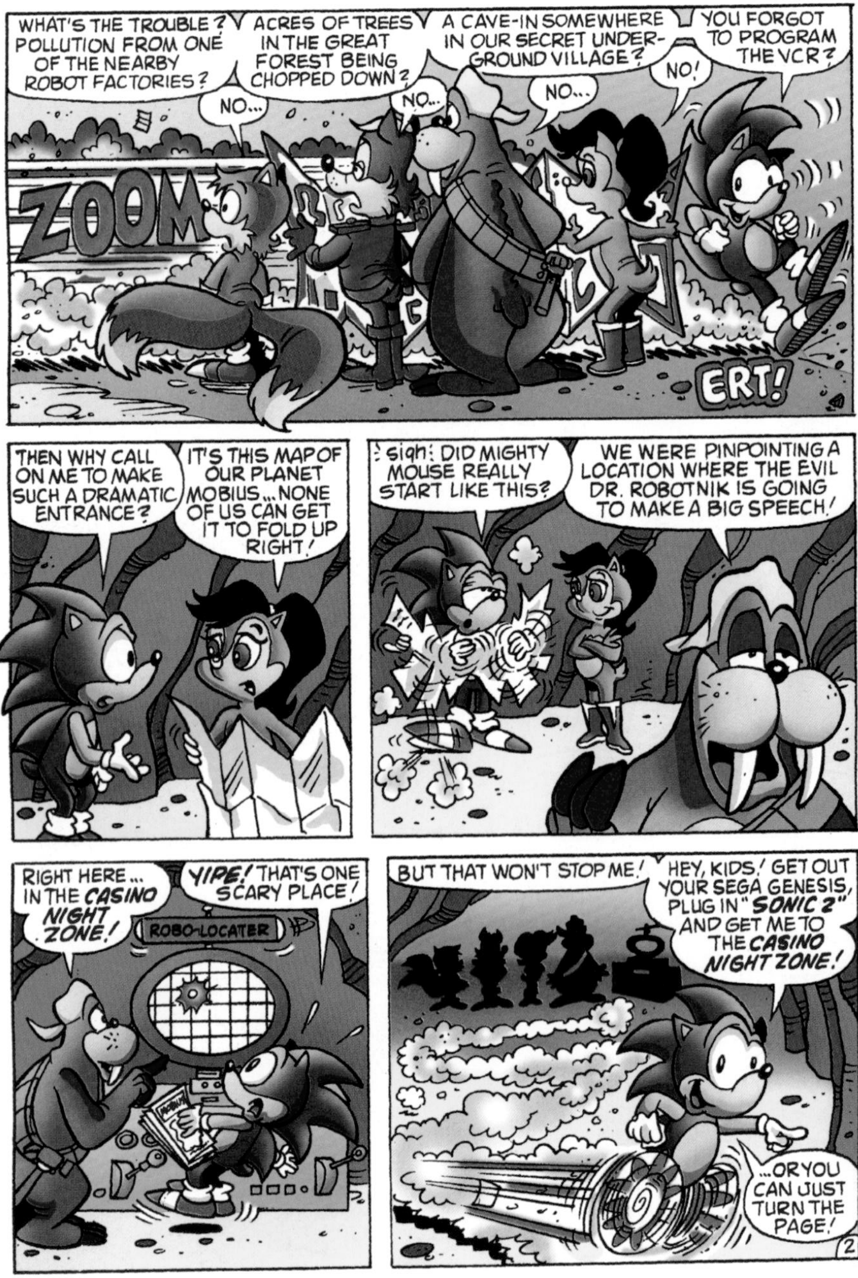
WHAT'S THE TROUBLE? POLLUTION FROM ONE OF THE NEARBY ROBOT FACTORIES?
NO...
ACRES OF TREES IN THE GREAT FOREST BEING CHOPPED DOWN?
NO...
A CAVE-IN SOMEWHERE IN OUR SECRET UNDER-GROUND VILLAGE?
NO...
YOU FORGOT TO PROGRAM THE VCR?
NO!
ZOOM
ERT!
THEN WHY CALL ON ME TO MAKE SUCH A DRAMATIC ENTRANCE?
IT'S THIS MAP OF OUR PLANET MOBIUS... NONE OF US CAN GET IT TO FOLD UP RIGHT!
:sigh: DID MIGHTY MOUSE REALLY START LIKE THIS?
WE WERE PINPOINTING A LOCATION WHERE THE EVIL DR. ROBOTNIK IS GOING TO MAKE A BIG SPEECH!
RIGHT HERE... IN THE CASINO NIGHT ZONE!
YIPE! THAT'S ONE SCARY PLACE!
ROBO-LOCATER
BUT THAT WON'T STOP ME!
HEY, KIDS! GET OUT YOUR SEGA GENESIS, PLUG IN "SONIC 2" AND GET ME TO THE CASINO NIGHT ZONE!
...OR YOU CAN JUST TURN THE PAGE!

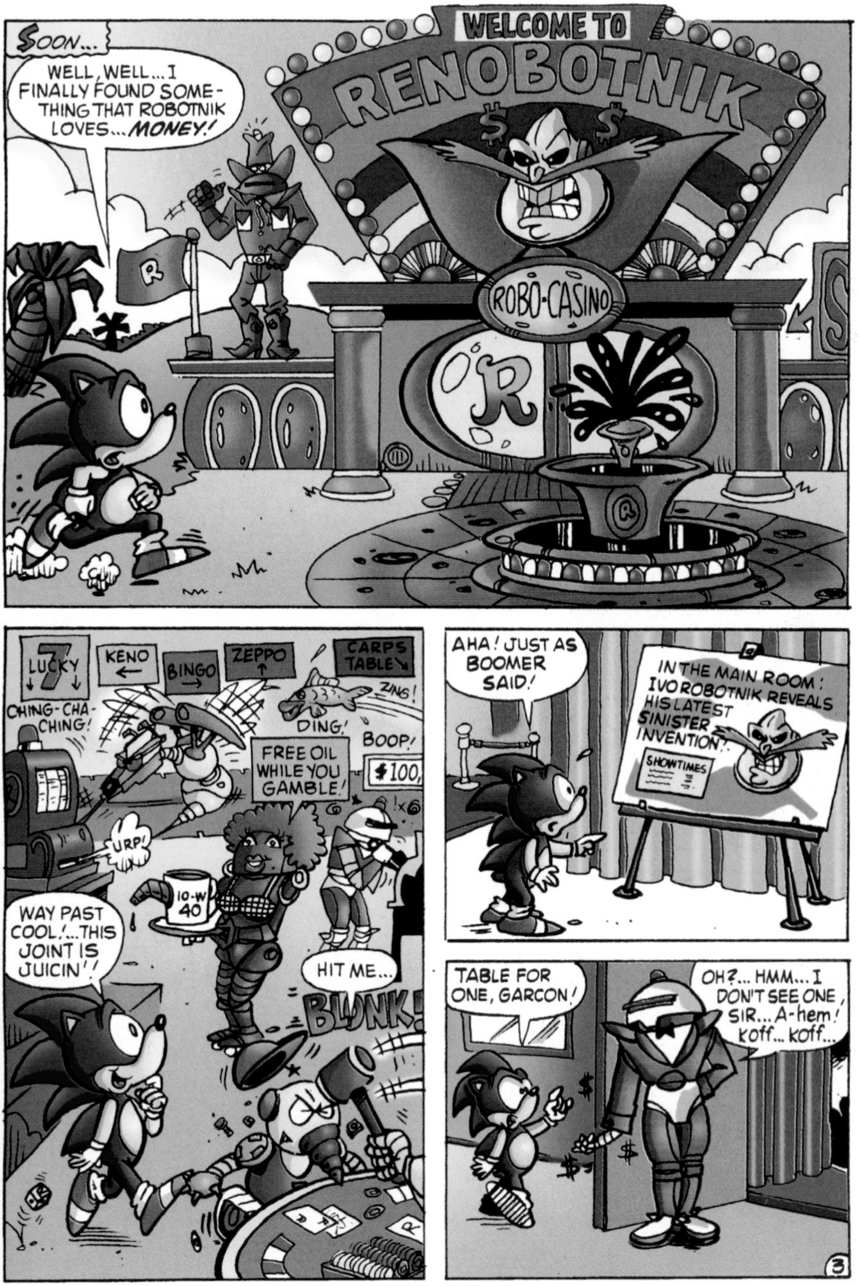
SOON...
WELL, WELL... I FINALLY FOUND SOME-THING THAT ROBOTNIK LOVES... MONEY!
WELCOME TO
RENOBOTNIK
ROBO-CASINO
LUCKY 7
KENO
BINGO
ZEPPO
CARPS TABLE
CHING-CHA-CHING!
ZING!
DING!
BOOP!
FREE OIL WHILE YOU GAMBLE!
$100
URP!
10-W 40
WAY PAST COOL!... THIS JOINT IS JUICIN'!
HIT ME...
BLUNK!
AHA! JUST AS BOOMER SAID!
IN THE MAIN ROOM: IVO ROBOTNIK REVEALS HIS LATEST SINISTER INVENTION!
SHOWTIMES
TABLE FOR ONE, GARCON!
OH?... HMM... I DON'T SEE ONE, SIR... A-hem! koff... koff...
3

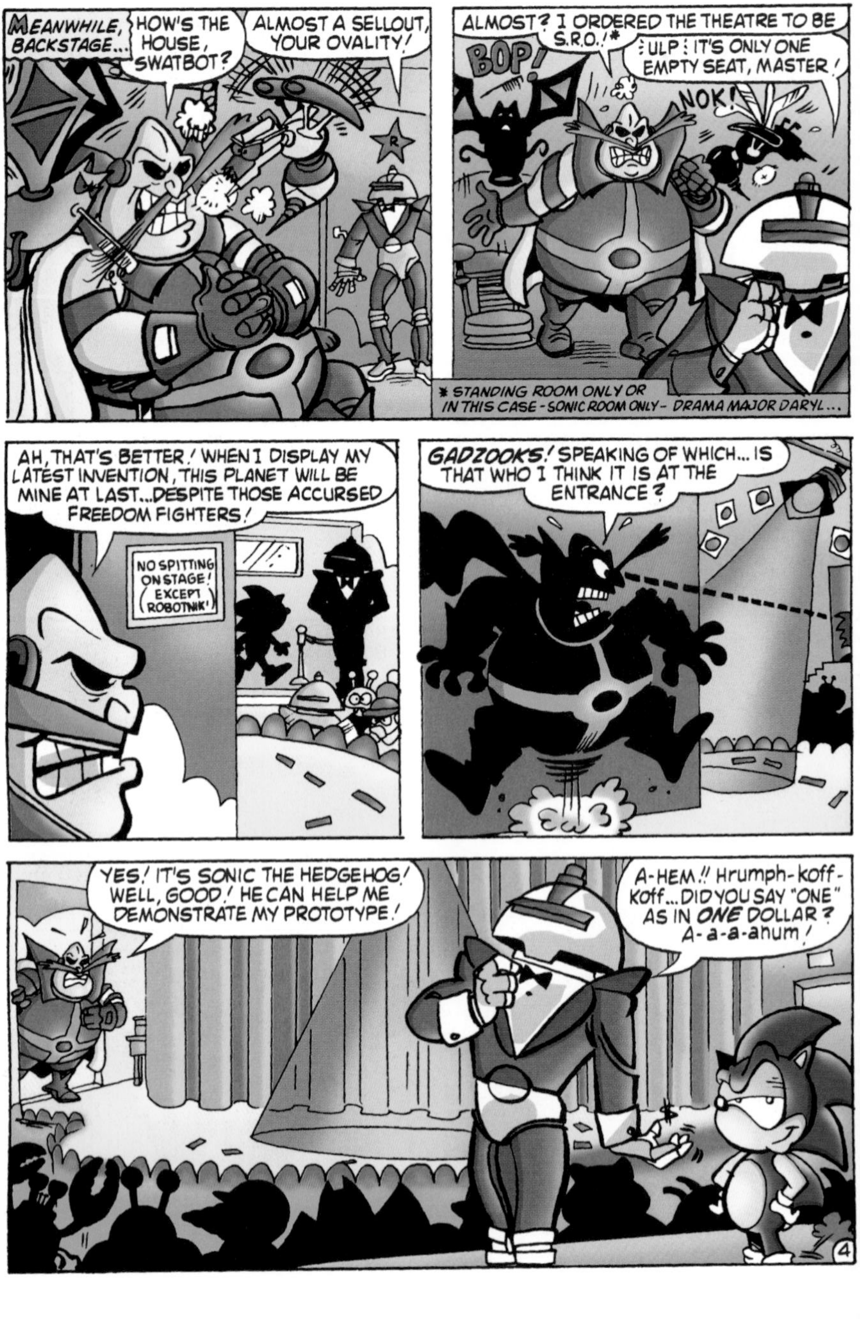
MEANWHILE, BACKSTAGE...
HOW'S THE HOUSE, SWATBOT?
ALMOST A SELLOUT, YOUR OVALITY!
ALMOST? I ORDERED THE THEATRE TO BE S.R.O.!*
BOP!
ULP! IT'S ONLY ONE EMPTY SEAT, MASTER!
NOK!
* STANDING ROOM ONLY OR IN THIS CASE - SONIC ROOM ONLY - DRAMA MAJOR DARYL...
AH, THAT'S BETTER! WHEN I DISPLAY MY LATEST INVENTION, THIS PLANET WILL BE MINE AT LAST...DESPITE THOSE ACCURSED FREEDOM FIGHTERS!
NO SPITTING ON STAGE! (EXCEPT ROBOTNIK!)
GADZOOKS! SPEAKING OF WHICH... IS THAT WHO I THINK IT IS AT THE ENTRANCE?
YES! IT'S SONIC THE HEDGEHOG! WELL, GOOD! HE CAN HELP ME DEMONSTRATE MY PROTOTYPE!
A-HEM!! Hrumph-koff-koff...DID YOU SAY "ONE" AS IN ONE DOLLAR? A-a-a-ahum!
4

GET REAL, BUCKETHEAD... YOU WANT A TIP?...*CROSS AT THE GREEN, NOT-IN-BETWEEN!*

squawk!

(whirr...whirl...whir...)

ZOOM

ALL RIGHT! FRONT AND CENTER!

LADIES AND GENTLEBOTS!... LET'S HEAR IT FOR OUR FEARLESS, FLABBY LEADER... *ROBOTNIK!*

THANKEW! WOTTA CROWD! THE LAST PLACE I PLAYED WAS SO SMALL, THE DOUBLE 'A' BATTERIES WERE STOOP-SHOULDERED! BUT SERIOUSLY, FOLKS...

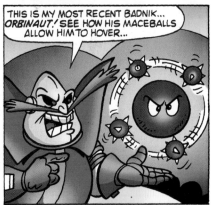

THIS IS MY MOST RECENT BADNIK... *ORBINAUT!* SEE HOW HIS MACEBALLS ALLOW HIM TO HOVER...

BEST OF ALL, THEY CAN BE LAUNCHED WITH DEADLY ACCURACY AT AN ENEMY!... FOR EXAMPLE, *SONIC THE HEDGEHOG!*

fling!

NOK!

OW!

END of Part 1

5

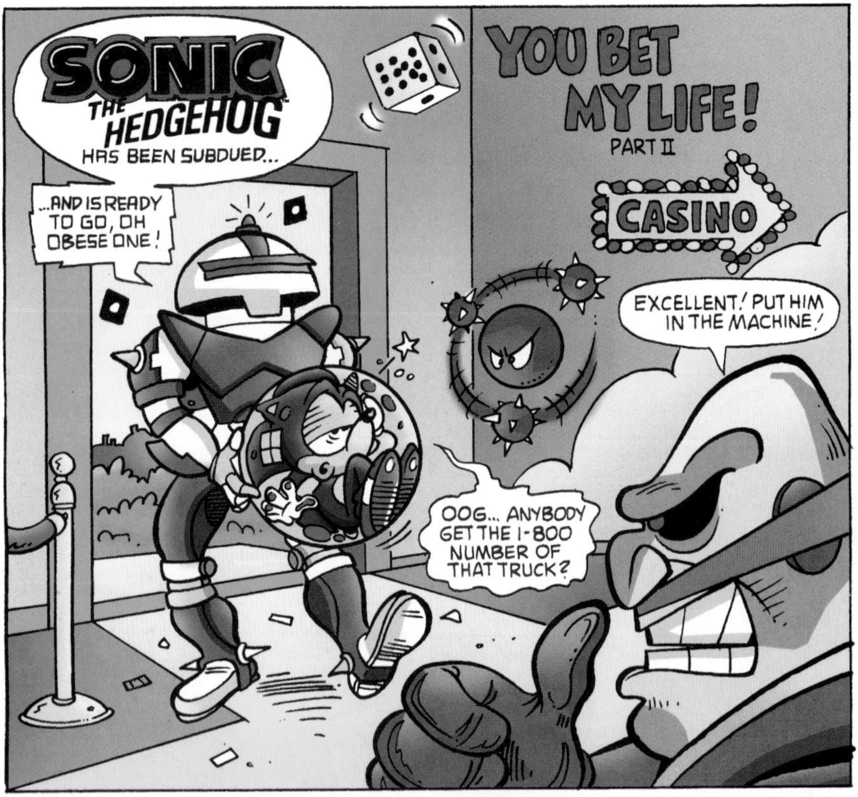
SONIC THE HEDGEHOG™ HAS BEEN SUBDUED...
YOU BET MY LIFE!
PART II
CASINO
...AND IS READY TO GO, OH OBESE ONE!
EXCELLENT! PUT HIM IN THE MACHINE!
OOG... ANYBODY GET THE 1-800 NUMBER OF THAT TRUCK?

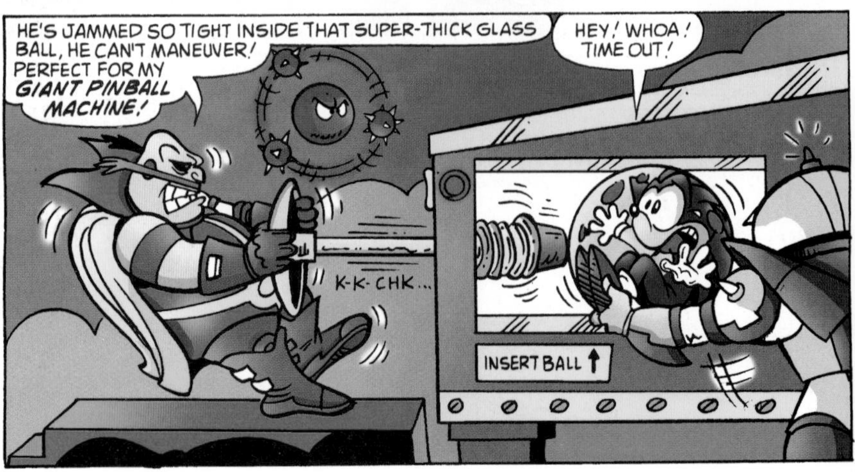
HE'S JAMMED SO TIGHT INSIDE THAT SUPER-THICK GLASS BALL, HE CAN'T MANEUVER! PERFECT FOR MY GIANT PINBALL MACHINE!
HEY! WHOA! TIME OUT!
K-K-CHK...
INSERT BALL

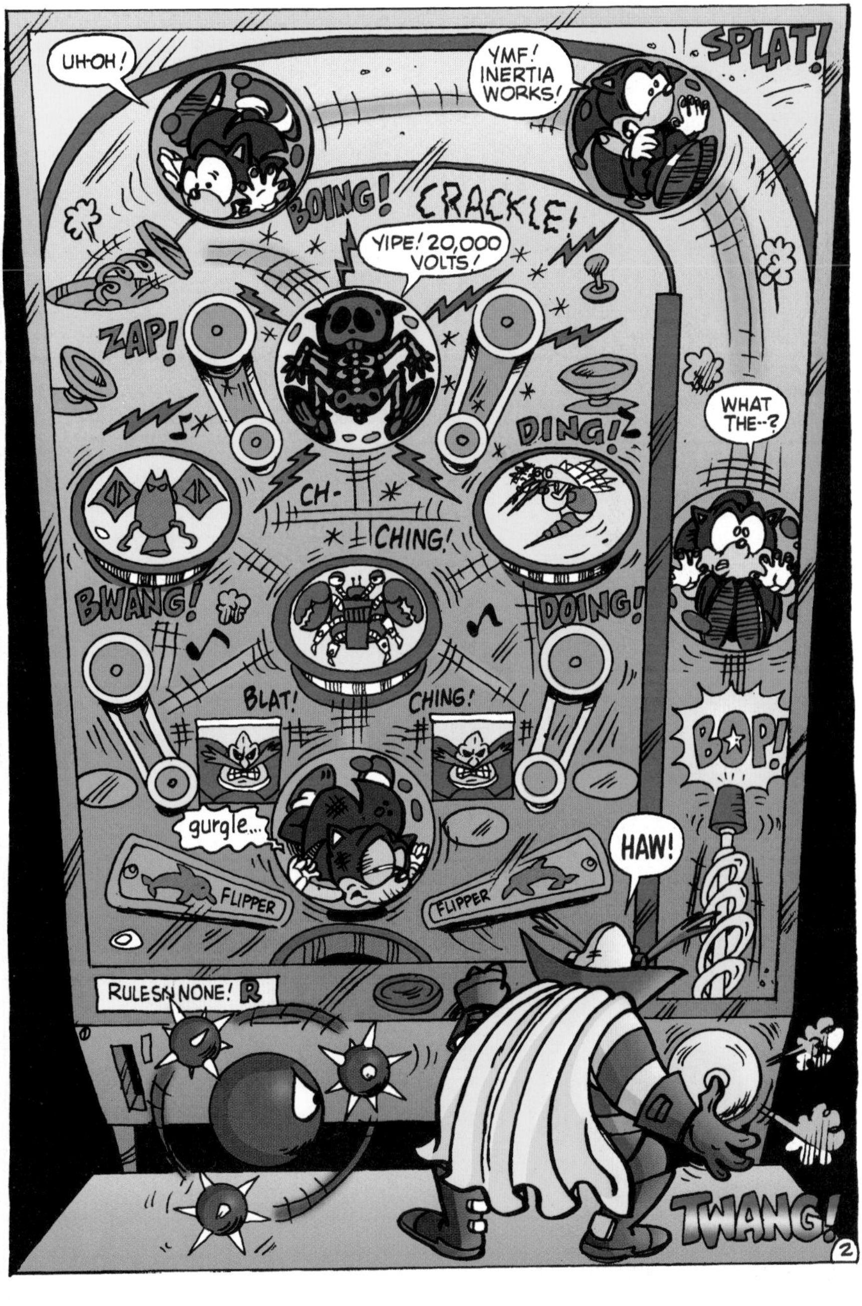
UH-OH!
YMF! INERTIA WORKS!
SPLAT!
BOING!
CRACKLE!
YIPE! 20,000 VOLTS!
ZAP!
DING!
WHAT THE--?
CH-
CHING!
BWANG!
DOING!
BLAT!
CHING!
BOP!
gurgle...
HAW!
FLIPPER
FLIPPER
RULES?! NONE! R
TWANG!

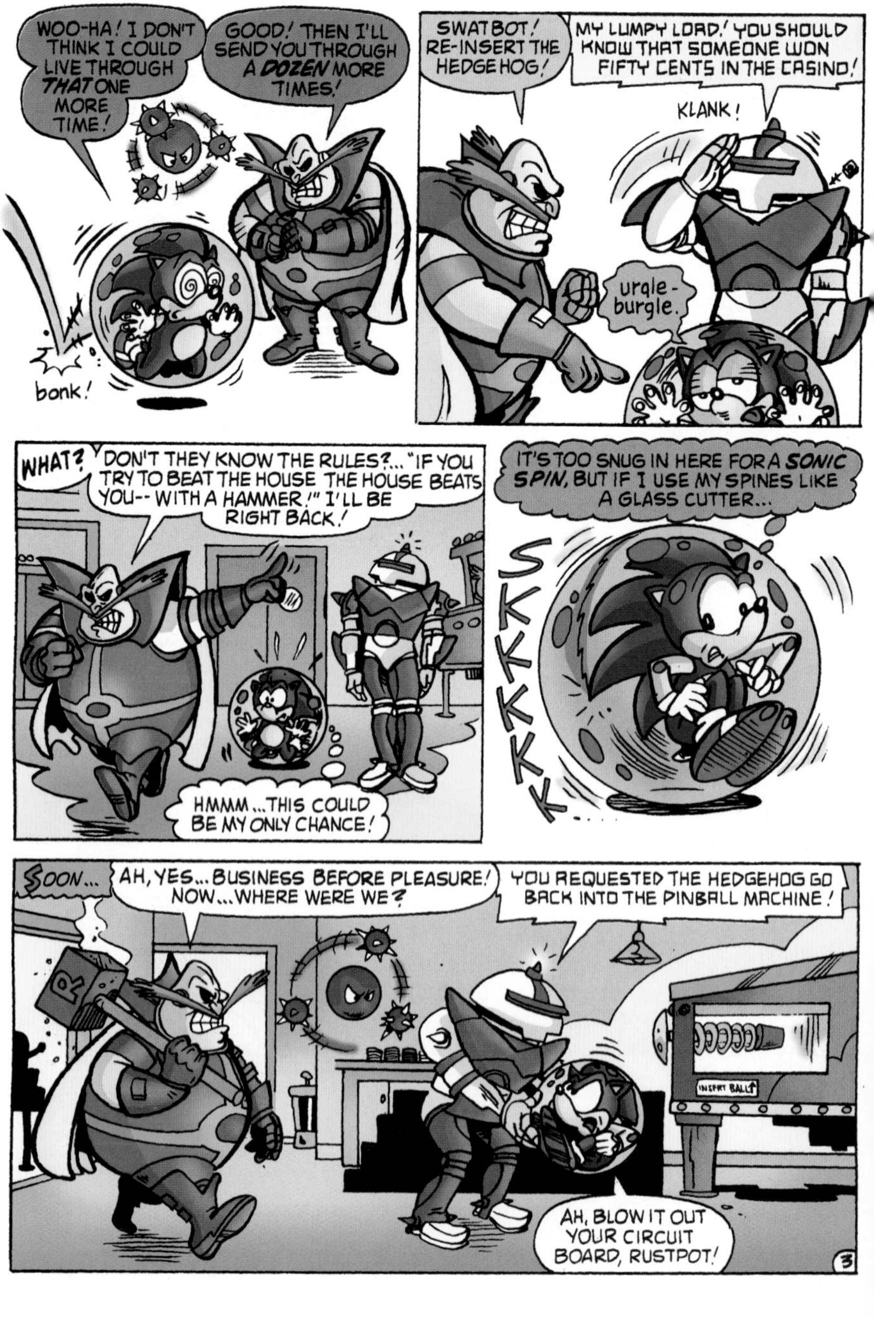
WOO-HA! I DON'T THINK I COULD LIVE THROUGH THAT ONE MORE TIME!
GOOD! THEN I'LL SEND YOU THROUGH A DOZEN MORE TIMES!
bonk!
SWATBOT! RE-INSERT THE HEDGEHOG!
MY LUMPY LORD! YOU SHOULD KNOW THAT SOMEONE WON FIFTY CENTS IN THE CASINO!
KLANK!
urgle-burgle.
WHAT?
DON'T THEY KNOW THE RULES?... "IF YOU TRY TO BEAT THE HOUSE THE HOUSE BEATS YOU-- WITH A HAMMER!" I'LL BE RIGHT BACK!
HMMM...THIS COULD BE MY ONLY CHANCE!
IT'S TOO SNUG IN HERE FOR A SONIC SPIN, BUT IF I USE MY SPINES LIKE A GLASS CUTTER...
SKKKKKK
SOON...
AH, YES... BUSINESS BEFORE PLEASURE! NOW... WHERE WERE WE?
YOU REQUESTED THE HEDGEHOG GO BACK INTO THE PINBALL MACHINE!
INSERT BALL
AH, BLOW IT OUT YOUR CIRCUIT BOARD, RUSTPOT!
3

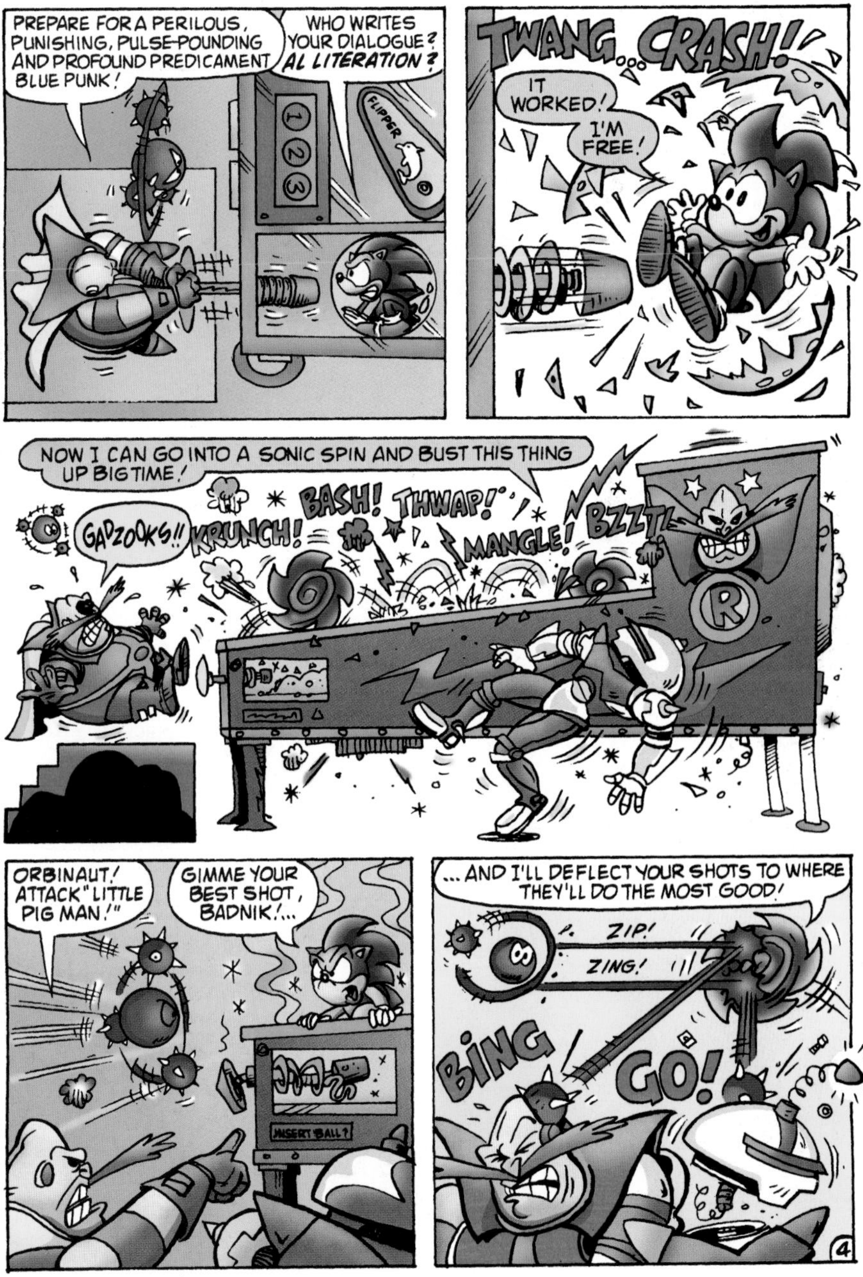
PREPARE FOR A PERILOUS, PUNISHING, PULSE-POUNDING AND PROFOUND PREDICAMENT BLUE PUNK!
WHO WRITES YOUR DIALOGUE? AL LITERATION?
FLIPPER
1
2
3
TWANG... CRASH!
IT WORKED!
I'M FREE!
NOW I CAN GO INTO A SONIC SPIN AND BUST THIS THING UP BIG TIME!
GADZOOKS!!
KRUNCH!
BASH!
THWAP!
MANGLE!
BZZT!
R
ORBINAUT! ATTACK "LITTLE PIG MAN!"
GIMME YOUR BEST SHOT, BADNIK!...
INSERT BALL?
...AND I'LL DEFLECT YOUR SHOTS TO WHERE THEY'LL DO THE MOST GOOD!
ZIP!
ZING!
BING
GO!

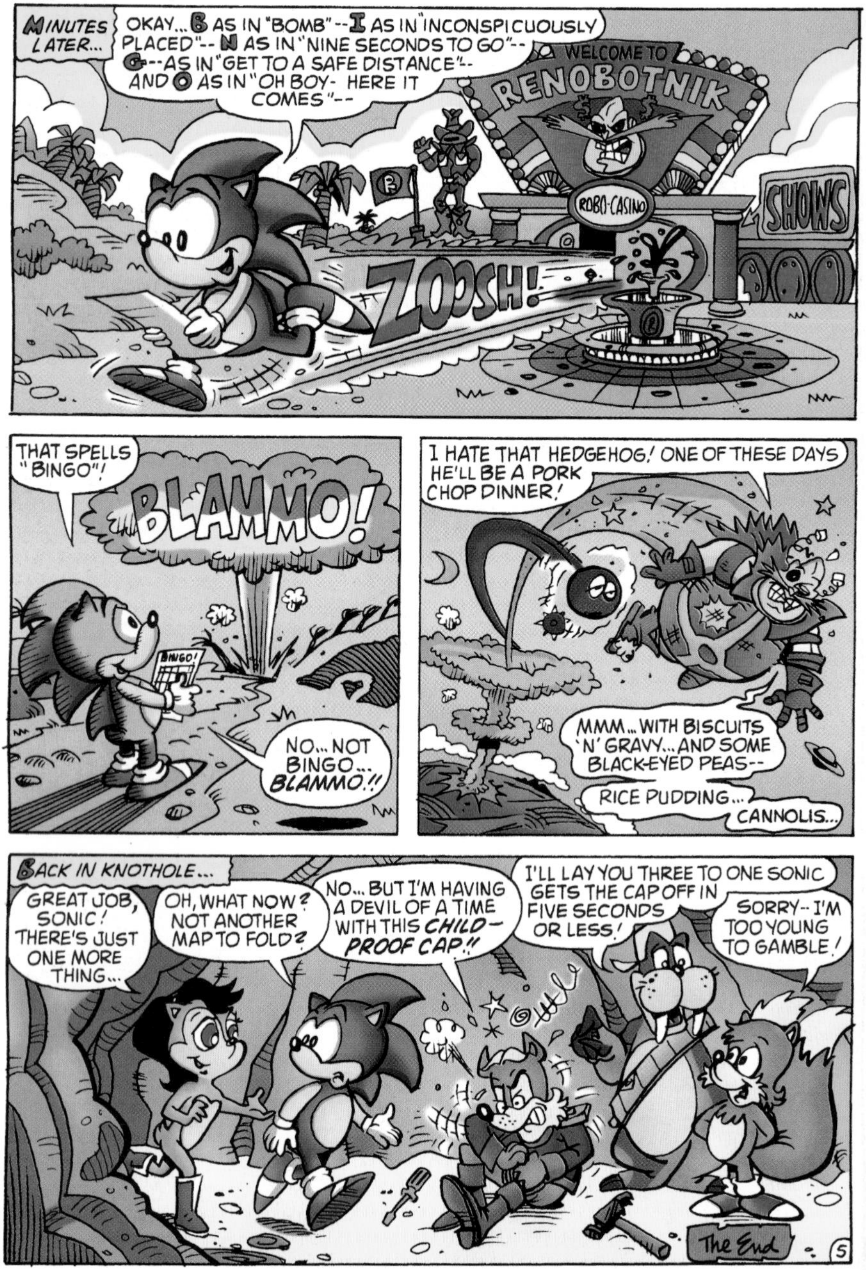

MINUTES LATER...
OKAY... B AS IN "BOMB" -- I AS IN "INCONSPICUOUSLY PLACED" -- N AS IN "NINE SECONDS TO GO" -- G -- AS IN "GET TO A SAFE DISTANCE" -- AND O AS IN "OH BOY- HERE IT COMES" --
WELCOME TO
RENOBOTNIK
ROBO-CASINO
SHOWS
ZOOSH!
THAT SPELLS "BINGO"!
BLAMMO!
BINGO!
NO... NOT BINGO... BLAMMO!!
I HATE THAT HEDGEHOG! ONE OF THESE DAYS HE'LL BE A PORK CHOP DINNER!
MMM... WITH BISCUITS 'N' GRAVY... AND SOME BLACK-EYED PEAS--
RICE PUDDING...
CANNOLIS...
BACK IN KNOTHOLE...
GREAT JOB, SONIC! THERE'S JUST ONE MORE THING...
OH, WHAT NOW? NOT ANOTHER MAP TO FOLD?
NO... BUT I'M HAVING A DEVIL OF A TIME WITH THIS CHILD-PROOF CAP!!
I'LL LAY YOU THREE TO ONE SONIC GETS THE CAP OFF IN FIVE SECONDS OR LESS!
SORRY-- I'M TOO YOUNG TO GAMBLE!
The End

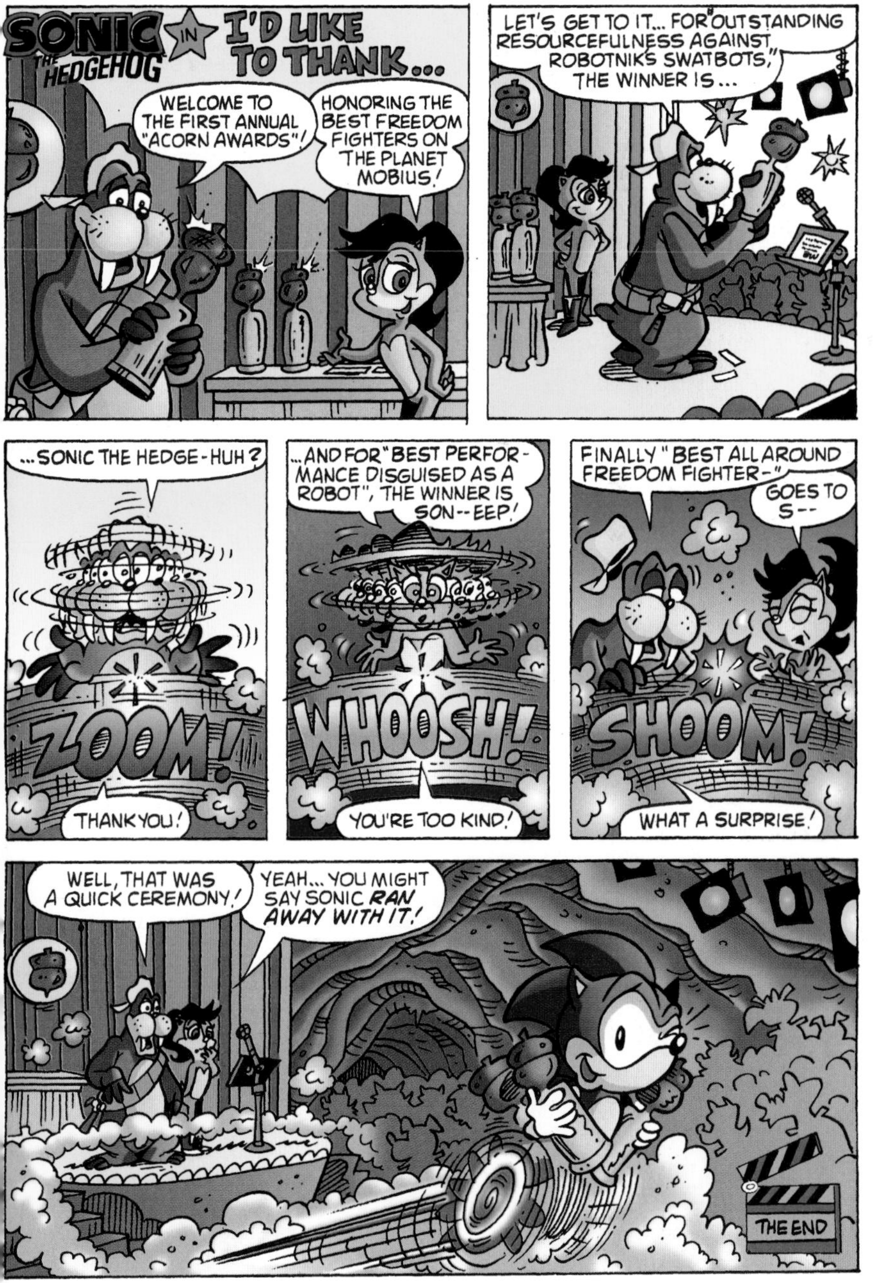
SONIC THE HEDGEHOG IN I'D LIKE TO THANK...
WELCOME TO THE FIRST ANNUAL "ACORN AWARDS"!
HONORING THE BEST FREEDOM FIGHTERS ON THE PLANET MOBIUS!
LET'S GET TO IT... FOR "OUTSTANDING RESOURCEFULNESS AGAINST ROBOTNIK'S SWATBOTS," THE WINNER IS...
...SONIC THE HEDGE-HUH?
ZOOM!
THANK YOU!
...AND FOR "BEST PERFORMANCE DISGUISED AS A ROBOT", THE WINNER IS SON--EEP!
WHOOSH!
YOU'RE TOO KIND!
FINALLY "BEST ALL AROUND FREEDOM FIGHTER-"
GOES TO S--
SHOOM!
WHAT A SURPRISE!
WELL, THAT WAS A QUICK CEREMONY!
YEAH... YOU MIGHT SAY SONIC RAN AWAY WITH IT!
THE END

SONIC THE HEDGEHOG in KEEP LOOKING UP!

HERE'S AN INTERESTING LETTER FROM J.R. KINCAID OF VERO BEACH, FL...

Dear Sonic,
At what speed do your legs disappear and become those blurry, spinning wheels? J.R.

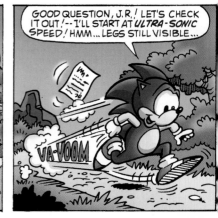

GOOD QUESTION, J.R.! LET'S CHECK IT OUT! -- I'LL START AT *ULTRA-SONIC* SPEED! HMM... LEGS STILL VISIBLE...

VA-VOOM

OKAY... I'LL MOVE TO *SUPER-SONIC!*

NOPE... NOT YET...

LET'S JUMP TO *TRANS-SONIC!*... OH, YEAH! NOW THEY'RE GETTING BLURRY...

T
W
A
C
K!

...AS A MATTER OF FACT, EVERYTHING LOOKS A LITTLE BLURRY...

The End

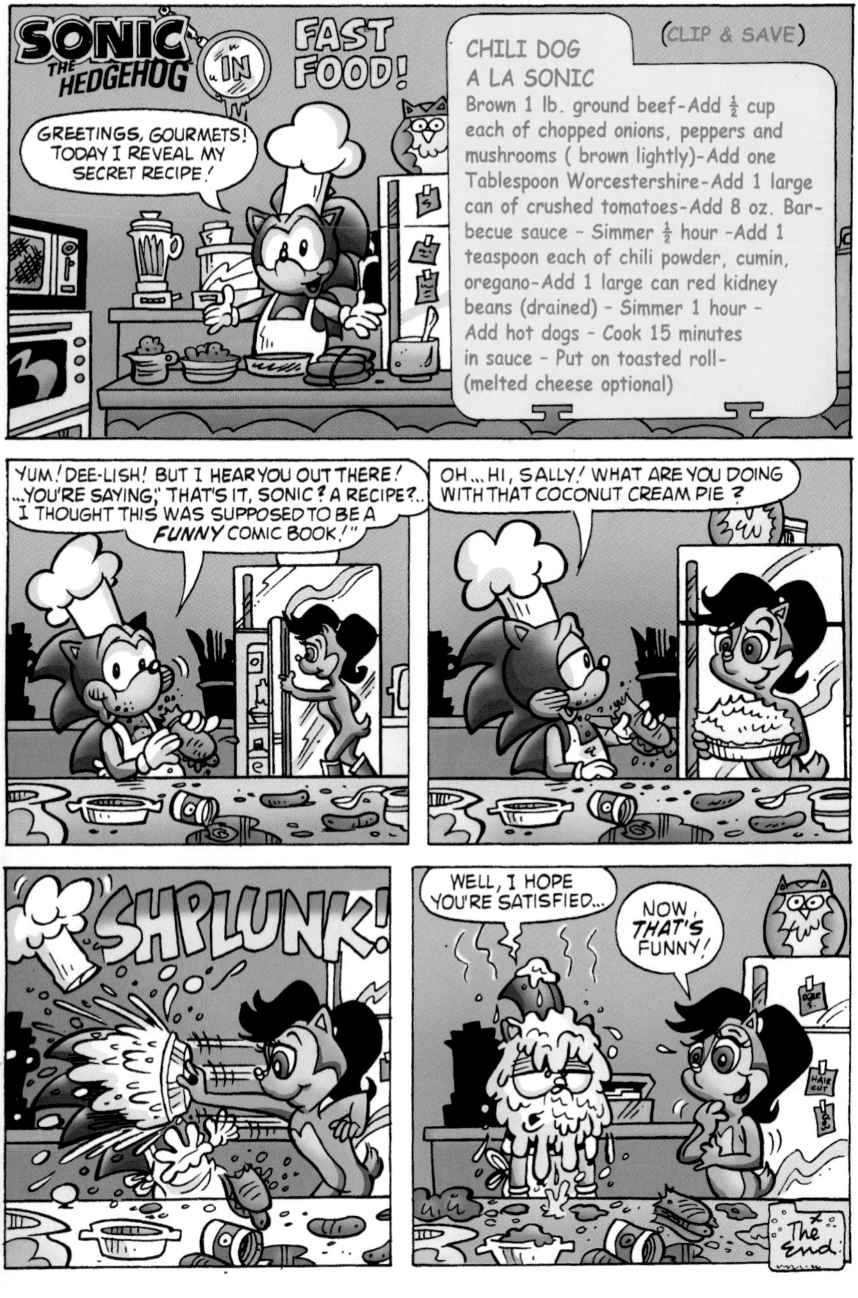
SONIC THE HEDGEHOG IN FAST FOOD!
(CLIP & SAVE)
CHILI DOG A LA SONIC
Brown 1 lb. ground beef-Add ½ cup each of chopped onions, peppers and mushrooms (brown lightly)-Add one Tablespoon Worcestershire-Add 1 large can of crushed tomatoes-Add 8 oz. Barbecue sauce - Simmer ½ hour -Add 1 teaspoon each of chili powder, cumin, oregano-Add 1 large can red kidney beans (drained) - Simmer 1 hour - Add hot dogs - Cook 15 minutes in sauce - Put on toasted roll- (melted cheese optional)
GREETINGS, GOURMETS! TODAY I REVEAL MY SECRET RECIPE!
YUM! DEE-LISH! BUT I HEAR YOU OUT THERE! ...YOU'RE SAYING," THAT'S IT, SONIC? A RECIPE?.. I THOUGHT THIS WAS SUPPOSED TO BE A FUNNY COMIC BOOK!"
OH... HI, SALLY! WHAT ARE YOU DOING WITH THAT COCONUT CREAM PIE?
SHPLUNK!
WELL, I HOPE YOU'RE SATISFIED...
NOW, THAT'S FUNNY!
The End

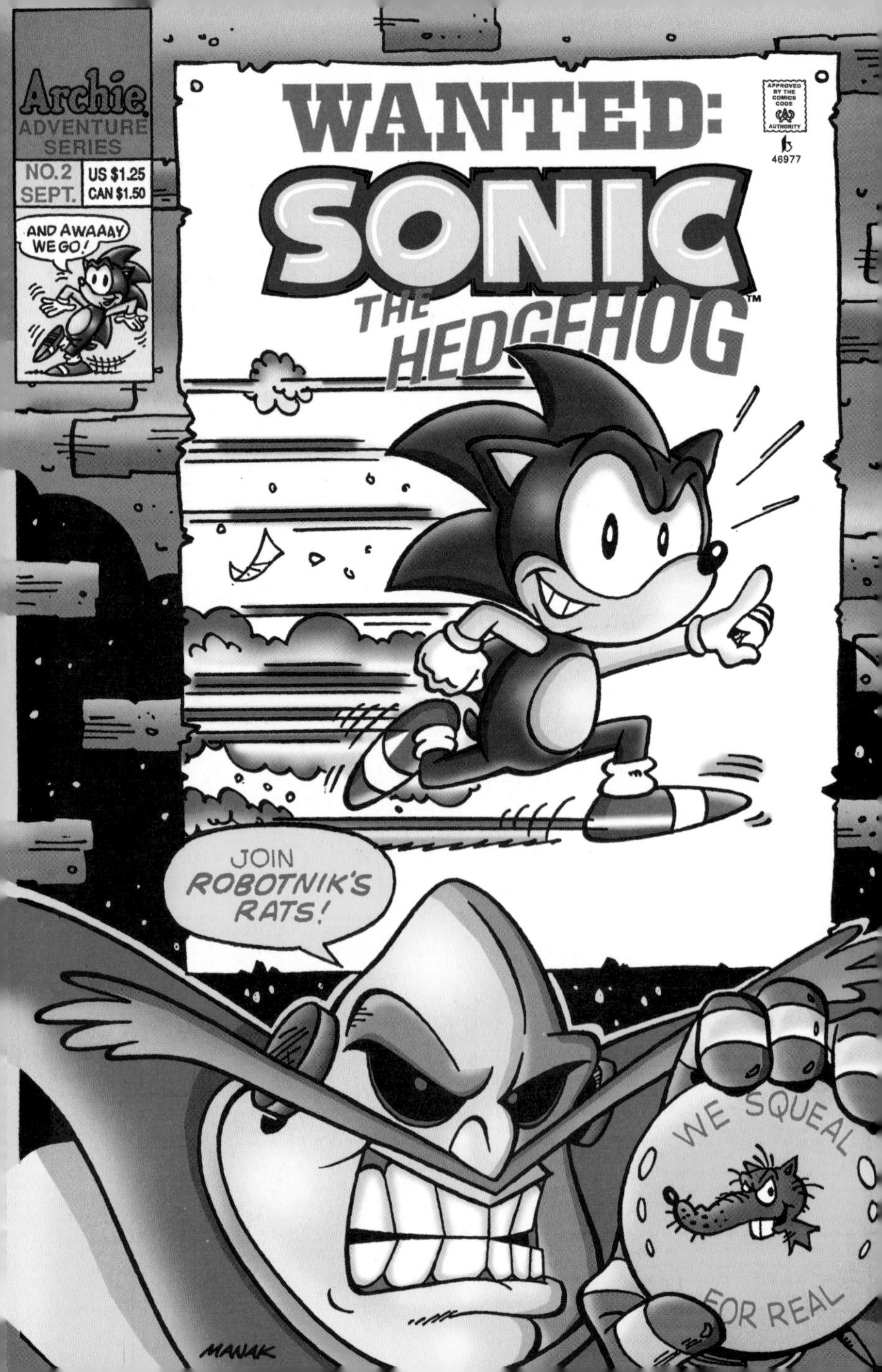
Archie
ADVENTURE SERIES
NO.2
SEPT.
US $1.25
CAN $1.50
AND AWAAAY WE GO!
WANTED:
SONIC THE HEDGEHOG™
APPROVED BY THE COMICS CODE AUTHORITY
46977
JOIN ROBOTNIK'S RATS!
WE SQUEAL FOR REAL
MANAK

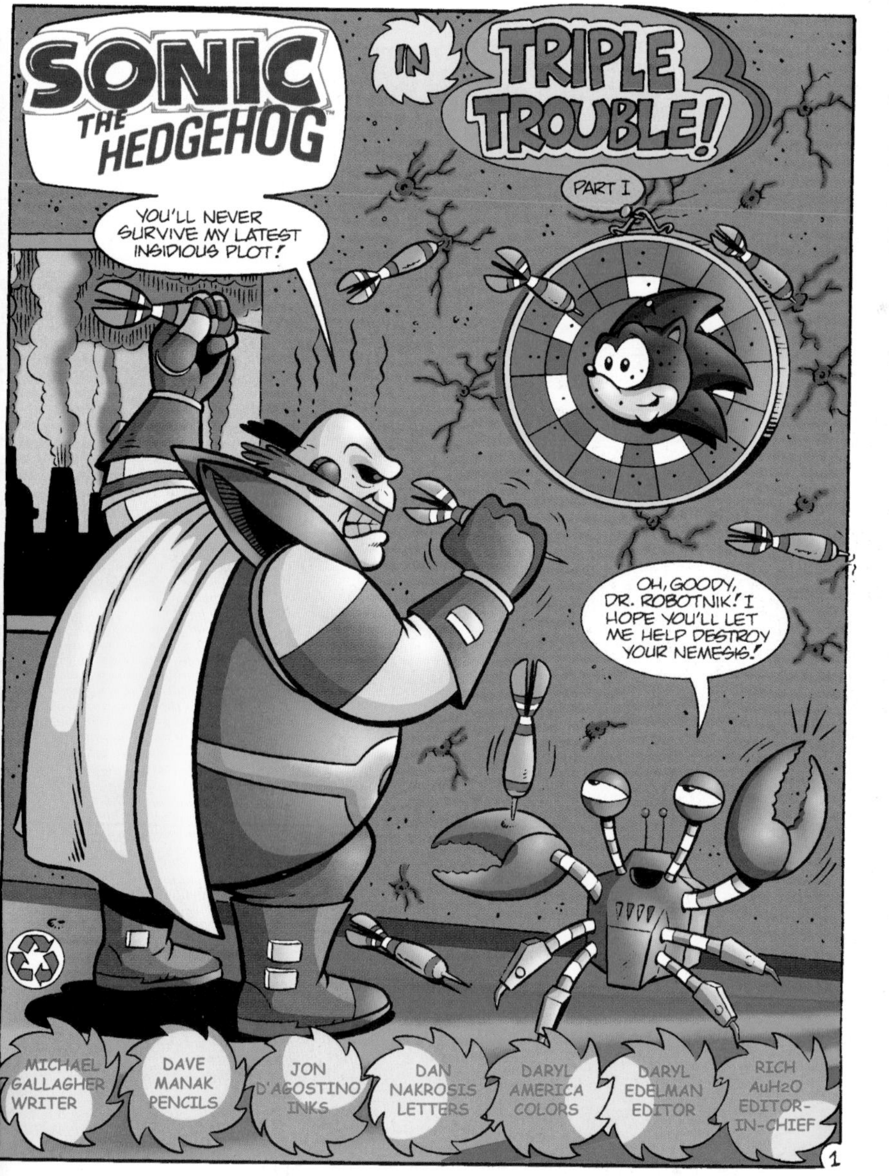
SONIC THE HEDGEHOG™
IN
TRIPLE TROUBLE!
PART I
YOU'LL NEVER SURVIVE MY LATEST INSIDIOUS PLOT!
OH, GOODY, DR. ROBOTNIK! I HOPE YOU'LL LET ME HELP DESTROY YOUR NEMESIS!
MICHAEL GALLAGHER WRITER
DAVE MANAK PENCILS
JON D'AGOSTINO INKS
DAN NAKROSIS LETTERS
DARYL AMERICA COLORS
DARYL EDELMAN EDITOR
RICH AuH2O EDITOR-IN-CHIEF

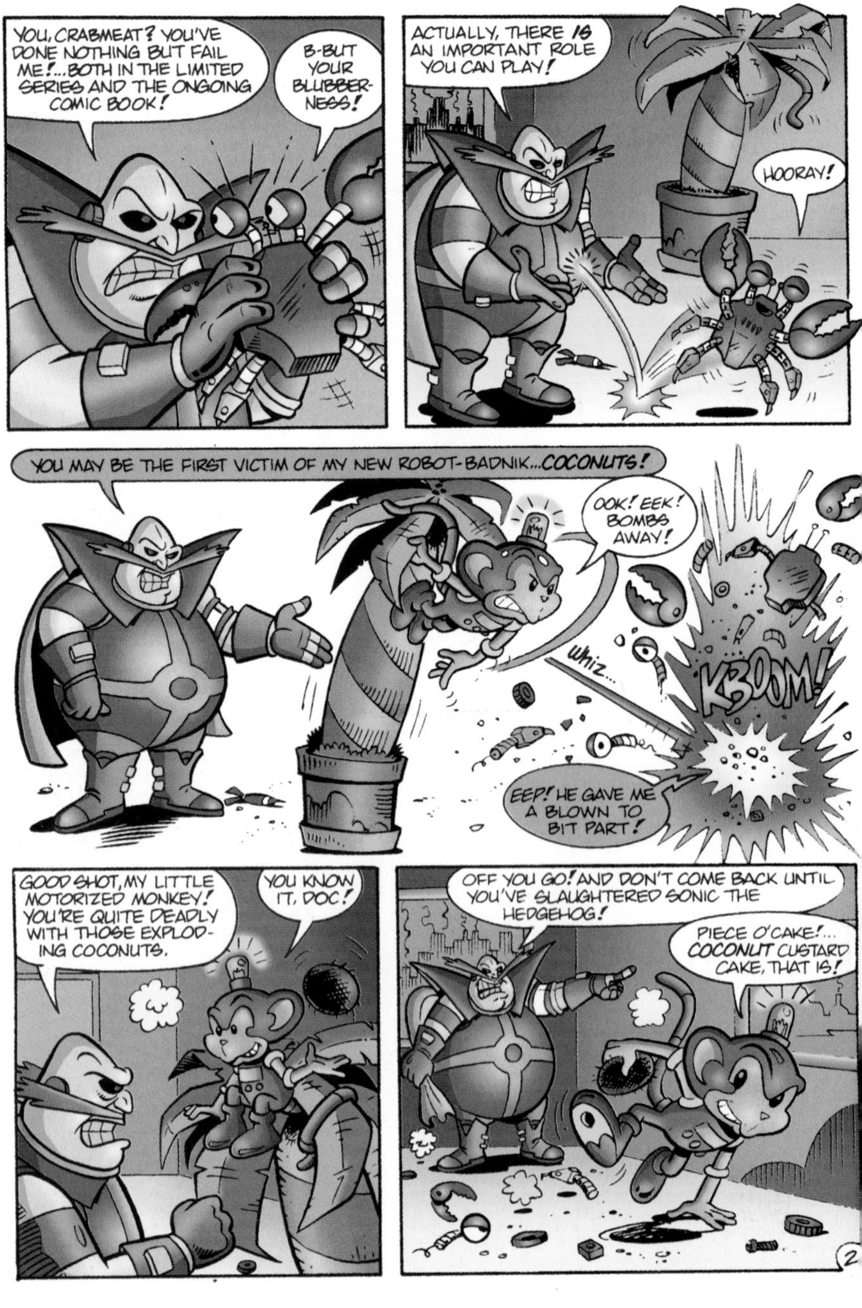
YOU, CRABMEAT? YOU'VE DONE NOTHING BUT FAIL ME!...BOTH IN THE LIMITED SERIES AND THE ONGOING COMIC BOOK!
B-BUT YOUR BLUBBER-NESS!
ACTUALLY, THERE IS AN IMPORTANT ROLE YOU CAN PLAY!
HOORAY!
YOU MAY BE THE FIRST VICTIM OF MY NEW ROBOT-BADNIK...COCONUTS!
OOK! EEK! BOMBS AWAY!
Whiz...
KBOOM!
EEP! HE GAVE ME A BLOWN TO BIT PART!
GOOD SHOT, MY LITTLE MOTORIZED MONKEY! YOU'RE QUITE DEADLY WITH THOSE EXPLODING COCONUTS.
YOU KNOW IT, DOC!
OFF YOU GO! AND DON'T COME BACK UNTIL YOU'VE SLAUGHTERED SONIC THE HEDGEHOG!
PIECE O'CAKE!... COCONUT CUSTARD CAKE, THAT IS!

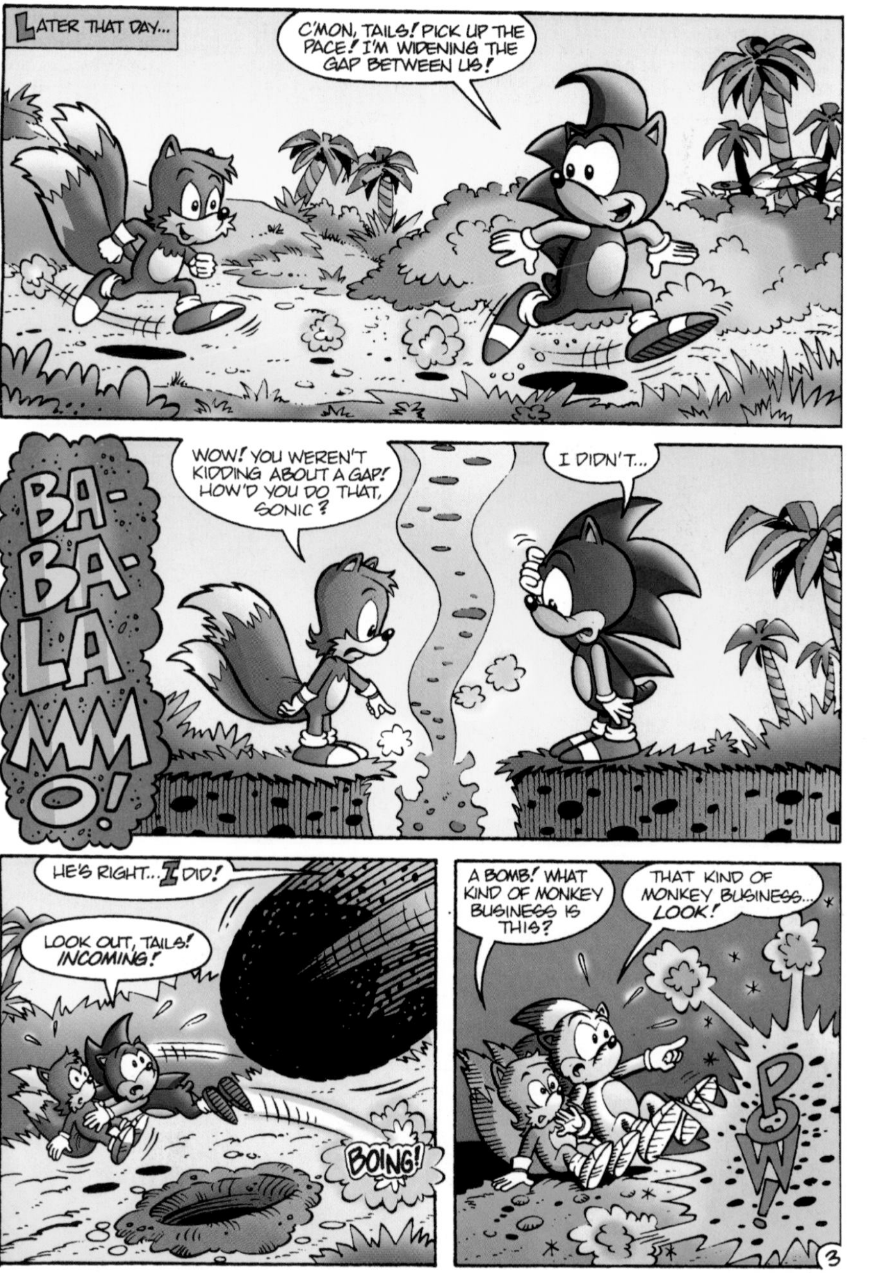
LATER THAT DAY...
C'MON, TAILS! PICK UP THE PACE! I'M WIDENING THE GAP BETWEEN US!
BA-BA-LAMMMO!
WOW! YOU WEREN'T KIDDING ABOUT A GAP! HOW'D YOU DO THAT, SONIC?
I DIDN'T...
HE'S RIGHT... I DID!
LOOK OUT, TAILS! INCOMING!
BOING!
A BOMB! WHAT KIND OF MONKEY BUSINESS IS THIS?
THAT KIND OF MONKEY BUSINESS... LOOK!
POW!
3

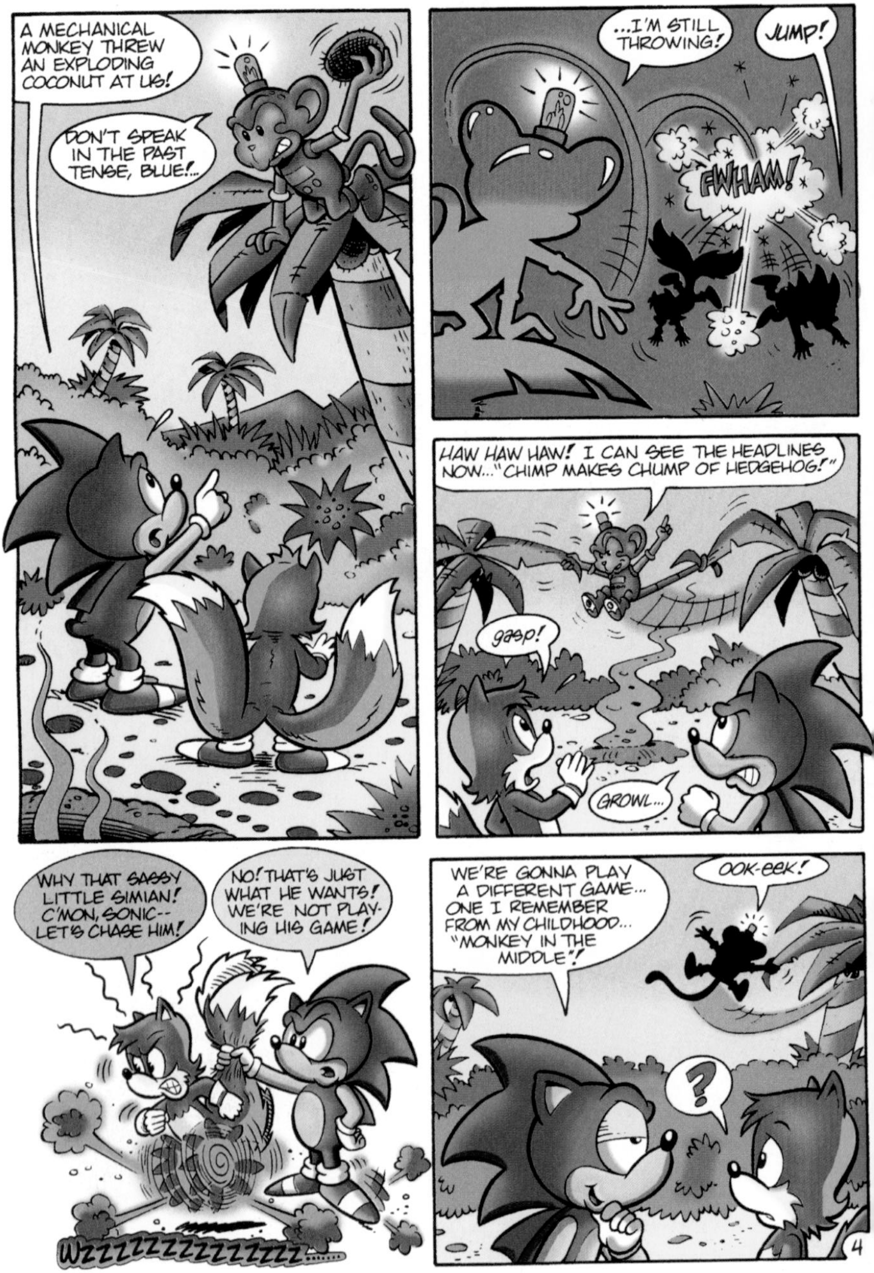

A MECHANICAL MONKEY THREW AN EXPLODING COCONUT AT US!
DON'T SPEAK IN THE PAST TENSE, BLUE!...
...I'M STILL THROWING!
JUMP!
FWHAM!
HAW HAW HAW! I CAN SEE THE HEADLINES NOW..."CHIMP MAKES CHUMP OF HEDGEHOG!"
gasp!
GROWL...
WHY THAT SASSY LITTLE SIMIAN! C'MON, SONIC-- LET'S CHASE HIM!
NO! THAT'S JUST WHAT HE WANTS! WE'RE NOT PLAYING HIS GAME!
WZZZZZZZZZZZZZZ
WE'RE GONNA PLAY A DIFFERENT GAME... ONE I REMEMBER FROM MY CHILDHOOD... "MONKEY IN THE MIDDLE"!
OOK-eek!
?

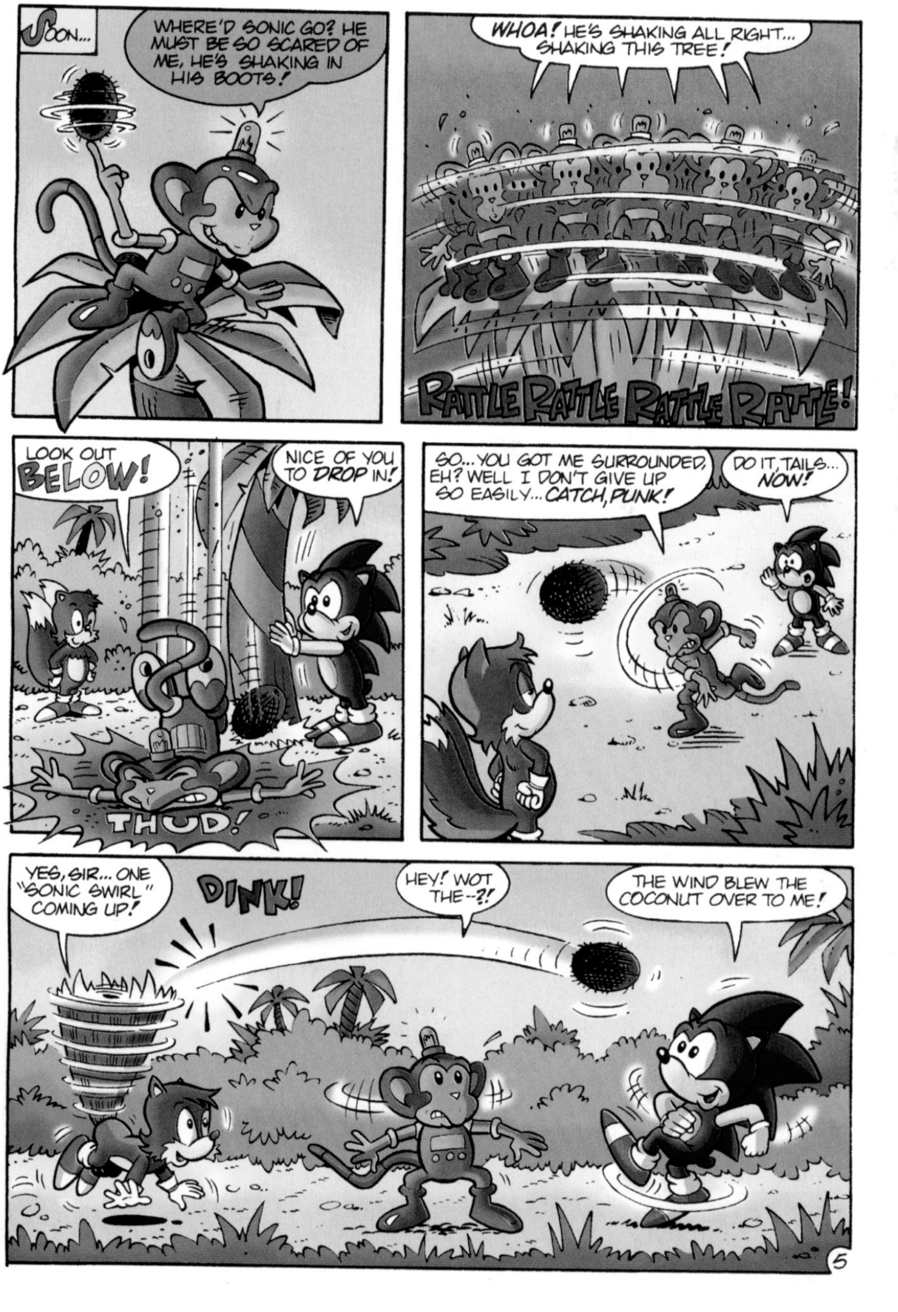
SOON...
WHERE'D SONIC GO? HE MUST BE SO SCARED OF ME, HE'S SHAKING IN HIS BOOTS!
WHOA! HE'S SHAKING ALL RIGHT... SHAKING THIS TREE!
RATTLE RATTLE RATTLE RATTLE!
LOOK OUT BELOW!
NICE OF YOU TO DROP IN!
THUD!
SO... YOU GOT ME SURROUNDED, EH? WELL I DON'T GIVE UP SO EASILY... CATCH, PUNK!
DO IT, TAILS... NOW!
YES, SIR... ONE "SONIC SWIRL" COMING UP!
DINK!
HEY! WOT THE--?!
THE WIND BLEW THE COCONUT OVER TO ME!

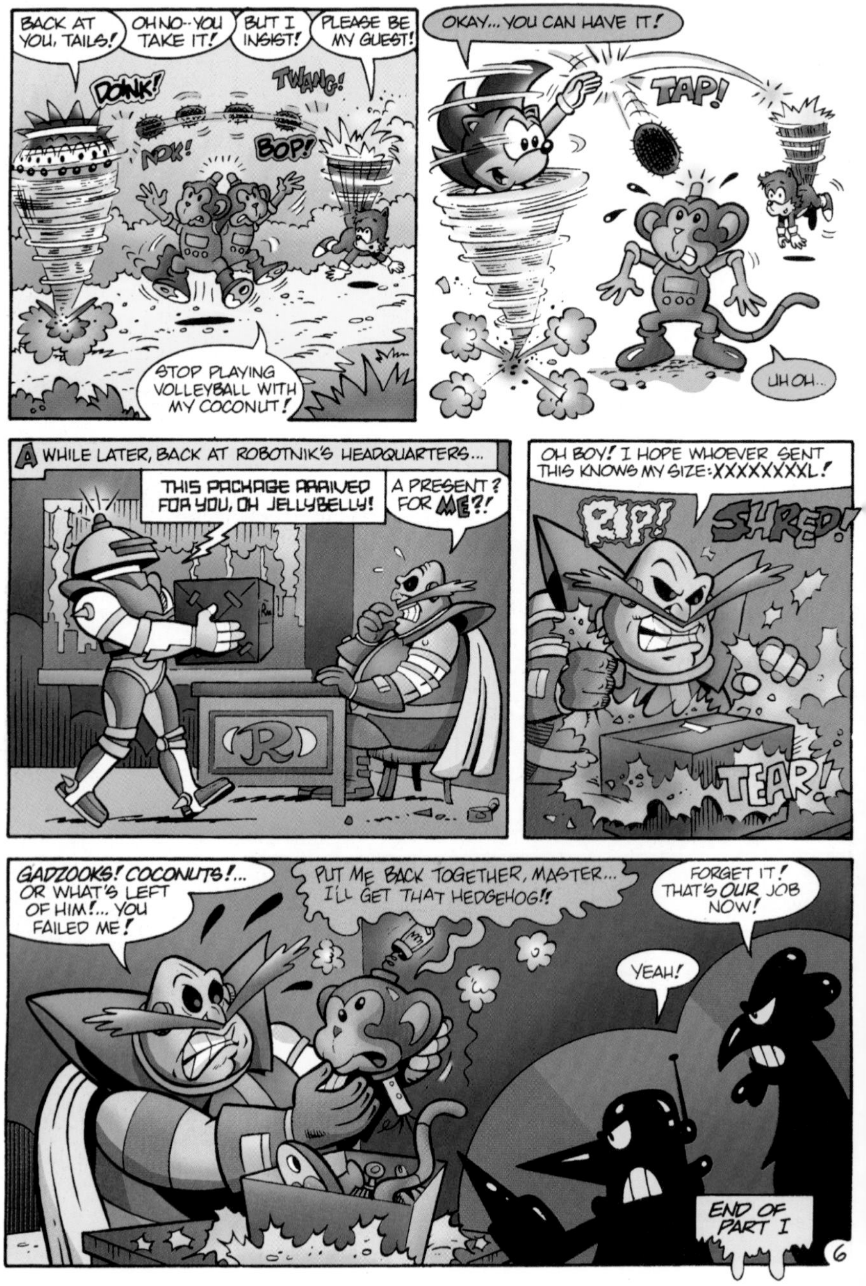
BACK AT YOU, TAILS!
OH NO-- YOU TAKE IT!
BUT I INSIST!
PLEASE BE MY GUEST!
DOINK!
TWANG!
NOK!
BOP!
STOP PLAYING VOLLEYBALL WITH MY COCONUT!
OKAY... YOU CAN HAVE IT!
TAP!
UH OH...
A WHILE LATER, BACK AT ROBOTNIK'S HEADQUARTERS...
THIS PACKAGE ARRIVED FOR YOU, OH JELLYBELLY!
A PRESENT? FOR ME?!
OH BOY! I HOPE WHOEVER SENT THIS KNOWS MY SIZE: XXXXXXXXL!
RIP!
SHRED!
TEAR!
GADZOOKS! COCONUTS!... OR WHAT'S LEFT OF HIM!... YOU FAILED ME!
PUT ME BACK TOGETHER, MASTER... I'LL GET THAT HEDGEHOG!!
FORGET IT! THAT'S OUR JOB NOW!
YEAH!
END OF PART I

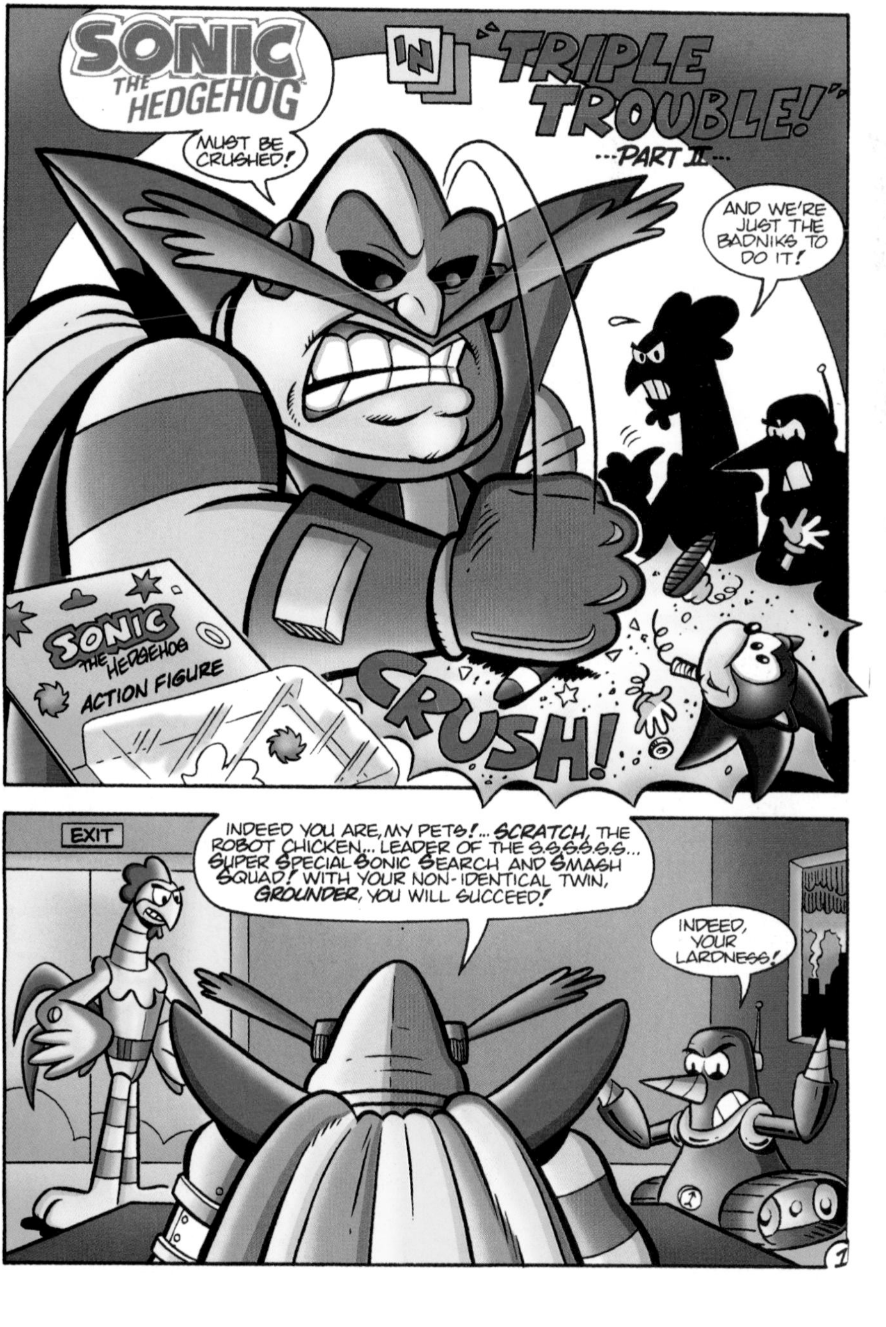
SONIC THE HEDGEHOG
MUST BE CRUSHED!
'IN' "TRIPLE TROUBLE!"
---PART II---
AND WE'RE JUST THE BADNIKS TO DO IT!
SONIC THE HEDGEHOG ACTION FIGURE
CRUSH!
EXIT
INDEED YOU ARE, MY PETS!... SCRATCH, THE ROBOT CHICKEN... LEADER OF THE S.S.S.S.S.S... SUPER SPECIAL SONIC SEARCH AND SMASH SQUAD! WITH YOUR NON-IDENTICAL TWIN, GROUNDER, YOU WILL SUCCEED!
INDEED, YOUR LARDNESS!

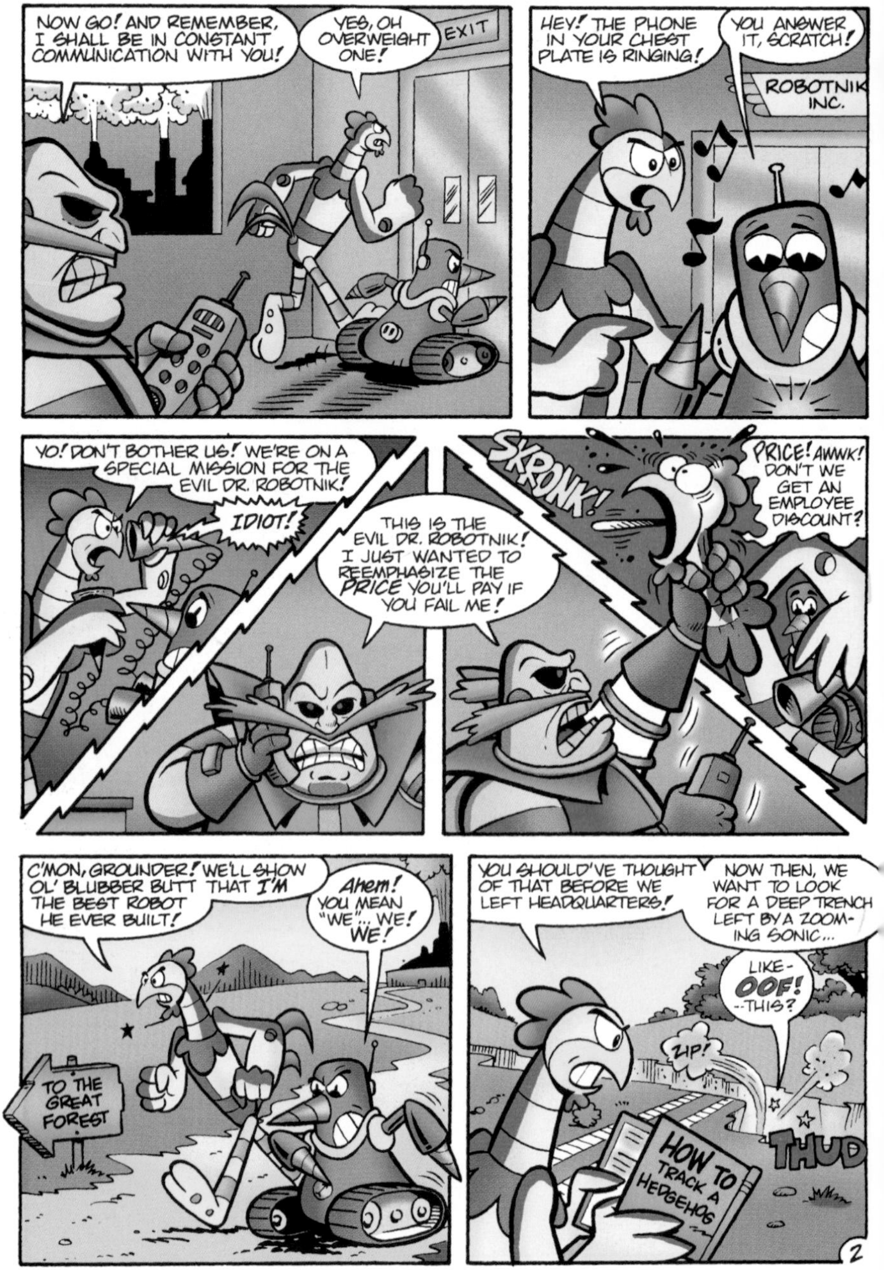
NOW GO! AND REMEMBER, I SHALL BE IN CONSTANT COMMUNICATION WITH YOU!
YES, OH OVERWEIGHT ONE!
EXIT
HEY! THE PHONE IN YOUR CHEST PLATE IS RINGING!
YOU ANSWER IT, SCRATCH!
ROBOTNIK INC.
YO! DON'T BOTHER US! WE'RE ON A SPECIAL MISSION FOR THE EVIL DR. ROBOTNIK!
IDIOT!
THIS IS THE EVIL DR. ROBOTNIK! I JUST WANTED TO REEMPHASIZE THE PRICE YOU'LL PAY IF YOU FAIL ME!
SKRONK!
PRICE! AWWK! DON'T WE GET AN EMPLOYEE DISCOUNT?
C'MON, GROUNDER! WE'LL SHOW OL' BLUBBER BUTT THAT I'M THE BEST ROBOT HE EVER BUILT!
Ahem! YOU MEAN "WE"... WE! WE!
TO THE GREAT FOREST
YOU SHOULD'VE THOUGHT OF THAT BEFORE WE LEFT HEADQUARTERS!
NOW THEN, WE WANT TO LOOK FOR A DEEP TRENCH LEFT BY A ZOOMING SONIC...
LIKE- OOF! --THIS?
ZIP!
THUD
HOW TO TRACK A HEDGEHOG

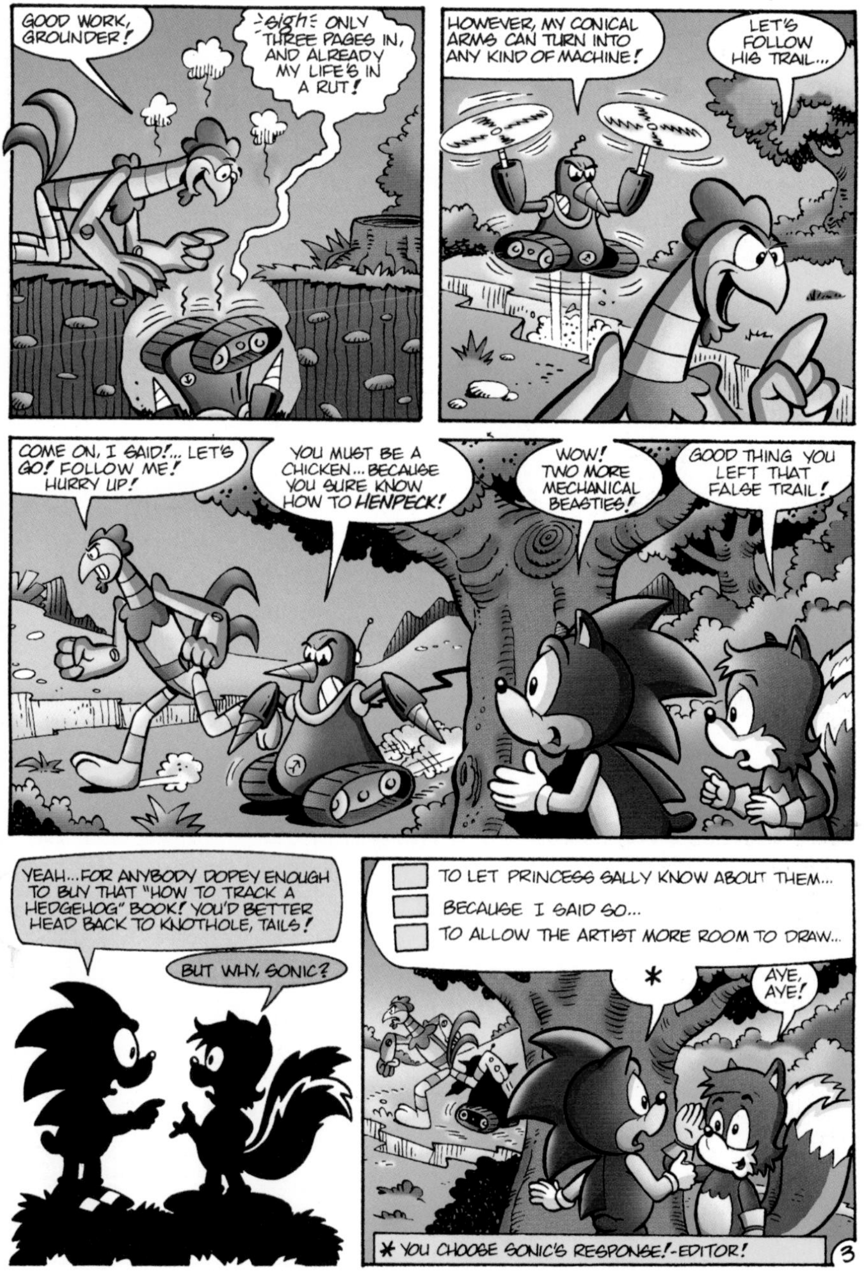
GOOD WORK, GROUNDER!
sigh ONLY THREE PAGES IN, AND ALREADY MY LIFE'S IN A RUT!
HOWEVER, MY CONICAL ARMS CAN TURN INTO ANY KIND OF MACHINE!
LET'S FOLLOW HIS TRAIL...
COME ON, I SAID!... LET'S GO! FOLLOW ME! HURRY UP!
YOU MUST BE A CHICKEN... BECAUSE YOU SURE KNOW HOW TO HENPECK!
WOW! TWO MORE MECHANICAL BEASTIES!
GOOD THING YOU LEFT THAT FALSE TRAIL!
YEAH... FOR ANYBODY DOPEY ENOUGH TO BUY THAT "HOW TO TRACK A HEDGEHOG" BOOK! YOU'D BETTER HEAD BACK TO KNOTHOLE, TAILS!
BUT WHY, SONIC?
TO LET PRINCESS SALLY KNOW ABOUT THEM...
BECAUSE I SAID SO...
TO ALLOW THE ARTIST MORE ROOM TO DRAW...
*
AYE, AYE!
* YOU CHOOSE SONIC'S RESPONSE! -EDITOR!

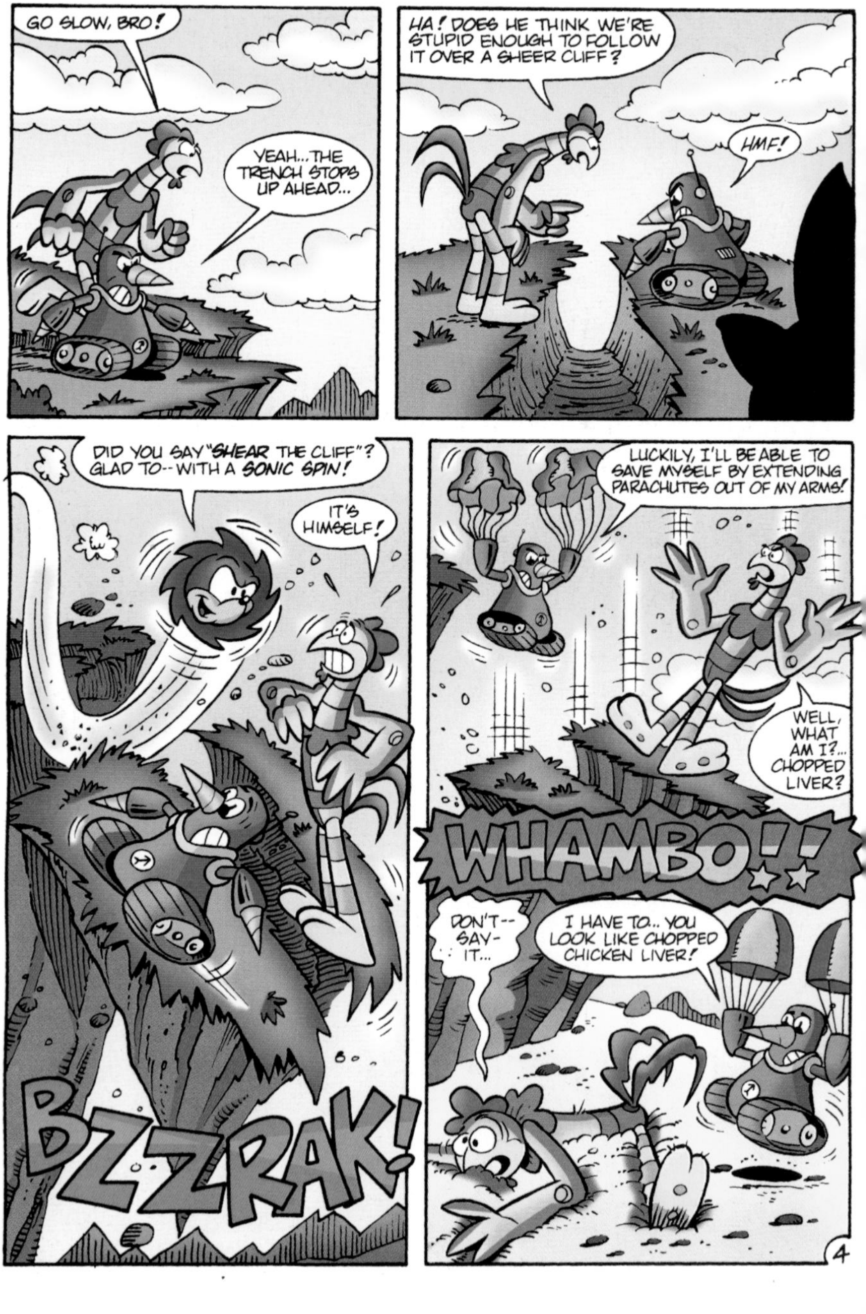

GO SLOW, BRO!
YEAH... THE TRENCH STOPS UP AHEAD...
HA! DOES HE THINK WE'RE STUPID ENOUGH TO FOLLOW IT OVER A SHEER CLIFF?
HMF!
DID YOU SAY "SHEAR THE CLIFF"? GLAD TO-- WITH A SONIC SPIN!
IT'S HIMSELF!
BZZRAK!
LUCKILY, I'LL BE ABLE TO SAVE MYSELF BY EXTENDING PARACHUTES OUT OF MY ARMS!
WELL, WHAT AM I?... CHOPPED LIVER?
WHAMBO!!
DON'T-- SAY- IT...
I HAVE TO... YOU LOOK LIKE CHOPPED CHICKEN LIVER!

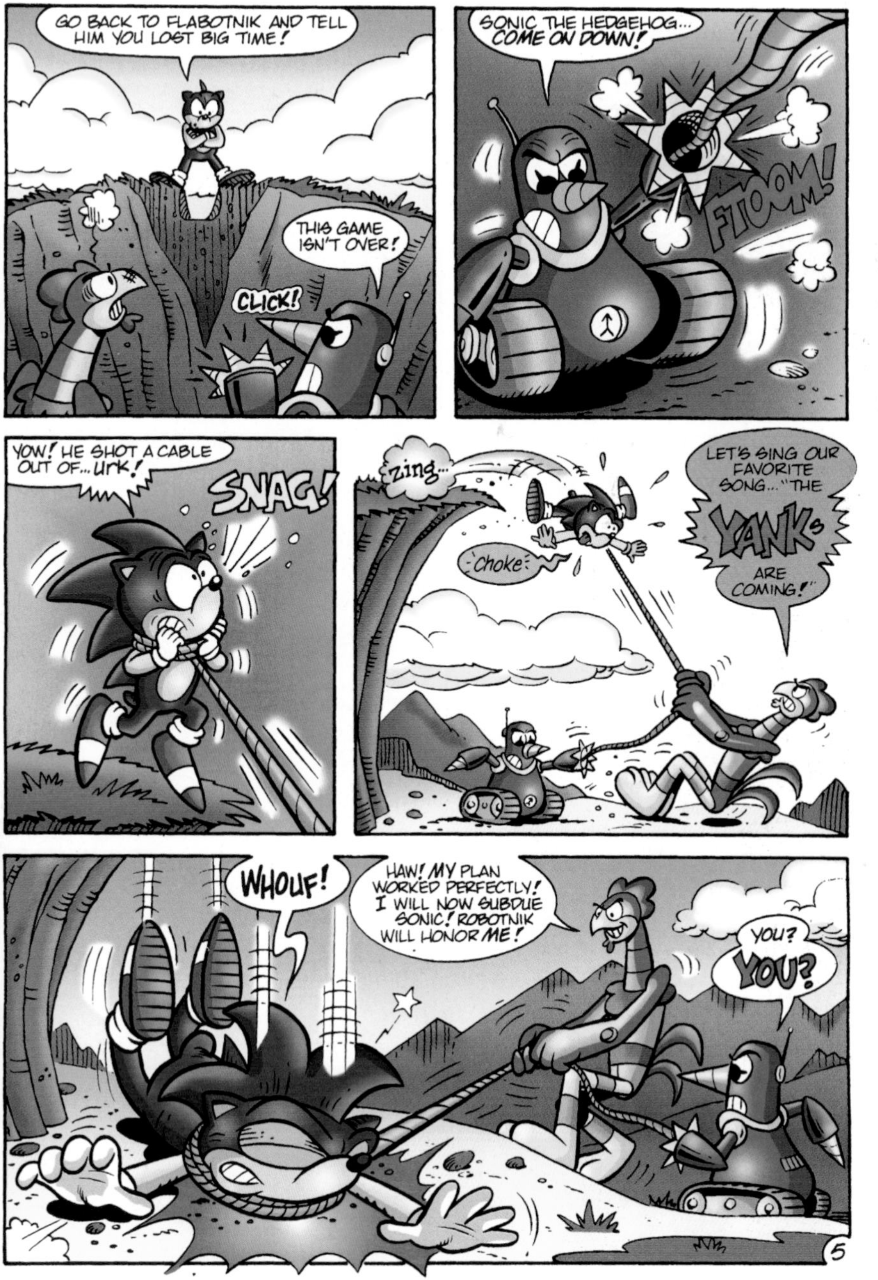
GO BACK TO FLABOTNIK AND TELL HIM YOU LOST BIG TIME!
THIS GAME ISN'T OVER!
CLICK!
SONIC THE HEDGEHOG... COME ON DOWN!
FTOOM!
YOW! HE SHOT A CABLE OUT OF... urk!
SNAG!
zing...
LET'S SING OUR FAVORITE SONG... "THE YANKs ARE COMING!"
Choke
WHOUF!
HAW! MY PLAN WORKED PERFECTLY! I WILL NOW SUBDUE SONIC! ROBOTNIK WILL HONOR ME!
YOU? YOU?
5

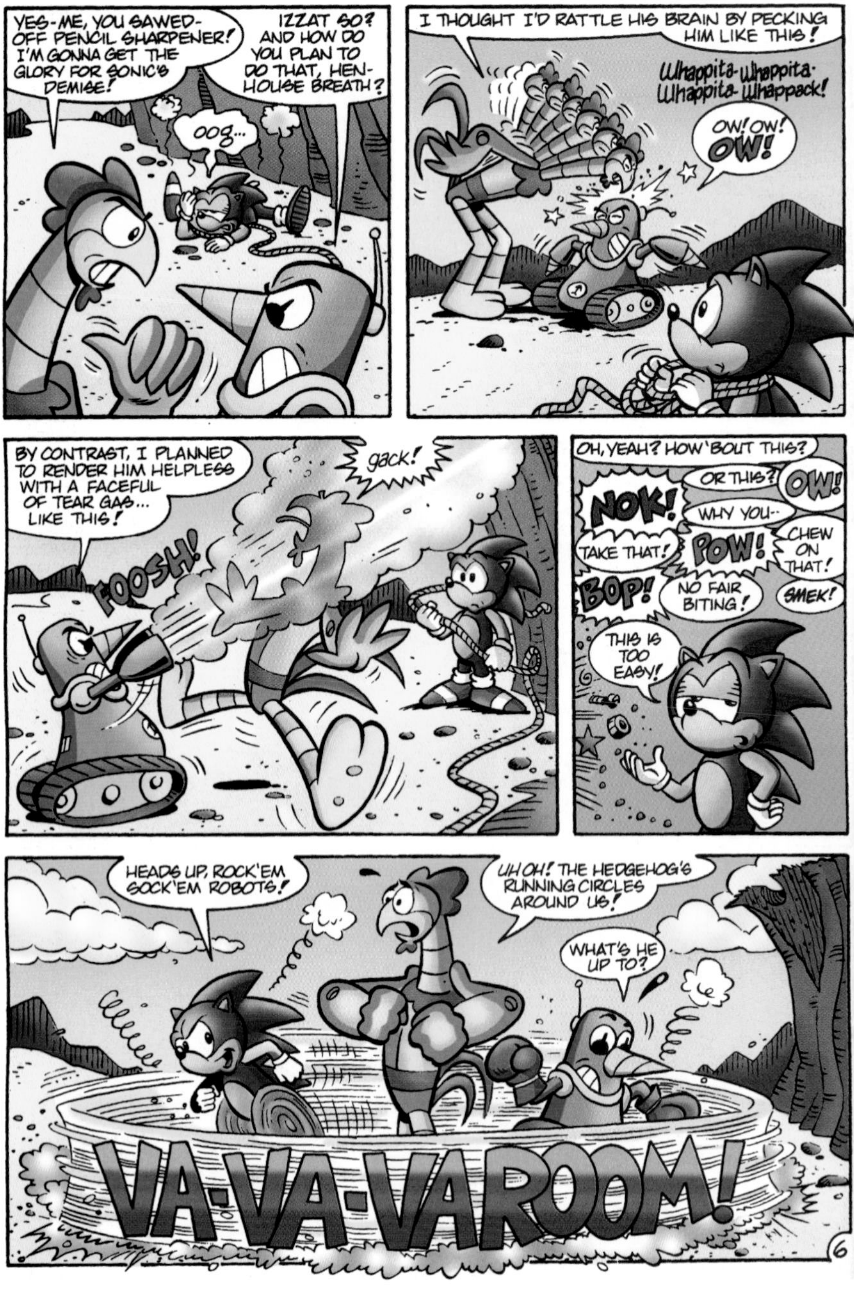

YES-ME, YOU SAWED-OFF PENCIL SHARPENER! I'M GONNA GET THE GLORY FOR SONIC'S DEMISE!
IZZAT SO? AND HOW DO YOU PLAN TO DO THAT, HEN-HOUSE BREATH?
OOG...
I THOUGHT I'D RATTLE HIS BRAIN BY PECKING HIM LIKE THIS!
Whappita-Whappita-Whappita-Whappack!
OW! OW! OW!
BY CONTRAST, I PLANNED TO RENDER HIM HELPLESS WITH A FACEFUL OF TEAR GAS... LIKE THIS!
gack!
FOOSH!
OH, YEAH? HOW 'BOUT THIS?
OR THIS?
OW!
NOK!
WHY YOU--
TAKE THAT!
POW!
CHEW ON THAT!
BOP!
NO FAIR BITING!
SMEK!
THIS IS TOO EASY!
HEADS UP, ROCK 'EM SOCK 'EM ROBOTS!
UH OH! THE HEDGEHOG'S RUNNING CIRCLES AROUND US!
WHAT'S HE UP TO?
VA-VA-VAROOM!

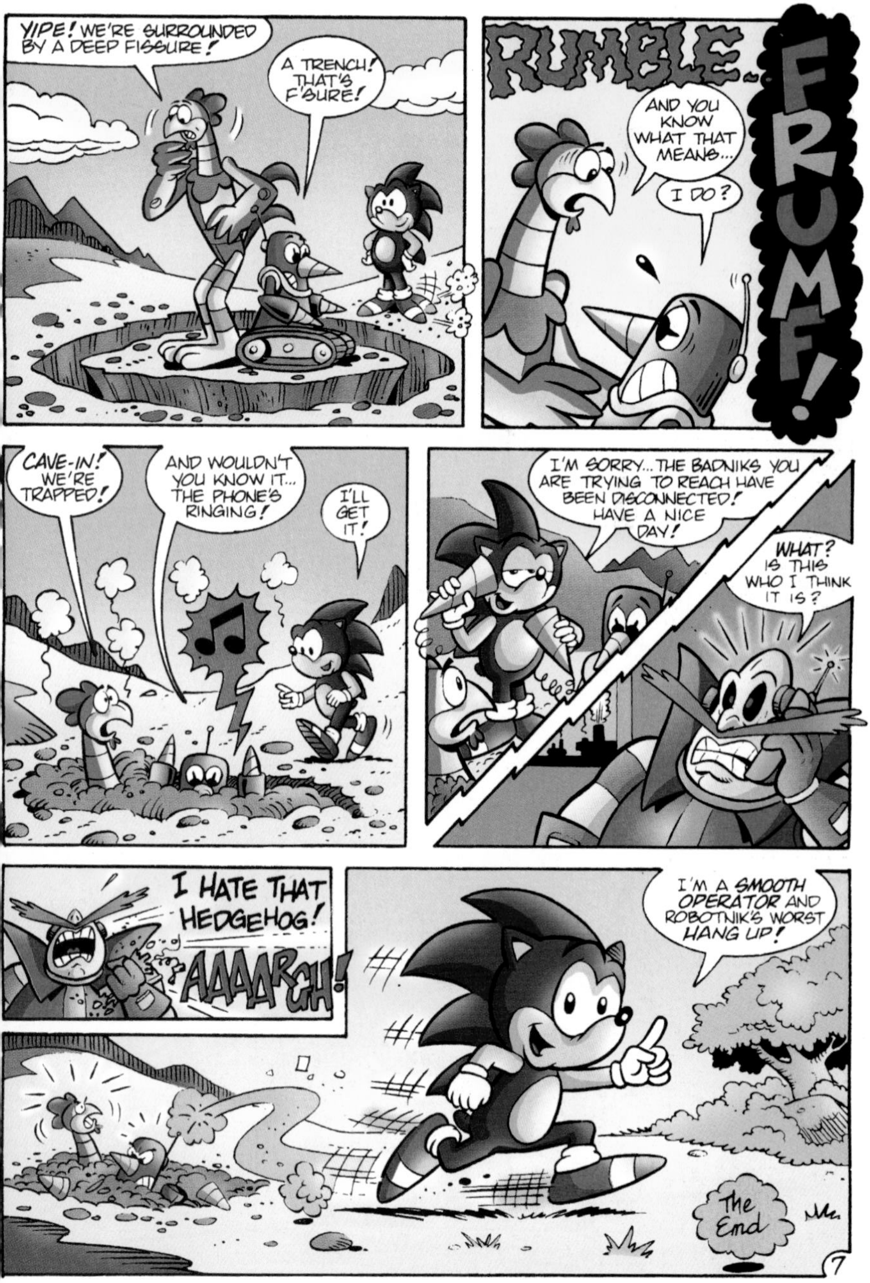

YIPE! WE'RE SURROUNDED BY A DEEP FISSURE!
A TRENCH! THAT'S F'SURE!
RUMBLE...
AND YOU KNOW WHAT THAT MEANS...
I DO?
FRUMF!
CAVE-IN! WE'RE TRAPPED!
AND WOULDN'T YOU KNOW IT... THE PHONE'S RINGING!
I'LL GET IT!
I'M SORRY... THE BADNIKS YOU ARE TRYING TO REACH HAVE BEEN DISCONNECTED! HAVE A NICE DAY!
WHAT? IS THIS WHO I THINK IT IS?
I HATE THAT HEDGEHOG!
AAAARGH!
I'M A SMOOTH OPERATOR AND ROBOTNIK'S WORST HANG UP!
The End

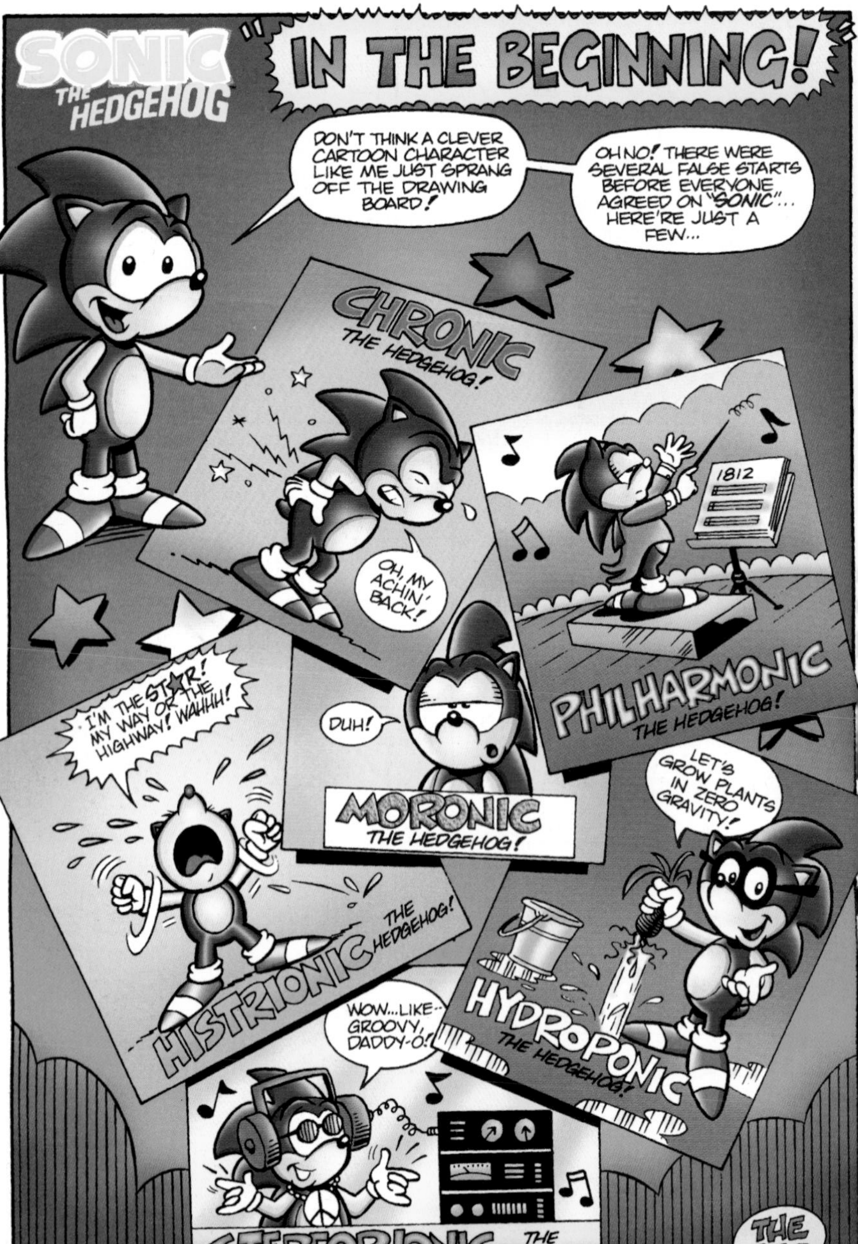
SONIC THE HEDGEHOG
"IN THE BEGINNING!"
DON'T THINK A CLEVER CARTOON CHARACTER LIKE ME JUST SPRANG OFF THE DRAWING BOARD!
OH NO! THERE WERE SEVERAL FALSE STARTS BEFORE EVERYONE AGREED ON "SONIC"... HERE'RE JUST A FEW...
CHRONIC THE HEDGEHOG!
OH, MY ACHIN' BACK!
1812
PHILHARMONIC THE HEDGEHOG!
I'M THE STAR! MY WAY OR THE HIGHWAY! WAHHH!
DUH!
MORONIC THE HEDGEHOG!
HISTRIONIC THE HEDGEHOG!
LET'S GROW PLANTS IN ZERO GRAVITY!
HYDROPONIC THE HEDGEHOG!
WOW...LIKE... GROOVY, DADDY-O!
STEREOPHONIC THE HEDGEHOG!
THE END

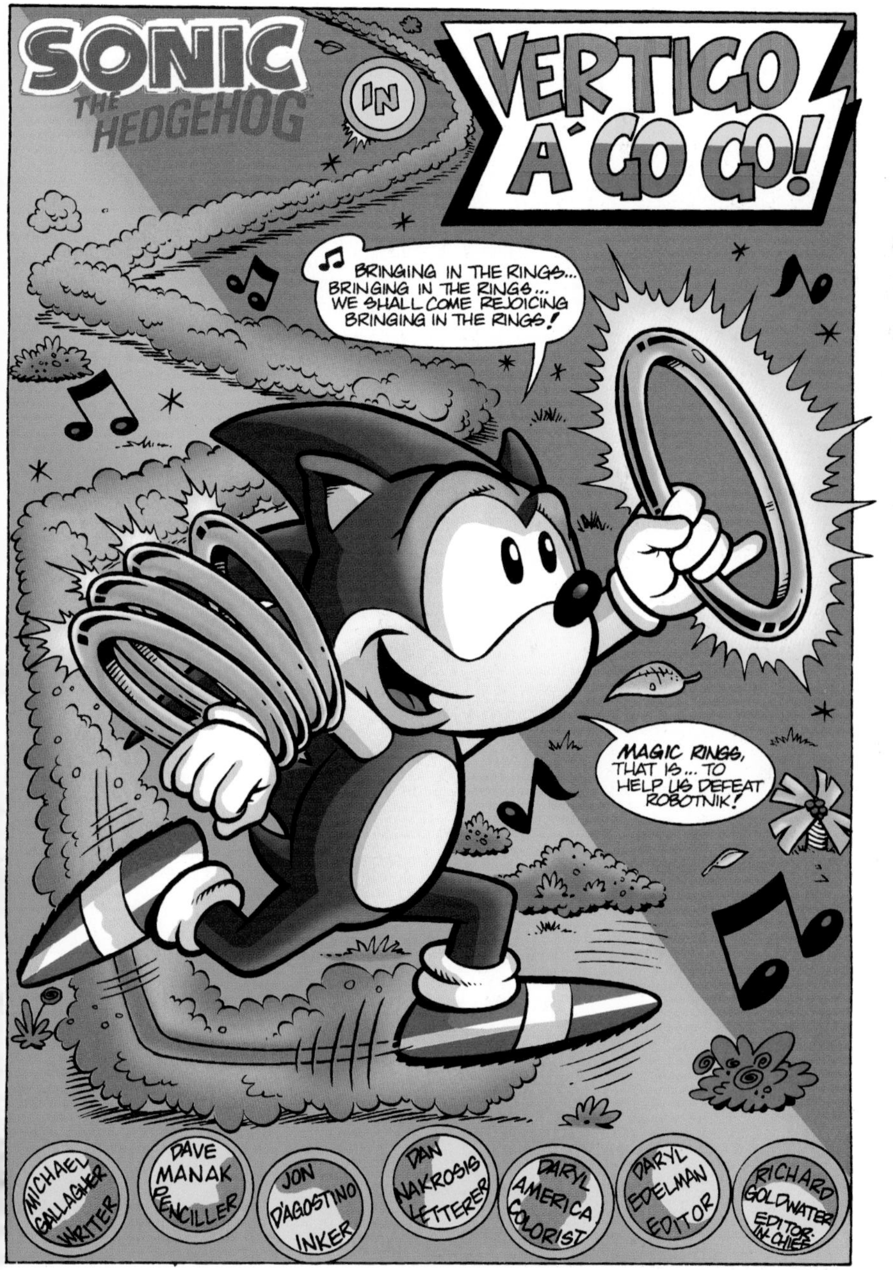
SONIC THE HEDGEHOG
IN
VERTIGO A'GO GO!
BRINGING IN THE RINGS... BRINGING IN THE RINGS... WE SHALL COME REJOICING BRINGING IN THE RINGS!
MAGIC RINGS, THAT IS... TO HELP US DEFEAT ROBOTNIK!
MICHAEL GALLAGHER WRITER
DAVE MANAK PENCILLER
JON D'AGOSTINO INKER
DAN NAKROSIS LETTERER
DARYL AMERICA COLORIST
DARYL EDELMAN EDITOR
RICHARD GOLDWATER EDITOR-IN-CHIEF

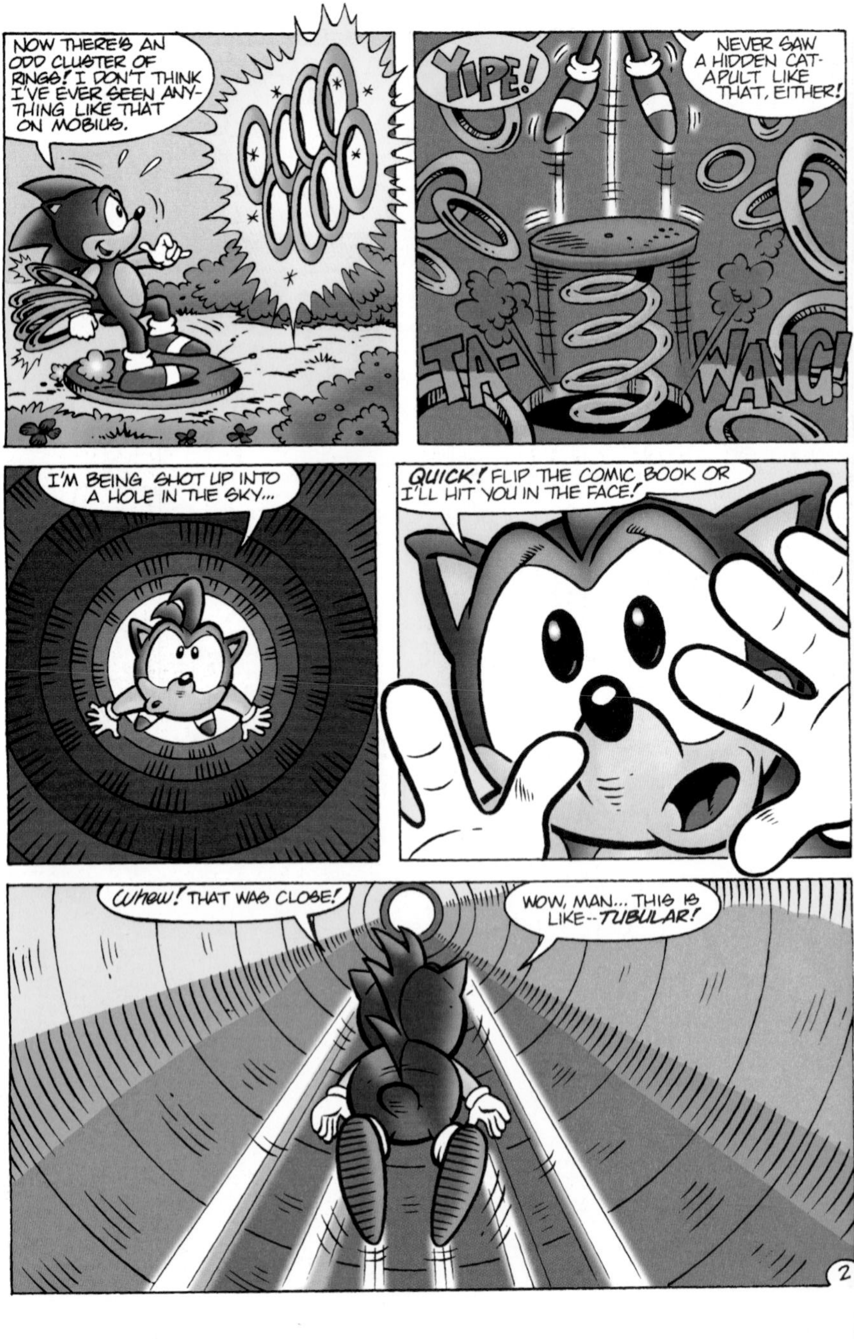

NOW THERE'S AN ODD CLUSTER OF RINGS! I DON'T THINK I'VE EVER SEEN ANYTHING LIKE THAT ON MOBIUS.
YIPE!
NEVER SAW A HIDDEN CATAPULT LIKE THAT, EITHER!
TA-WANG!
I'M BEING SHOT UP INTO A HOLE IN THE SKY...
QUICK! FLIP THE COMIC BOOK OR I'LL HIT YOU IN THE FACE!
Whew! THAT WAS CLOSE!
WOW, MAN... THIS IS LIKE--TUBULAR!

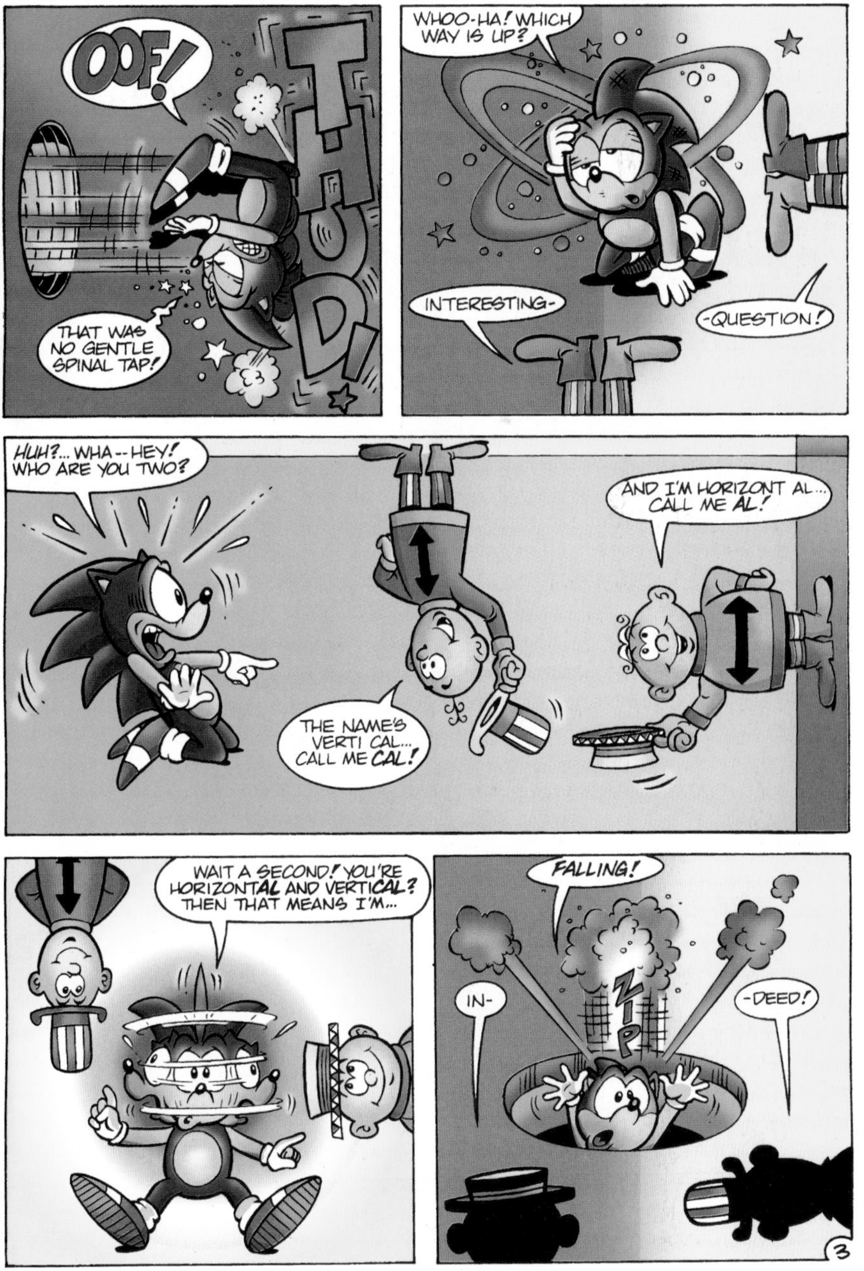
OOF!
THUD!
THAT WAS NO GENTLE SPINAL TAP!
WHOO-HA! WHICH WAY IS UP?
INTERESTING-
-QUESTION!
HUH?... WHA--HEY! WHO ARE YOU TWO?
THE NAME'S VERTI CAL... CALL ME CAL!
AND I'M HORIZONT AL... CALL ME AL!
WAIT A SECOND! YOU'RE HORIZONTAL AND VERTICAL? THEN THAT MEANS I'M...
FALLING!
IN-
ZIP
-DEED!

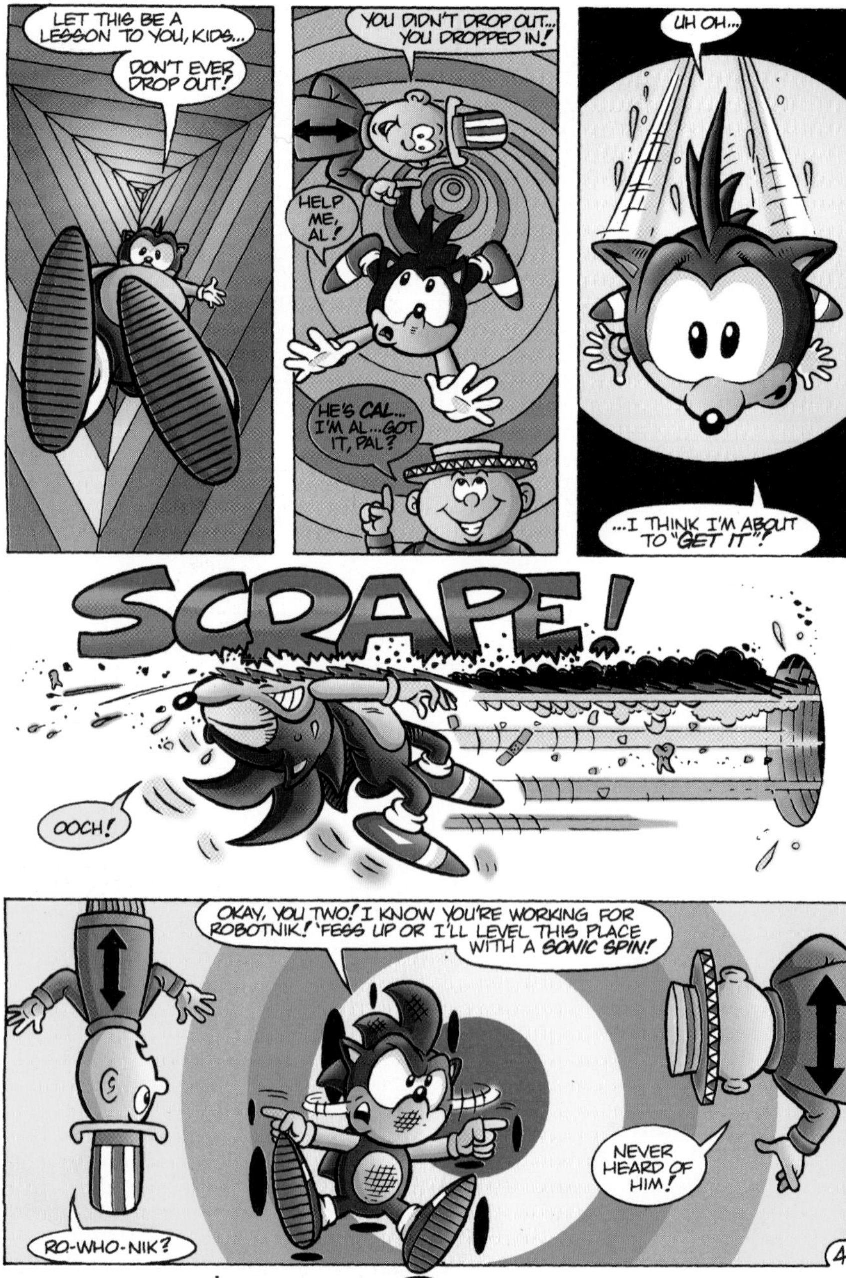
LET THIS BE A LESSON TO YOU, KIDS...
DON'T EVER DROP OUT!
YOU DIDN'T DROP OUT... YOU DROPPED IN!
HELP ME, AL!
HE'S CAL... I'M AL... GOT IT, PAL?
UH OH...
...I THINK I'M ABOUT TO "GET IT"!
SCRAPE!
OOCH!
OKAY, YOU TWO! I KNOW YOU'RE WORKING FOR ROBOTNIK! 'FESS UP OR I'LL LEVEL THIS PLACE WITH A SONIC SPIN!
NEVER HEARD OF HIM!
RO-WHO-NIK?

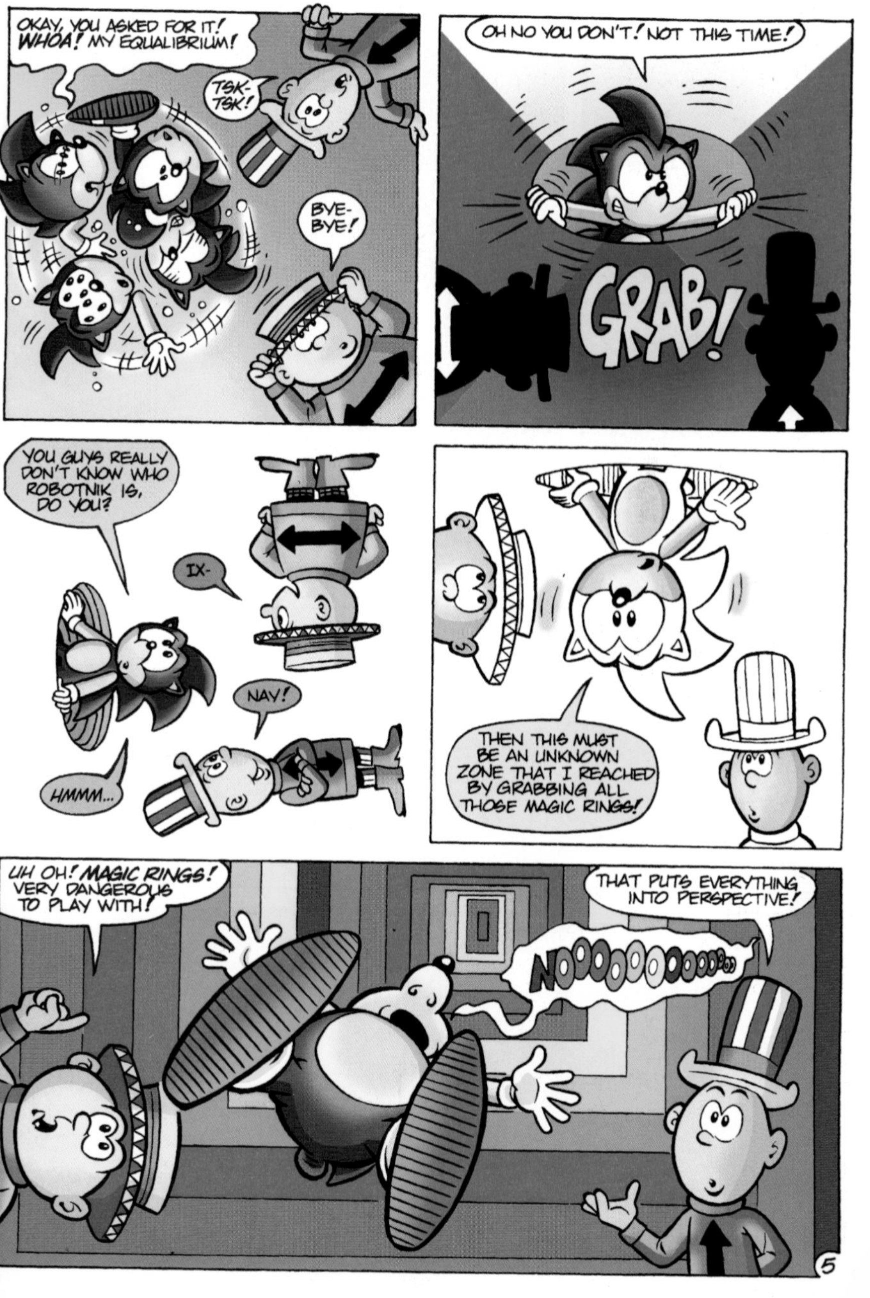
OKAY, YOU ASKED FOR IT! WHOA! MY EQUALIBRIUM!
TSK-TSK!
BYE-BYE!
OH NO YOU DON'T! NOT THIS TIME!
GRAB!
YOU GUYS REALLY DON'T KNOW WHO ROBOTNIK IS, DO YOU?
IX-
NAY!
HMMM...
THEN THIS MUST BE AN UNKNOWN ZONE THAT I REACHED BY GRABBING ALL THOSE MAGIC RINGS!
UH OH! MAGIC RINGS! VERY DANGEROUS TO PLAY WITH!
THAT PUTS EVERYTHING INTO PERSPECTIVE!
NOOOOOOOOOOOoo

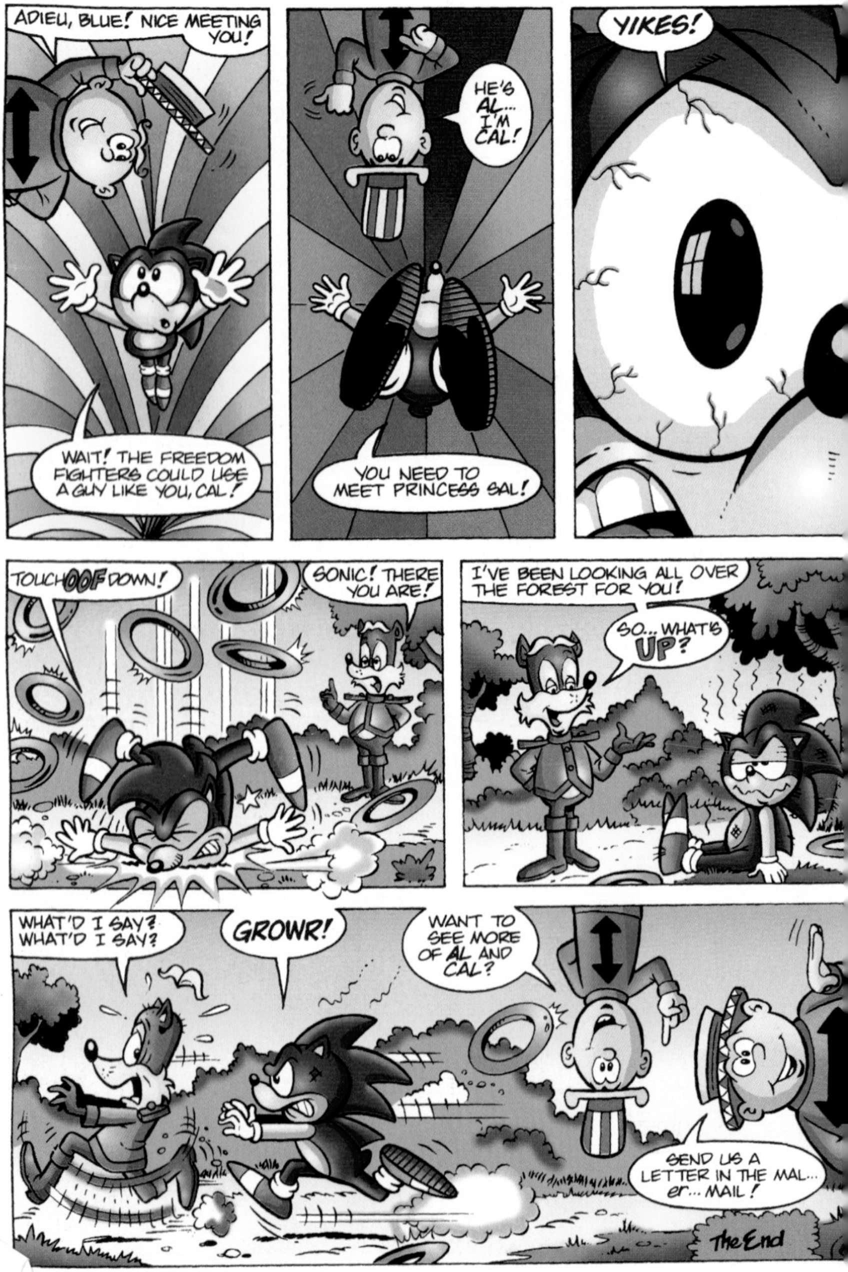
ADIEU, BLUE! NICE MEETING YOU!
WAIT! THE FREEDOM FIGHTERS COULD USE A GUY LIKE YOU, CAL!
HE'S AL... I'M CAL!
YOU NEED TO MEET PRINCESS SAL!
YIKES!
TOUCHOOFDOWN!
SONIC! THERE YOU ARE!
I'VE BEEN LOOKING ALL OVER THE FOREST FOR YOU!
SO... WHAT'S UP?
WHAT'D I SAY? WHAT'D I SAY?
GROWR!
WANT TO SEE MORE OF AL AND CAL?
SEND US A LETTER IN THE MAL... er... MAIL!
The End

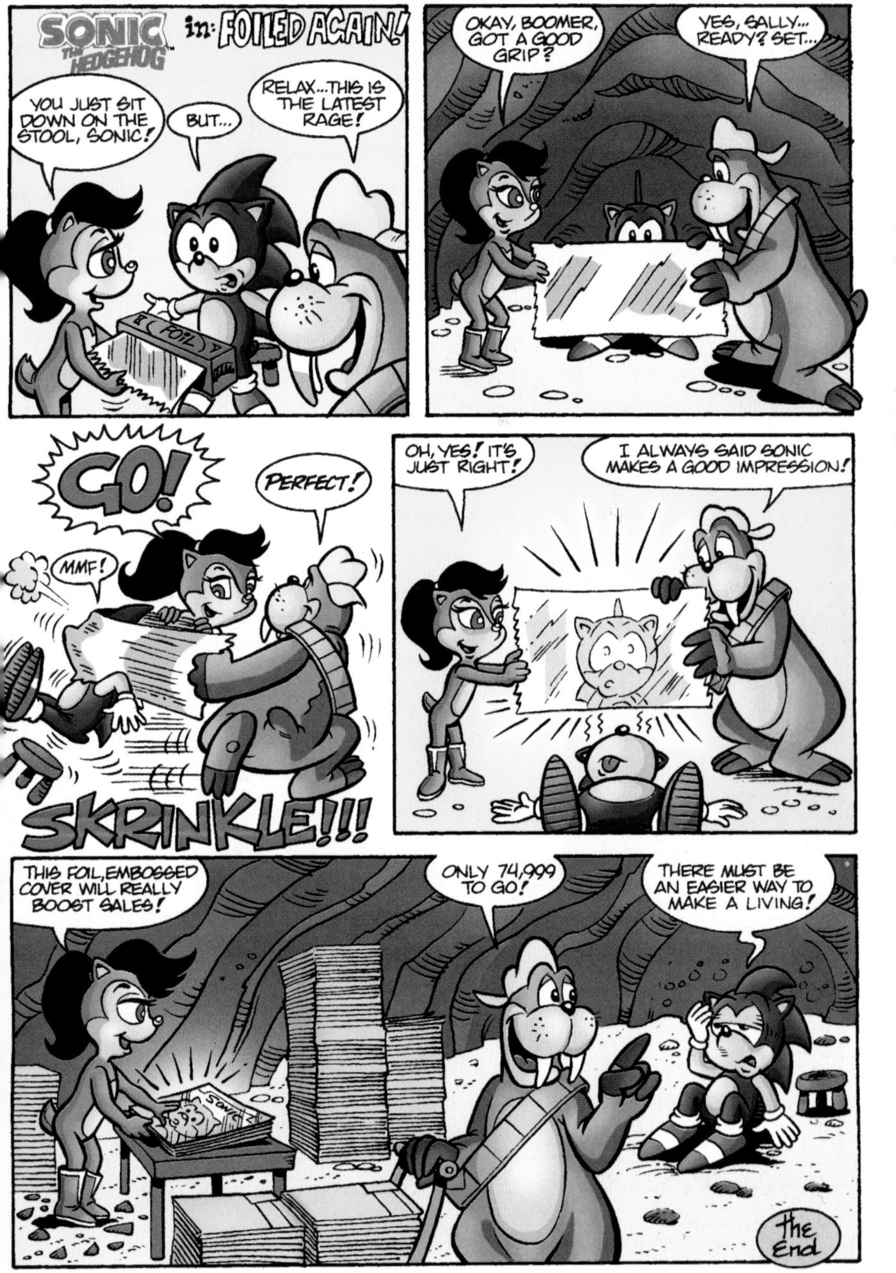
SONIC THE HEDGEHOG in: FOILED AGAIN!
YOU JUST SIT DOWN ON THE STOOL, SONIC!
BUT...
RELAX...THIS IS THE LATEST RAGE!
FOIL
OKAY, BOOMER, GOT A GOOD GRIP?
YES, SALLY... READY? SET...
GO!
PERFECT!
MMF!
SKRINKLE!!!
OH, YES! IT'S JUST RIGHT!
I ALWAYS SAID SONIC MAKES A GOOD IMPRESSION!
THIS FOIL, EMBOSSED COVER WILL REALLY BOOST SALES!
ONLY 74,999 TO GO!
THERE MUST BE AN EASIER WAY TO MAKE A LIVING!
SONIC
the End

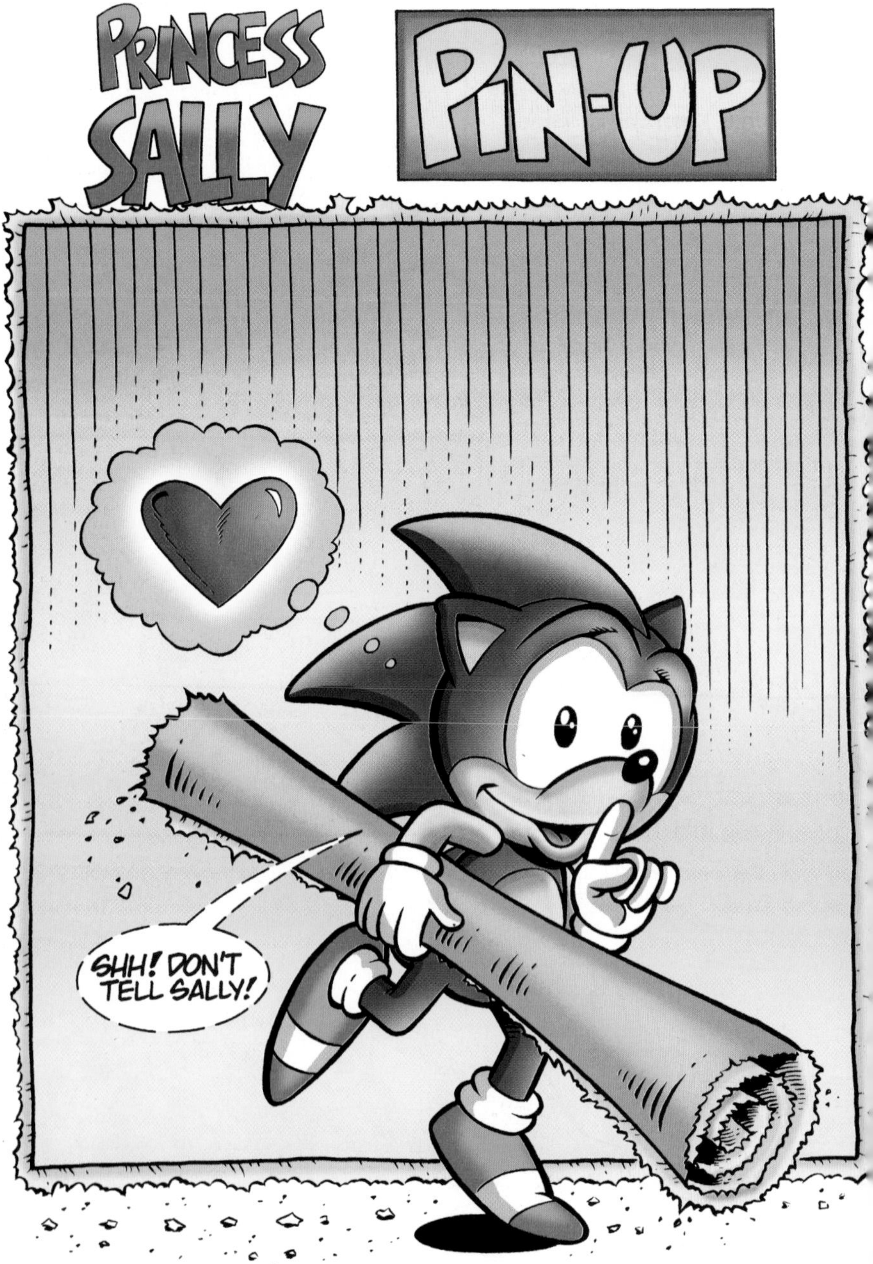
PRINCESS SALLY
PIN-UP
SHH! DON'T TELL SALLY!

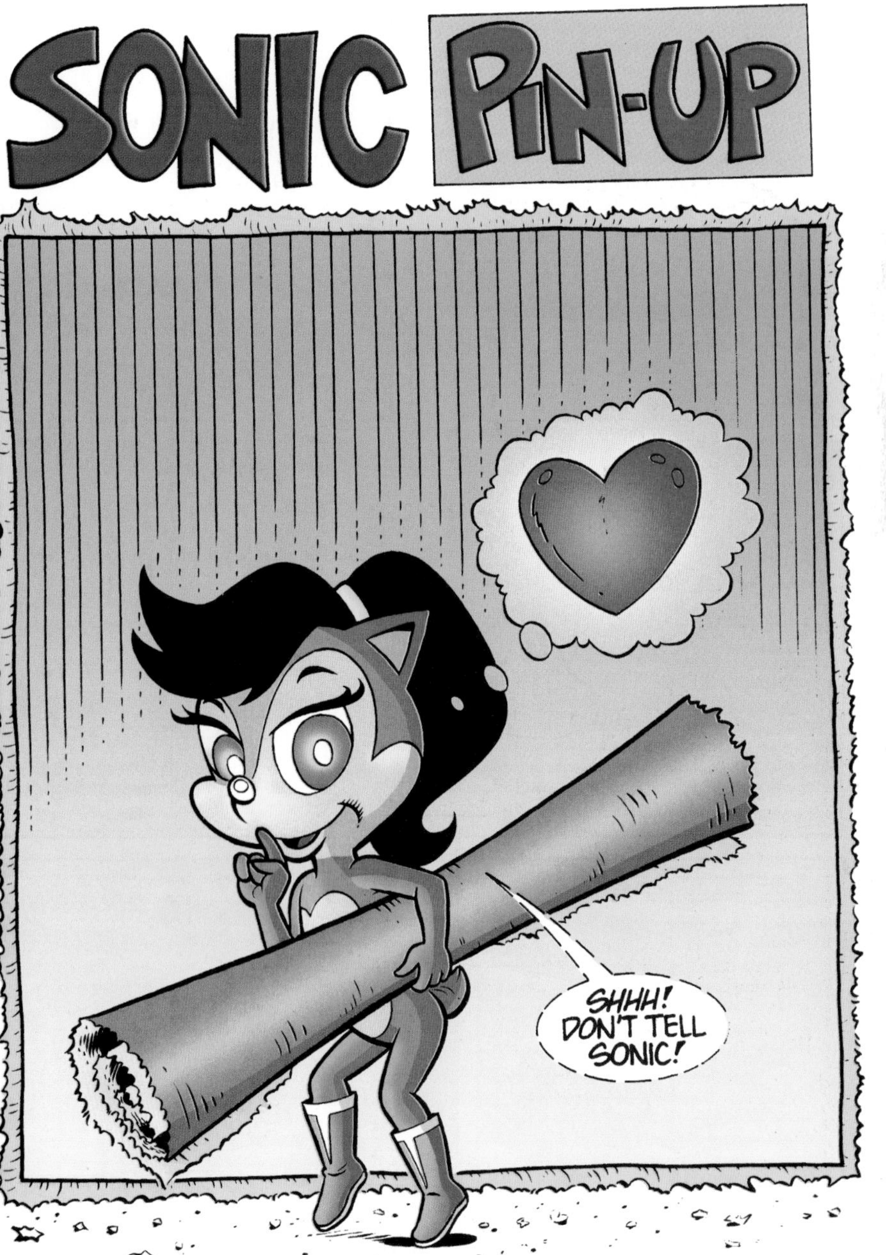
SONIC PIN-UP
SHHH! DON'T TELL SONIC!

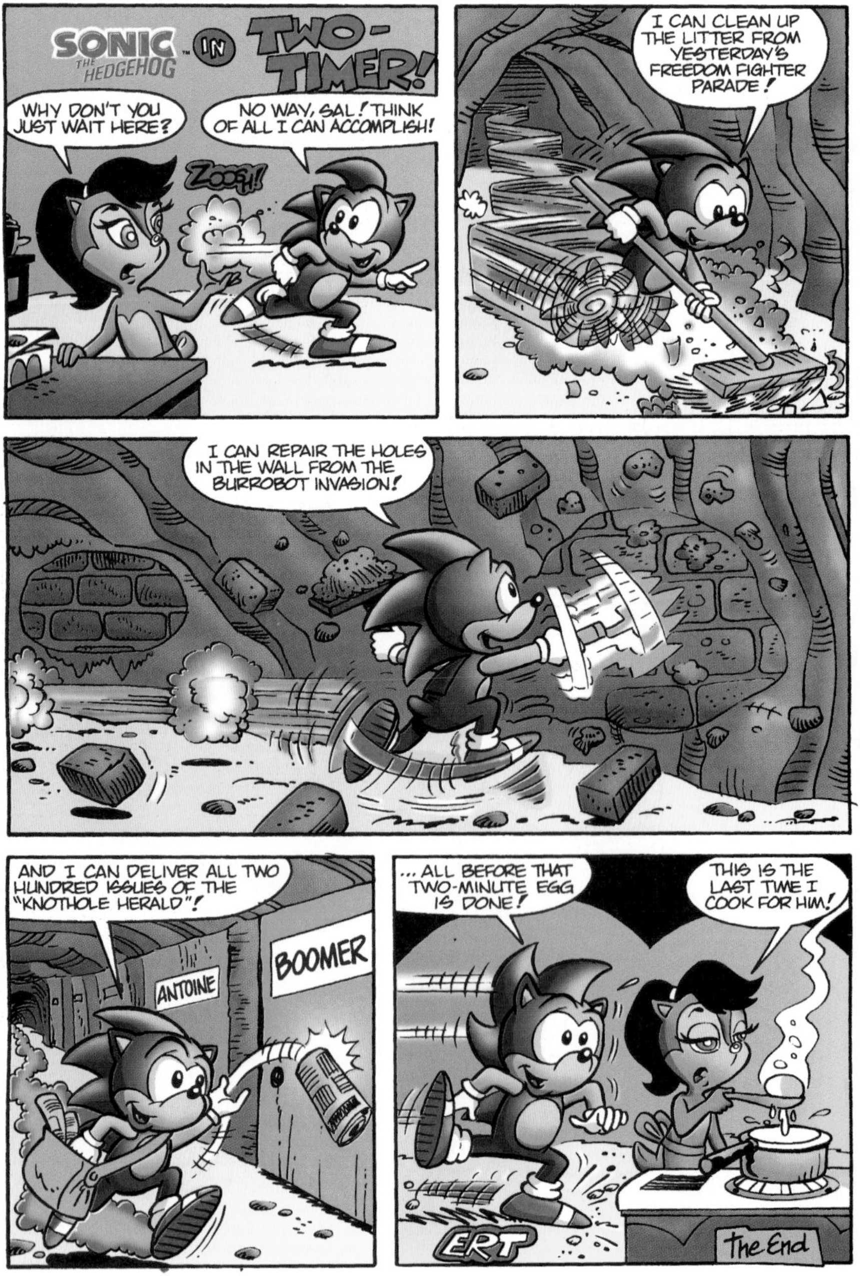
SONIC THE HEDGEHOG™ IN TWO-TIMER!
WHY DON'T YOU JUST WAIT HERE?
NO WAY, SAL! THINK OF ALL I CAN ACCOMPLISH!
ZOOSH!
I CAN CLEAN UP THE LITTER FROM YESTERDAY'S FREEDOM FIGHTER PARADE!
I CAN REPAIR THE HOLES IN THE WALL FROM THE BURROBOT INVASION!
AND I CAN DELIVER ALL TWO HUNDRED ISSUES OF THE "KNOTHOLE HERALD"!
ANTOINE
BOOMER
...ALL BEFORE THAT TWO-MINUTE EGG IS DONE!
THIS IS THE LAST TIME I COOK FOR HIM!
ERT
The End

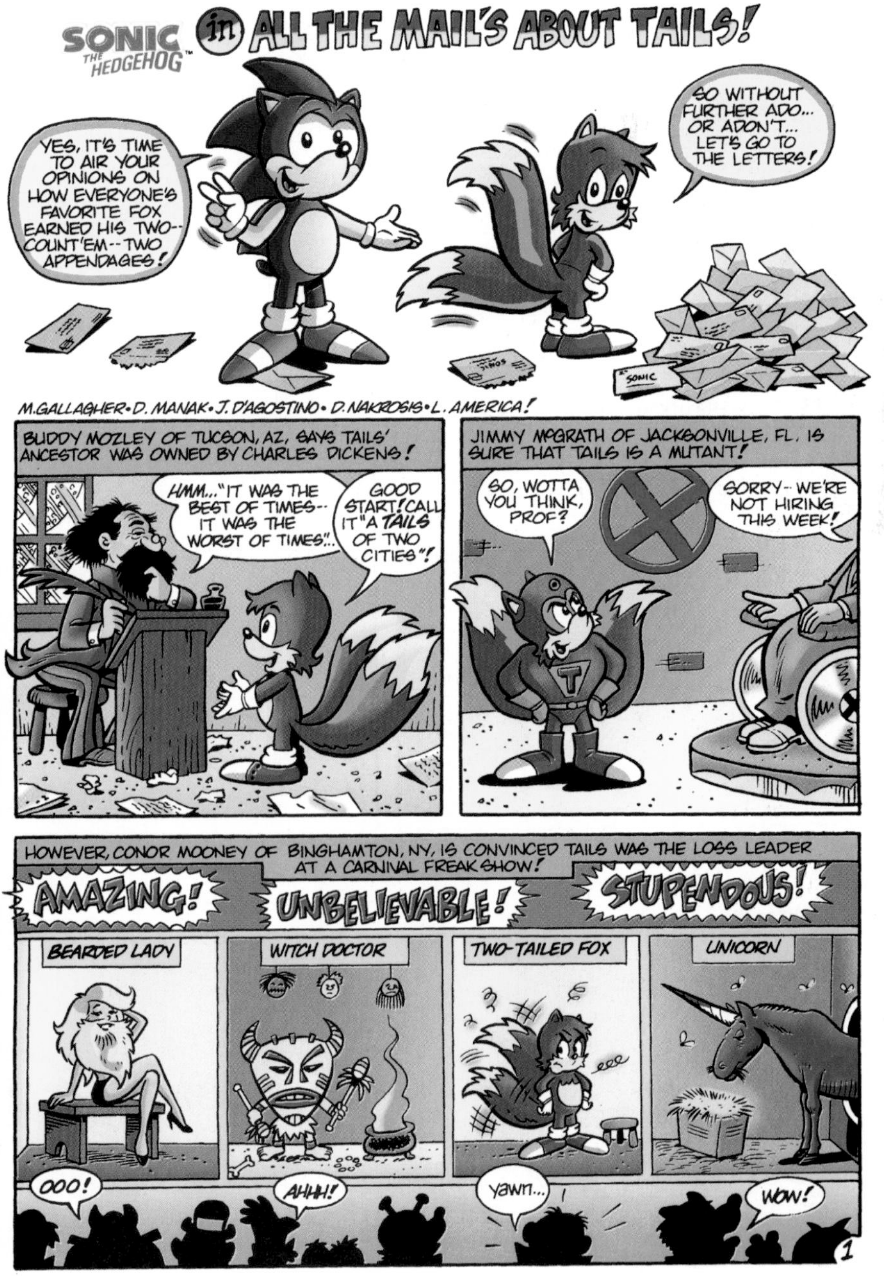
SONIC THE HEDGEHOG
in ALL THE MAIL'S ABOUT TAILS!
YES, IT'S TIME TO AIR YOUR OPINIONS ON HOW EVERYONE'S FAVORITE FOX EARNED HIS TWO-- COUNT'EM -- TWO APPENDAGES!
SO WITHOUT FURTHER ADO... OR ADON'T... LET'S GO TO THE LETTERS!
SONIC
M.GALLAGHER•D. MANAK•J. D'AGOSTINO•D. NAKROSIS•L. AMERICA!
BUDDY MOZLEY OF TUCSON, AZ, SAYS TAILS' ANCESTOR WAS OWNED BY CHARLES DICKENS!
HMM..."IT WAS THE BEST OF TIMES-- IT WAS THE WORST OF TIMES"...
GOOD START! CALL IT "A TAILS OF TWO CITIES"!
JIMMY McGRATH OF JACKSONVILLE, FL. IS SURE THAT TAILS IS A MUTANT!
SO, WOTTA YOU THINK, PROF?
SORRY-- WE'RE NOT HIRING THIS WEEK!
HOWEVER, CONOR MOONEY OF BINGHAMTON, NY, IS CONVINCED TAILS WAS THE LOSS LEADER AT A CARNIVAL FREAK SHOW!
AMAZING!
UNBELIEVABLE!
STUPENDOUS!
BEARDED LADY
WITCH DOCTOR
TWO-TAILED FOX
UNICORN
OOO!
AHHH!
yawn...
WOW!

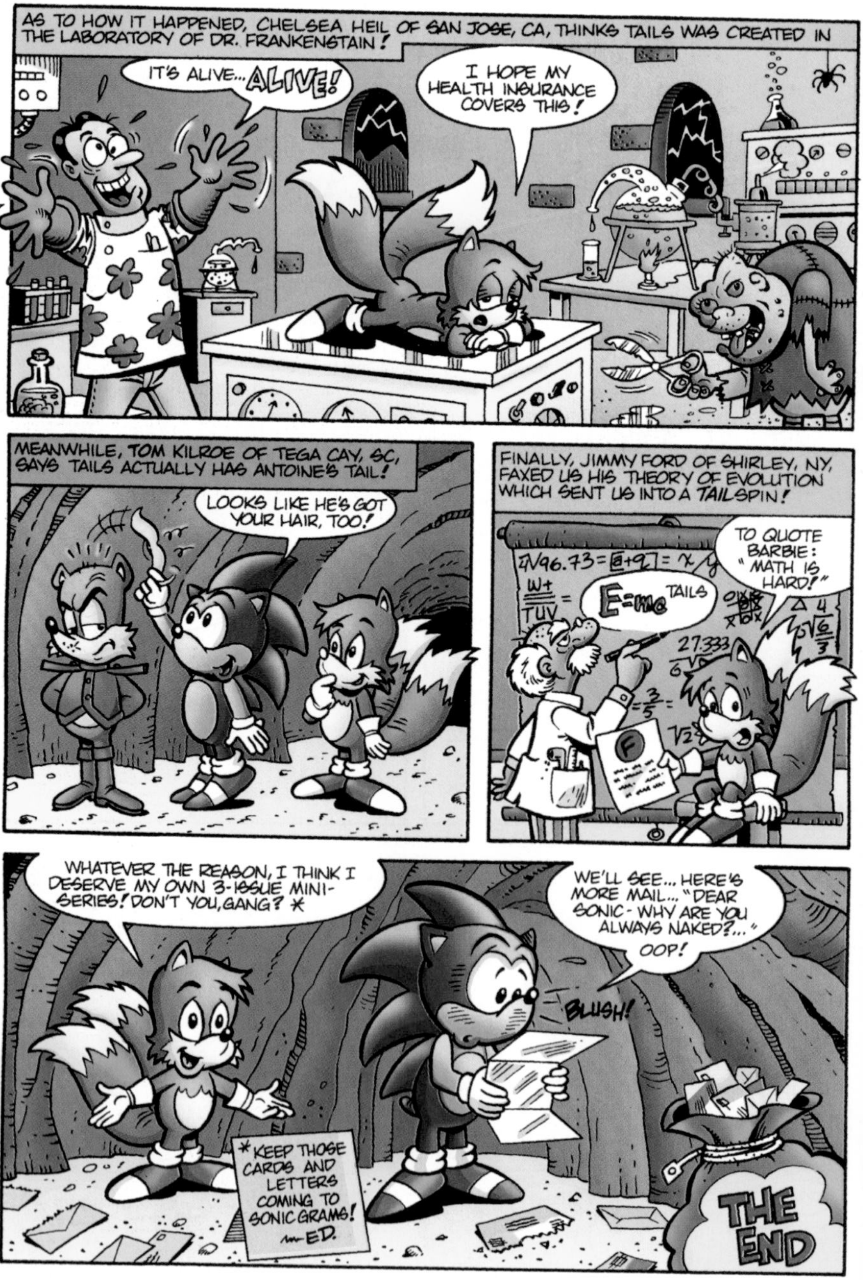
AS TO HOW IT HAPPENED, CHELSEA HEIL OF SAN JOSE, CA, THINKS TAILS WAS CREATED IN THE LABORATORY OF DR. FRANKENSTAIN!
IT'S ALIVE... ALIVE!
I HOPE MY HEALTH INSURANCE COVERS THIS!
MEANWHILE, TOM KILROE OF TEGA CAY, SC, SAYS TAILS ACTUALLY HAS ANTOINE'S TAIL!
LOOKS LIKE HE'S GOT YOUR HAIR, TOO!
FINALLY, JIMMY FORD OF SHIRLEY, NY, FAXED US HIS THEORY OF EVOLUTION WHICH SENT US INTO A TAILSPIN!
TO QUOTE BARBIE: "MATH IS HARD!"
E=mc TAILS
WHATEVER THE REASON, I THINK I DESERVE MY OWN 3-ISSUE MINI-SERIES! DON'T YOU, GANG? *
WE'LL SEE... HERE'S MORE MAIL... "DEAR SONIC- WHY ARE YOU ALWAYS NAKED?..." OOP!
BLUSH!
* KEEP THOSE CARDS AND LETTERS COMING TO SONIC GRAMS! —ED.
THE END

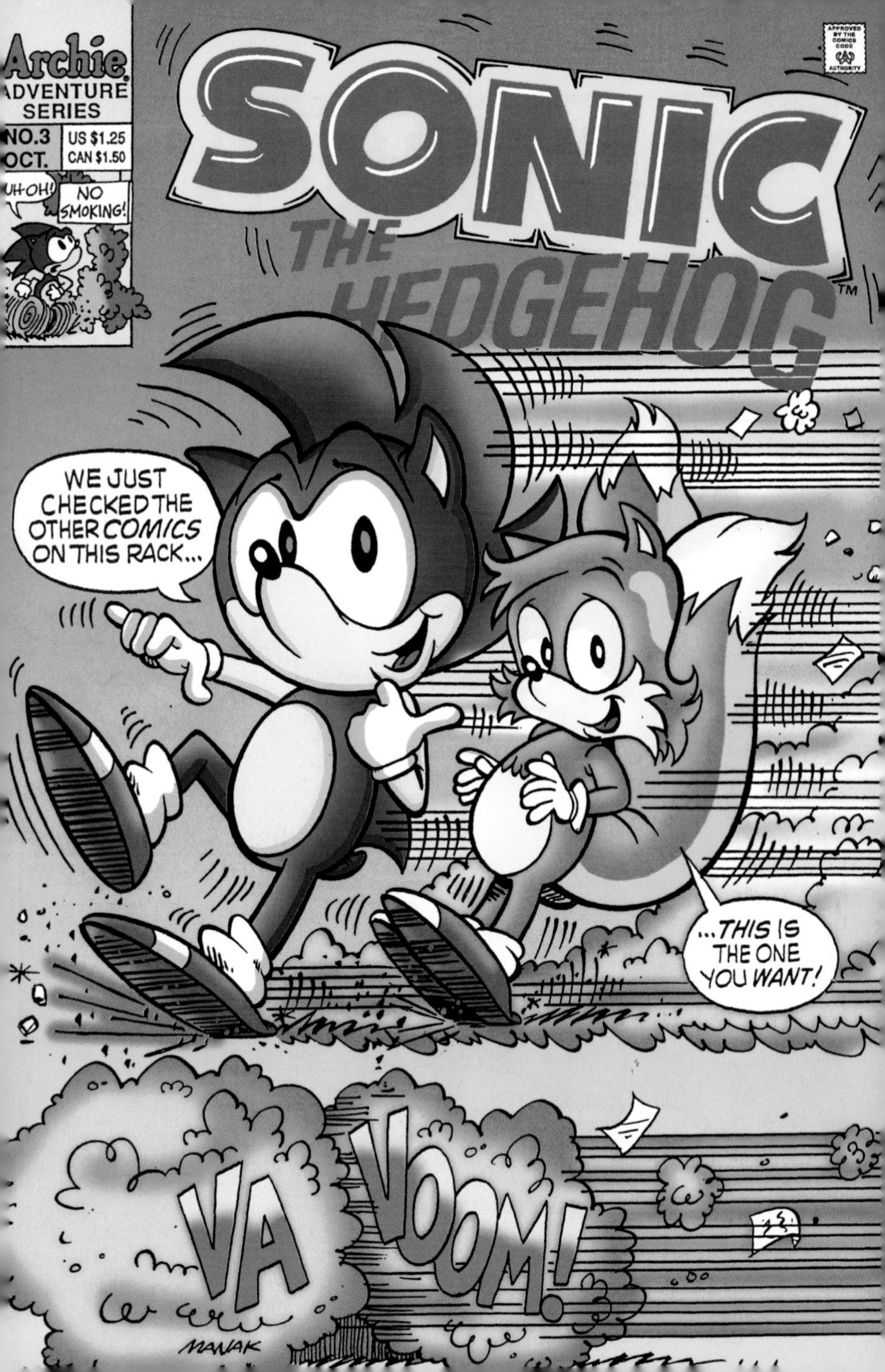
Archie
ADVENTURE SERIES
NO.3
OCT.
US $1.25
CAN $1.50
APPROVED BY THE COMICS CODE AUTHORITY
UH-OH!
NO SMOKING!
SONIC THE HEDGEHOG™
WE JUST CHECKED THE OTHER COMICS ON THIS RACK...
...THIS IS THE ONE YOU WANT!
VA VOOM!
MANAK

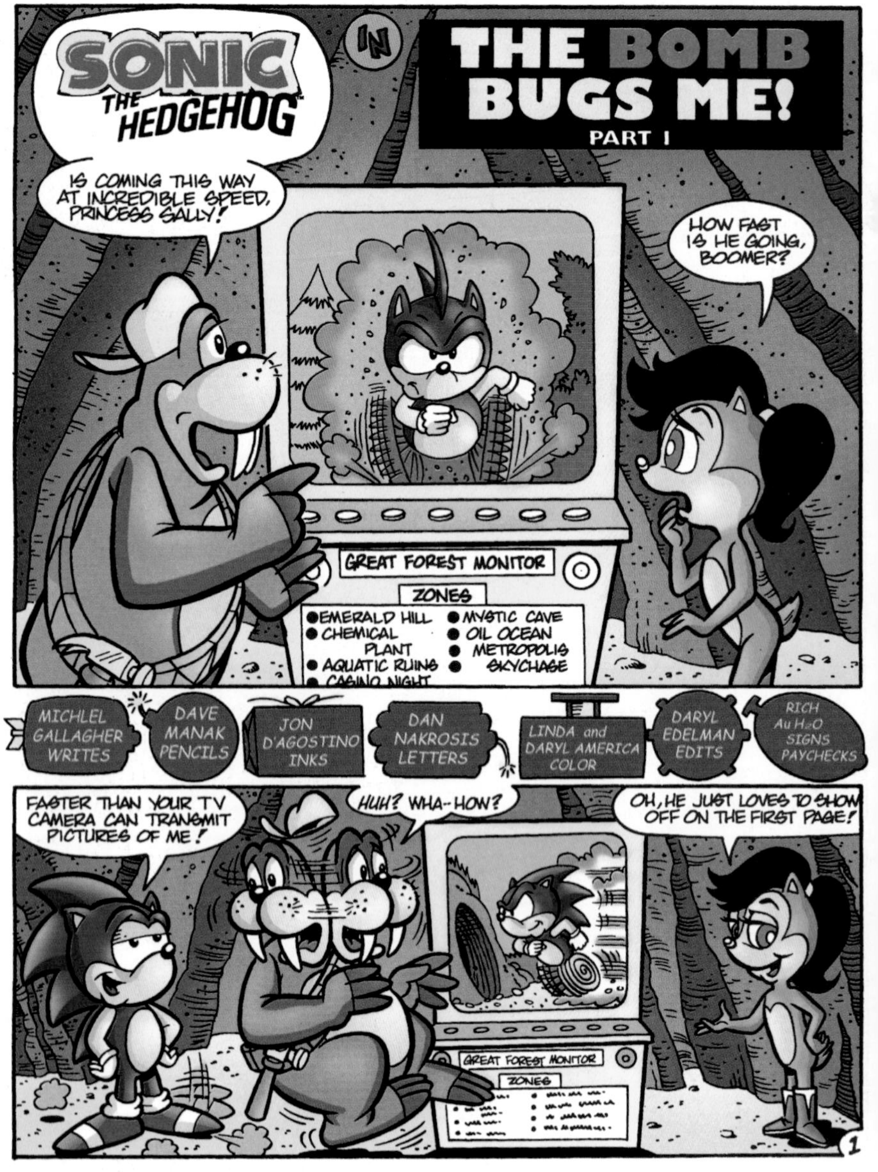
SONIC THE HEDGEHOG™
IN
THE BOMB BUGS ME!
PART I
IS COMING THIS WAY AT INCREDIBLE SPEED, PRINCESS SALLY!
HOW FAST IS HE GOING, BOOMER?
GREAT FOREST MONITOR
ZONES
EMERALD HILL
CHEMICAL PLANT
AQUATIC RUINS
CASINO NIGHT
MYSTIC CAVE
OIL OCEAN
METROPOLIS
SKYCHASE
MICHLEL GALLAGHER WRITES
DAVE MANAK PENCILS
JON D'AGOSTINO INKS
DAN NAKROSIS LETTERS
LINDA and DARYL AMERICA COLOR
DARYL EDELMAN EDITS
RICH Au H2O SIGNS PAYCHECKS
FASTER THAN YOUR TV CAMERA CAN TRANSMIT PICTURES OF ME!
HUH? WHA--HOW?
OH, HE JUST LOVES TO SHOW OFF ON THE FIRST PAGE!
GREAT FOREST MONITOR
ZONES

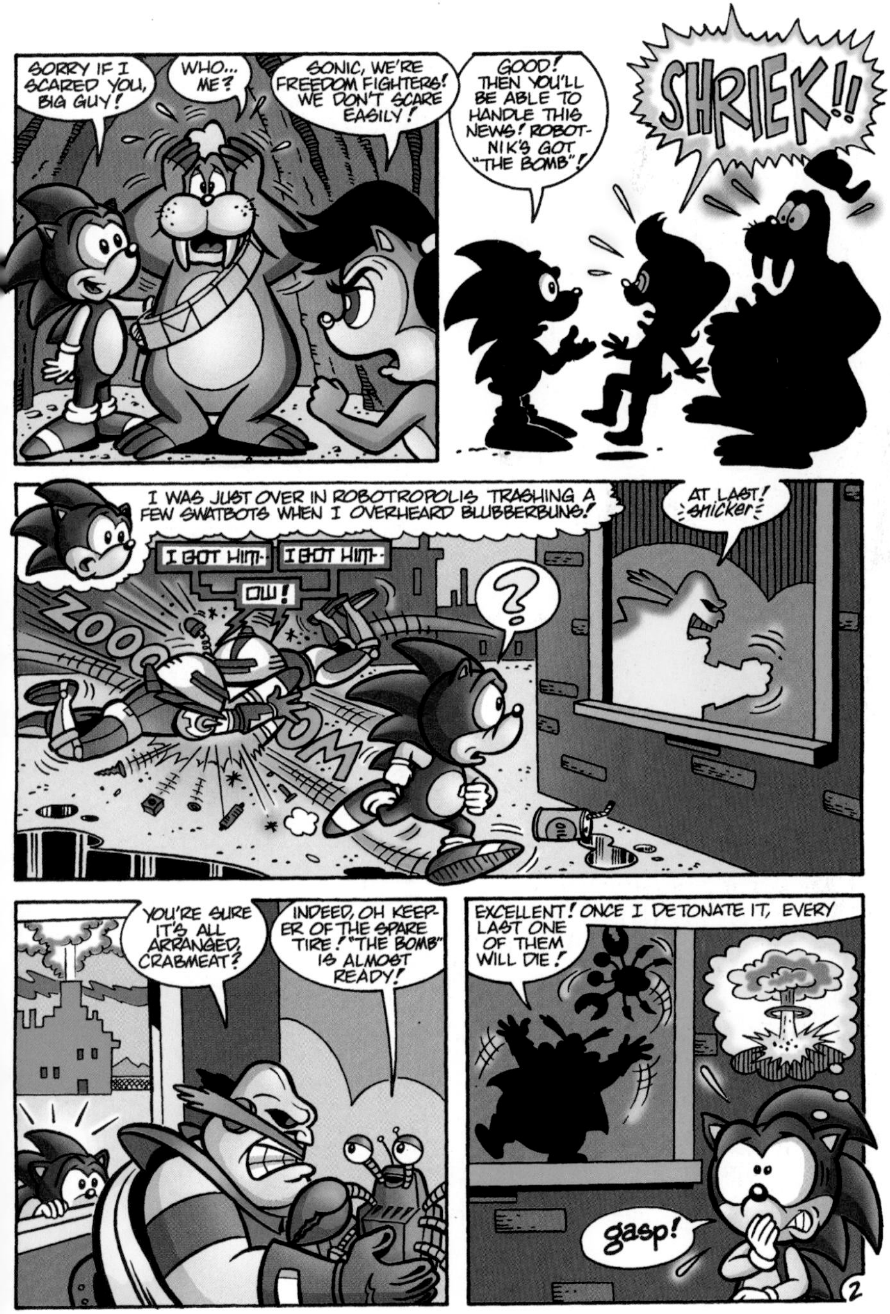
SORRY IF I SCARED YOU, BIG GUY!
WHO... ME?
SONIC, WE'RE FREEDOM FIGHTERS! WE DON'T SCARE EASILY!
GOOD! THEN YOU'LL BE ABLE TO HANDLE THIS NEWS! ROBOTNIK'S GOT "THE BOMB"!
SHRIEK!!
I WAS JUST OVER IN ROBOTROPOLIS TRASHING A FEW SWATBOTS WHEN I OVERHEARD BLUBBERBUNS!
I GOT HIM-
I GOT HIM-
OW!
ZOOOOM
?
AT LAST! snicker
YOU'RE SURE IT'S ALL ARRANGED, CRABMEAT?
INDEED, OH KEEPER OF THE SPARE TIRE! "THE BOMB" IS ALMOST READY!
EXCELLENT! ONCE I DETONATE IT, EVERY LAST ONE OF THEM WILL DIE!
gasp!

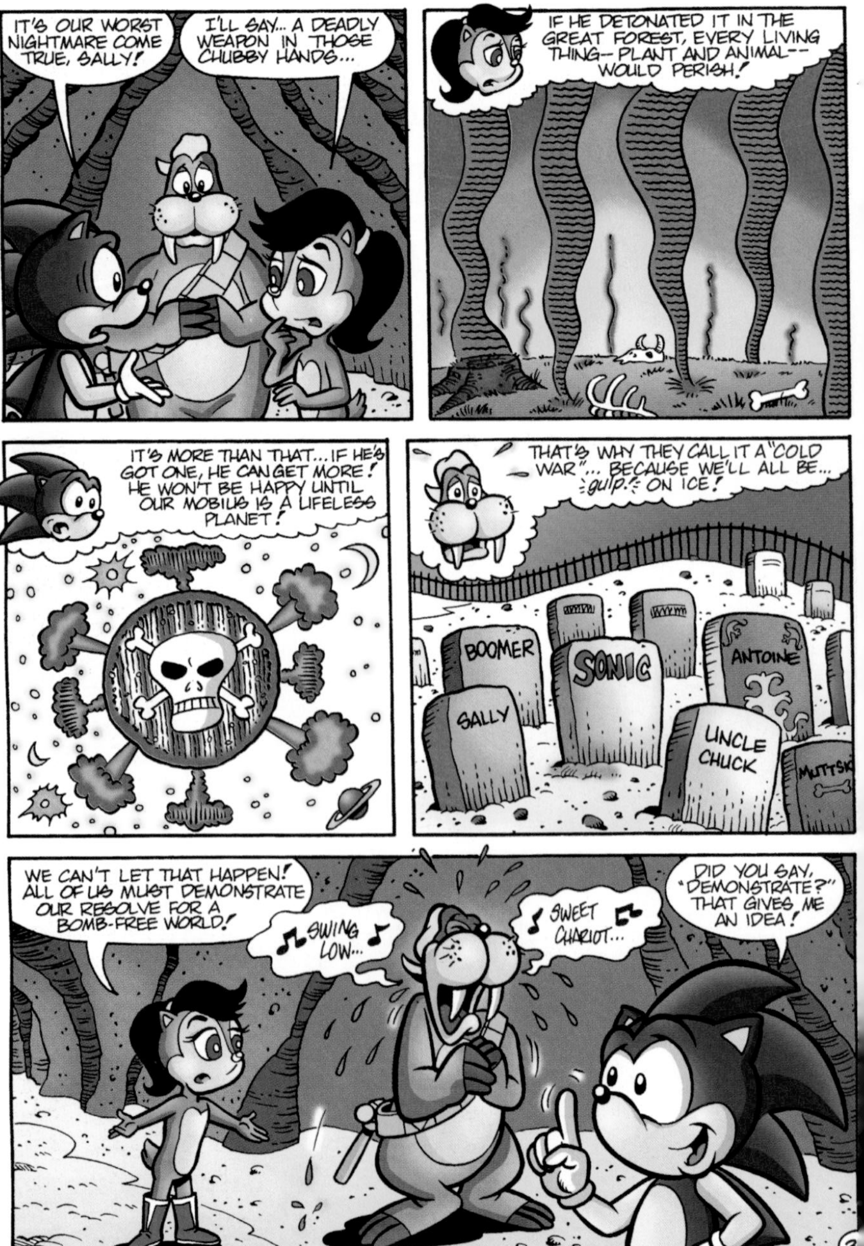
IT'S OUR WORST NIGHTMARE COME TRUE, SALLY!
I'LL SAY... A DEADLY WEAPON IN THOSE CHUBBY HANDS...
IF HE DETONATED IT IN THE GREAT FOREST, EVERY LIVING THING-- PLANT AND ANIMAL-- WOULD PERISH!
IT'S MORE THAN THAT... IF HE'S GOT ONE, HE CAN GET MORE! HE WON'T BE HAPPY UNTIL OUR MOBIUS IS A LIFELESS PLANET!
THAT'S WHY THEY CALL IT A "COLD WAR"... BECAUSE WE'LL ALL BE... gulp! ON ICE!
BOOMER
SONIC
ANTOINE
SALLY
UNCLE CHUCK
MUTTSKI
WE CAN'T LET THAT HAPPEN! ALL OF US MUST DEMONSTRATE OUR RESOLVE FOR A BOMB-FREE WORLD!
SWING LOW...
SWEET CHARIOT...
DID YOU SAY, "DEMONSTRATE?" THAT GIVES ME AN IDEA!

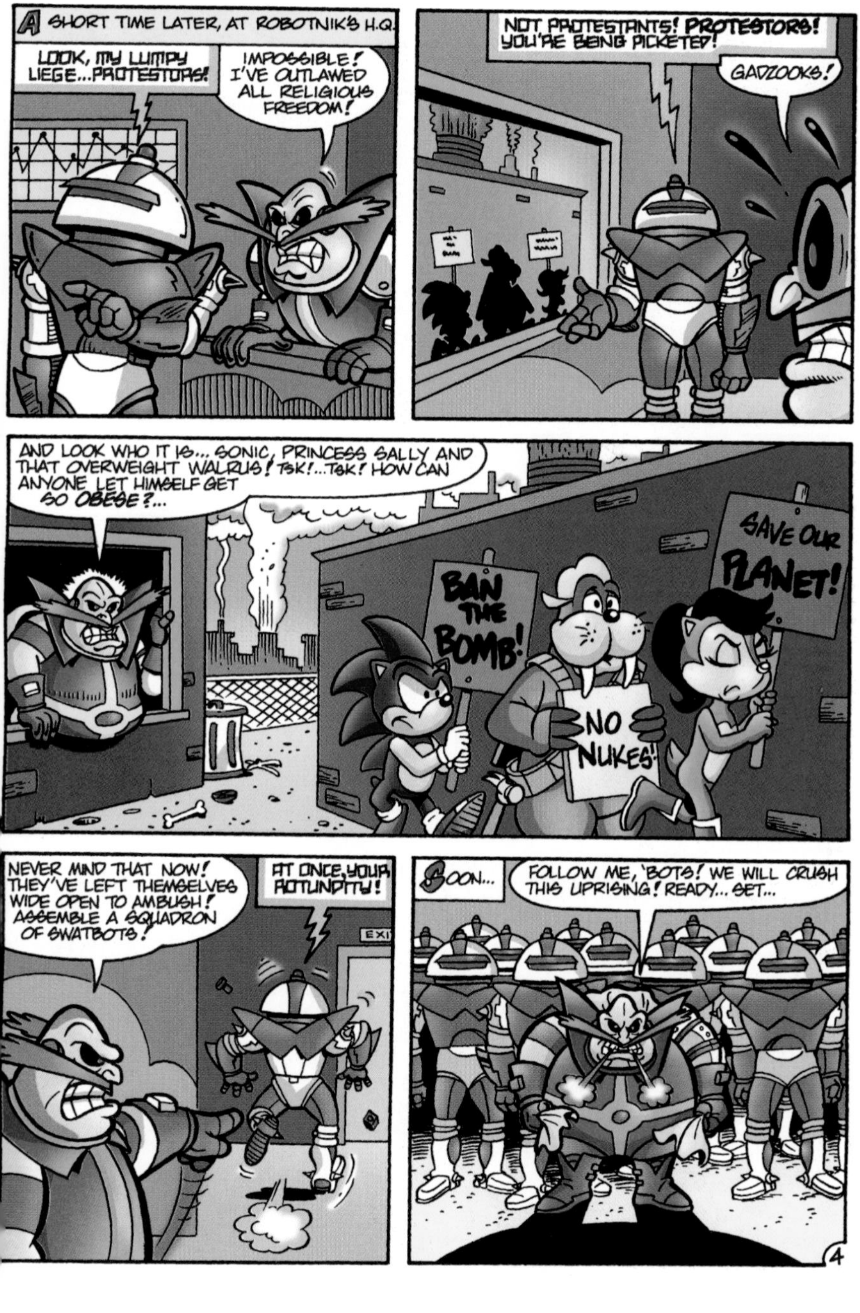
A SHORT TIME LATER, AT ROBOTNIK'S H.Q.
LOOK, MY LUMPY LIEGE...PROTESTORS!
IMPOSSIBLE! I'VE OUTLAWED ALL RELIGIOUS FREEDOM!
NOT PROTESTANTS! PROTESTORS! YOU'RE BEING PICKETED!
GADZOOKS!
AND LOOK WHO IT IS... SONIC, PRINCESS SALLY AND THAT OVERWEIGHT WALRUS! TSK!...TSK! HOW CAN ANYONE LET HIMSELF GET SO OBESE?...
BAN THE BOMB!
NO NUKES!
SAVE OUR PLANET!
NEVER MIND THAT NOW! THEY'VE LEFT THEMSELVES WIDE OPEN TO AMBUSH! ASSEMBLE A SQUADRON OF SWATBOTS!
AT ONCE, YOUR ROTUNDITY!
SOON...
FOLLOW ME, 'BOTS! WE WILL CRUSH THIS UPRISING! READY... SET...

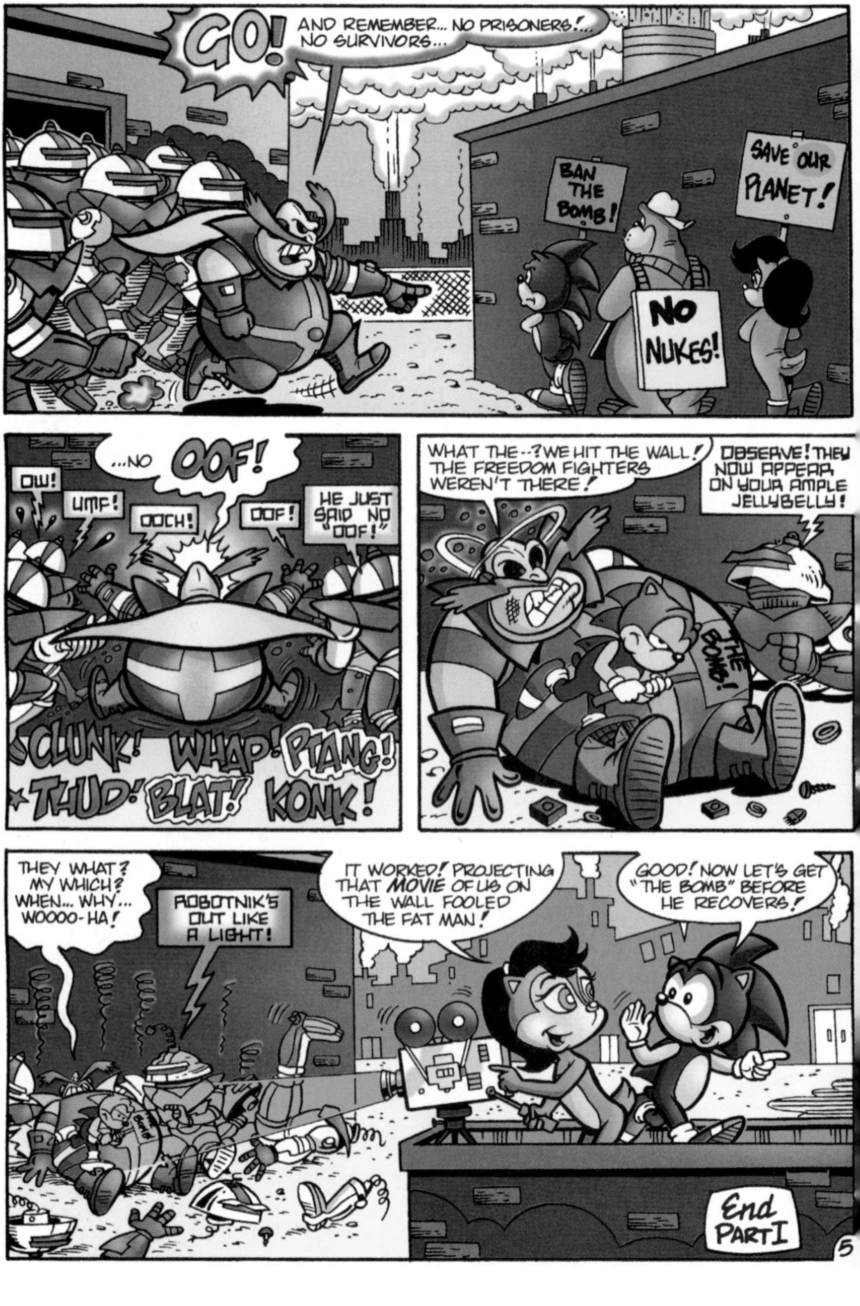
GO!
AND REMEMBER... NO PRISONERS!... NO SURVIVORS...
BAN THE BOMB!
SAVE OUR PLANET!
NO NUKES!
...NO OOF!
OW!
UMF!
OOCH!
OOF!
HE JUST SAID NO "OOF!"
CLUNK! WHAP! PTANG!
THUD! BLAT! KONK!
WHAT THE--? WE HIT THE WALL! THE FREEDOM FIGHTERS WEREN'T THERE!
OBSERVE! THEY NOW APPEAR ON YOUR AMPLE JELLYBELLY!
THE BOMB!
THEY WHAT? MY WHICH? WHEN... WHY... WOOOO-HA!
ROBOTNIK'S OUT LIKE A LIGHT!
IT WORKED! PROJECTING THAT MOVIE OF US ON THE WALL FOOLED THE FAT MAN!
GOOD! NOW LET'S GET "THE BOMB" BEFORE HE RECOVERS!
End PART I

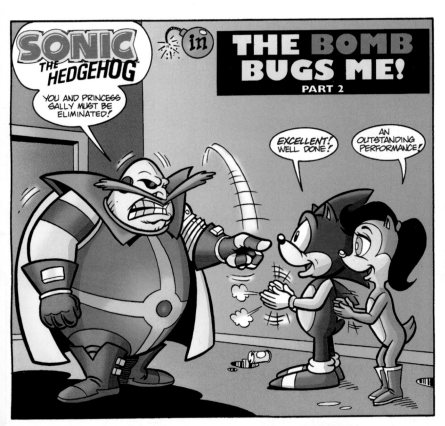

SONIC THE HEDGEHOG in **THE BOMB BUGS ME!** PART 2

YOU AND PRINCESS SALLY MUST BE ELIMINATED!

EXCELLENT! WELL DONE!

AN OUTSTANDING PERFORMANCE!

THANKS, YOUR MAJESTY!... I CAN DO OTHER VOICES BESIDES ROBOTNIK!... WANT TO HEAR MY JAMES CAGNEY?

NOT NOW, BOOMER... PUT THE MASK BACK ON!

YEAH... LET'S GET THIS SHOW ON THE ROAD!

1

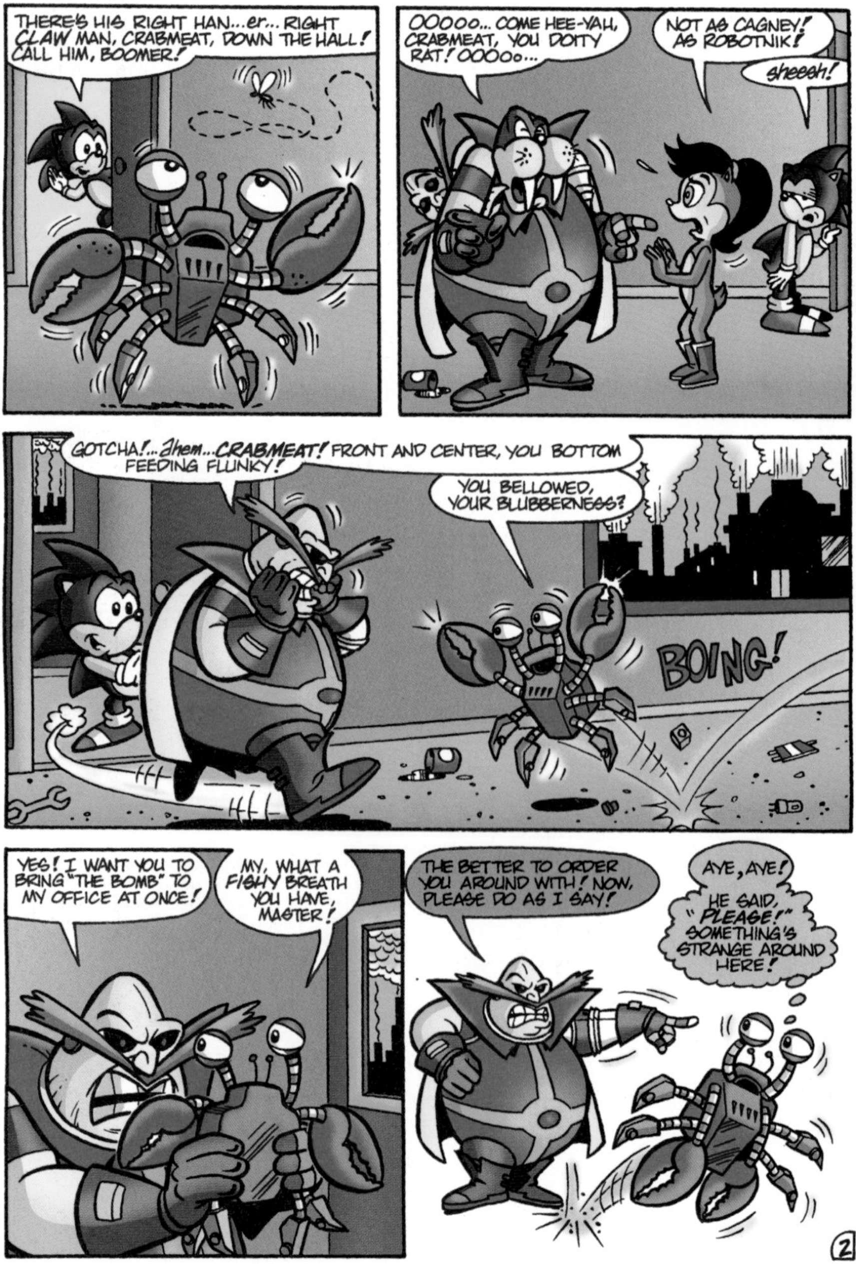
THERE'S HIS RIGHT HAN...er... RIGHT CLAW MAN, CRABMEAT, DOWN THE HALL! CALL HIM, BOOMER!
OOOOOo... COME HEE-YAH, CRABMEAT, YOU DOITY RAT! OOOOo...
NOT AS CAGNEY! AS ROBOTNIK!
sheesh!
GOTCHA!...ahem...CRABMEAT! FRONT AND CENTER, YOU BOTTOM FEEDING FLUNKY!
YOU BELLOWED, YOUR BLUBBERNESS?
BOING!
YES! I WANT YOU TO BRING "THE BOMB" TO MY OFFICE AT ONCE!
MY, WHAT A FISHY BREATH YOU HAVE, MASTER!
THE BETTER TO ORDER YOU AROUND WITH! NOW, PLEASE DO AS I SAY!
AYE, AYE!
HE SAID, "PLEASE!" SOMETHING'S STRANGE AROUND HERE!
2

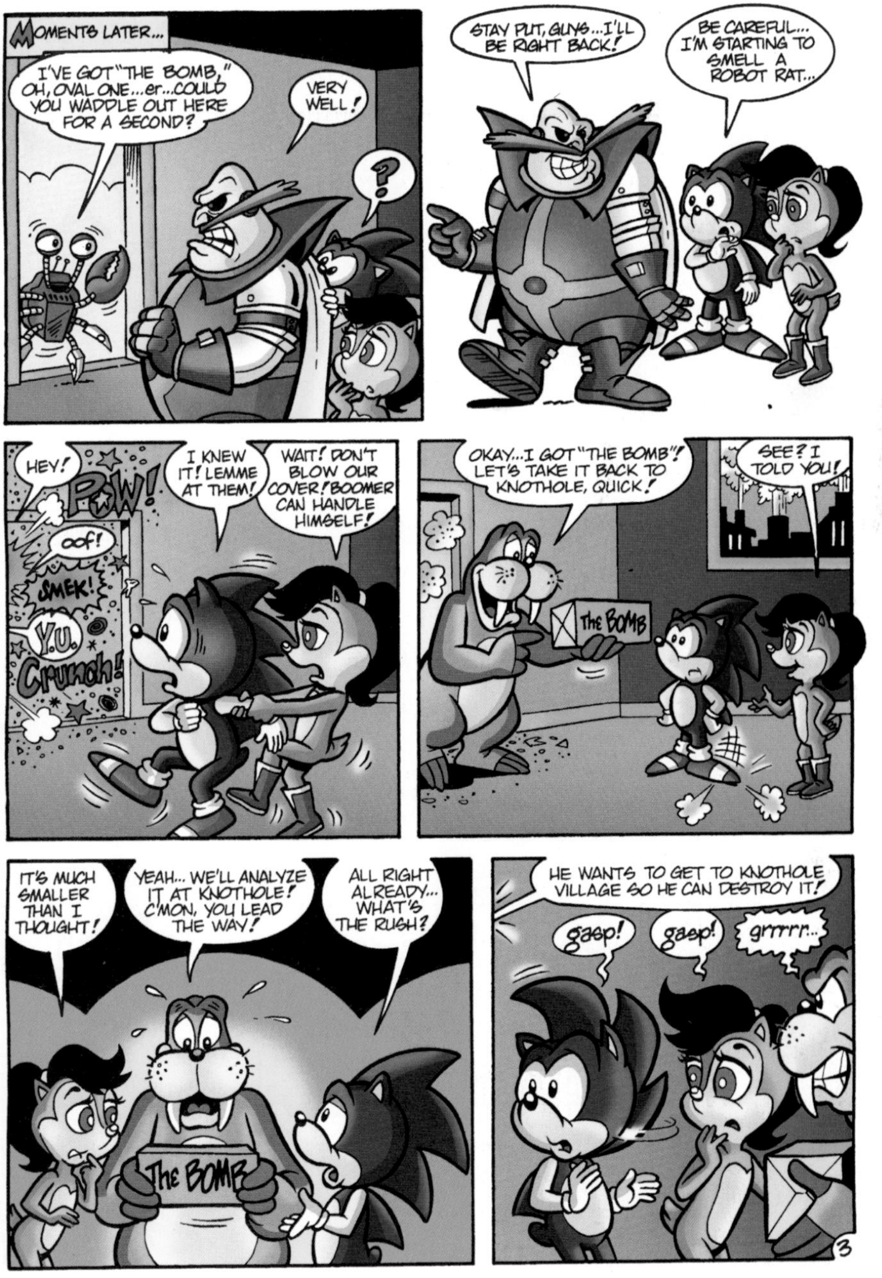
MOMENTS LATER...
I'VE GOT "THE BOMB," OH, OVAL ONE...er...COULD YOU WADDLE OUT HERE FOR A SECOND?
VERY WELL!
?
STAY PUT, GUYS...I'LL BE RIGHT BACK!
BE CAREFUL... I'M STARTING TO SMELL A ROBOT RAT...
HEY!
POW!
oof!
SMEK!
Y.U.
Crunch!
I KNEW IT! LEMME AT THEM!
WAIT! DON'T BLOW OUR COVER! BOOMER CAN HANDLE HIMSELF!
OKAY...I GOT "THE BOMB"! LET'S TAKE IT BACK TO KNOTHOLE, QUICK!
THE BOMB
SEE? I TOLD YOU!
IT'S MUCH SMALLER THAN I THOUGHT!
YEAH... WE'LL ANALYZE IT AT KNOTHOLE! C'MON, YOU LEAD THE WAY!
ALL RIGHT ALREADY... WHAT'S THE RUSH?
THE BOMB
HE WANTS TO GET TO KNOTHOLE VILLAGE SO HE CAN DESTROY IT!
gasp!
gasp!
grrrrr...

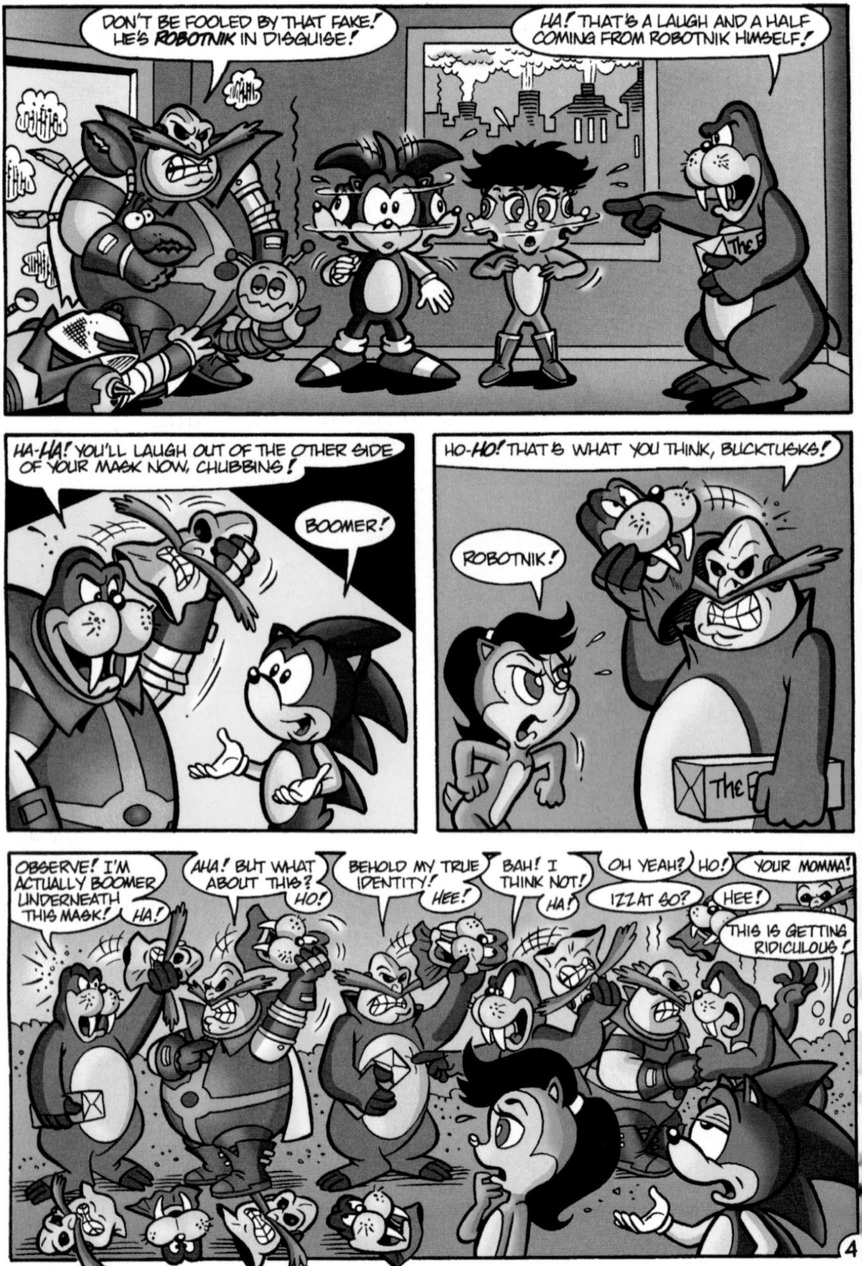
DON'T BE FOOLED BY THAT FAKE! HE'S ROBOTNIK IN DISGUISE!
HA! THAT'S A LAUGH AND A HALF COMING FROM ROBOTNIK HIMSELF!
HA-HA! YOU'LL LAUGH OUT OF THE OTHER SIDE OF YOUR MASK NOW, CHUBBINS!
BOOMER!
HO-HO! THAT'S WHAT YOU THINK, BUCKTUSKS!
ROBOTNIK!
OBSERVE! I'M ACTUALLY BOOMER UNDERNEATH THIS MASK!
HA!
AHA! BUT WHAT ABOUT THIS?
HO!
BEHOLD MY TRUE IDENTITY!
HEE!
BAH! I THINK NOT!
HA!
OH YEAH?
HO!
YOUR MOMMA!
IZZAT SO?
HEE!
THIS IS GETTING RIDICULOUS!

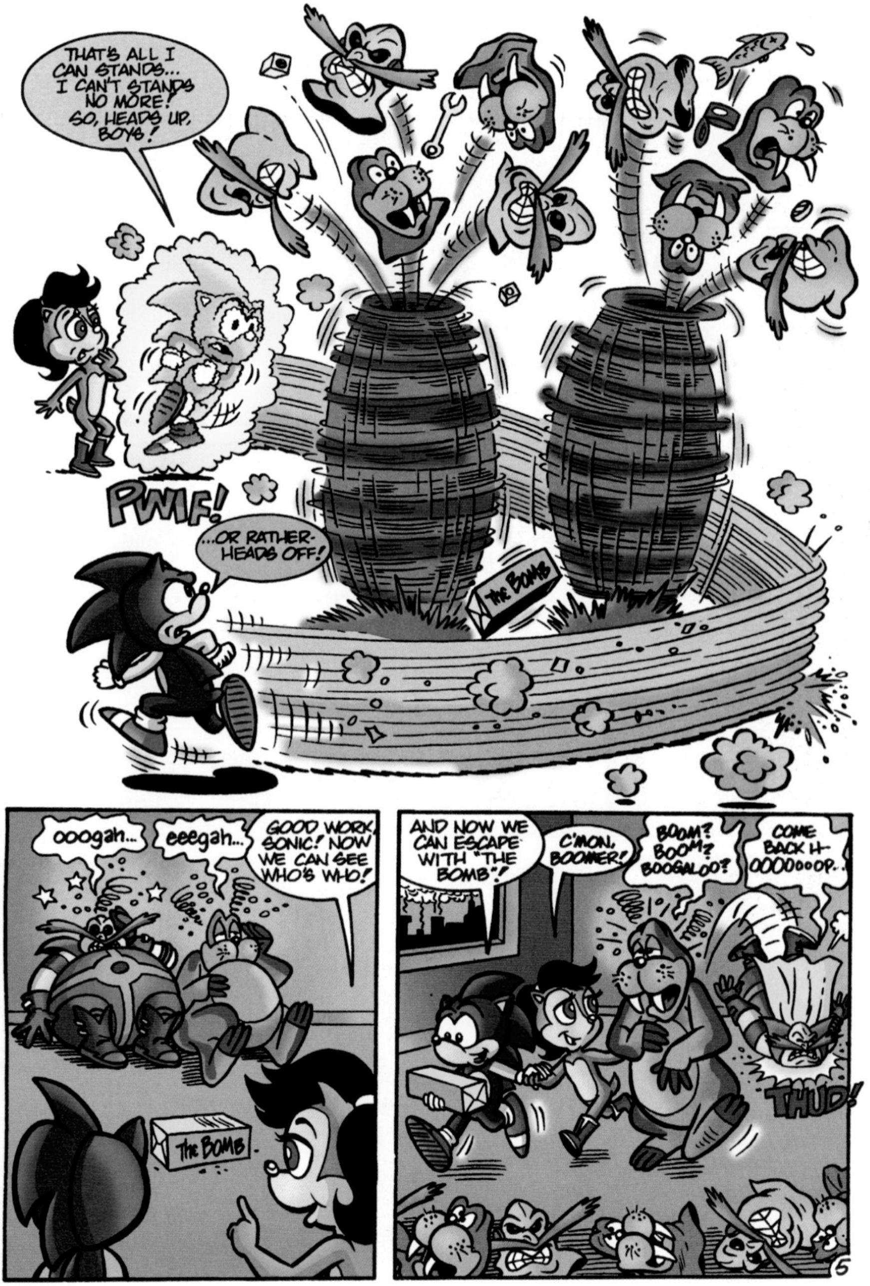
THAT'S ALL I CAN STANDS... I CAN'T STANDS NO MORE! SO, HEADS UP, BOYS!
PWIF!
...OR RATHER-HEADS OFF!
the BOMB
ooogah...
eeegah...
GOOD WORK, SONIC! NOW WE CAN SEE WHO'S WHO!
the BOMB
AND NOW WE CAN ESCAPE WITH "THE BOMB"!
C'MON, BOOMER!
BOOM? BOOM? BOOGALOO?
COME BACK H-OOOOooop..
THUD!

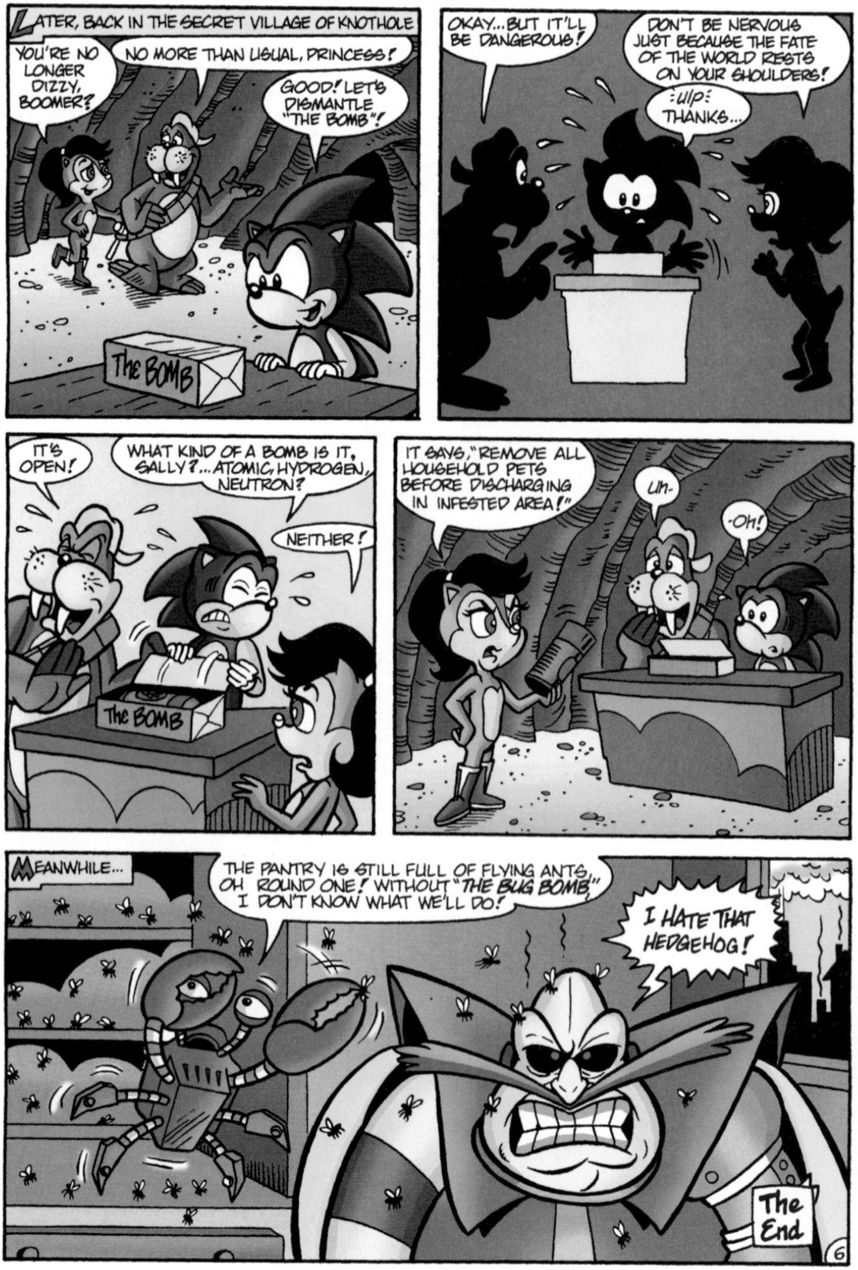
LATER, BACK IN THE SECRET VILLAGE OF KNOTHOLE
YOU'RE NO LONGER DIZZY, BOOMER?
NO MORE THAN USUAL, PRINCESS!
GOOD! LET'S DISMANTLE "THE BOMB"!
The BOMB
OKAY...BUT IT'LL BE DANGEROUS!
DON'T BE NERVOUS JUST BECAUSE THE FATE OF THE WORLD RESTS ON YOUR SHOULDERS!
ulp THANKS...
IT'S OPEN!
WHAT KIND OF A BOMB IS IT, SALLY?...ATOMIC, HYDROGEN, NEUTRON?
NEITHER!
The BOMB
IT SAYS, "REMOVE ALL HOUSEHOLD PETS BEFORE DISCHARGING IN INFESTED AREA!"
Uh-
-Oh!
MEANWHILE...
THE PANTRY IS STILL FULL OF FLYING ANTS, OH ROUND ONE! WITHOUT "THE BUG BOMB," I DON'T KNOW WHAT WE'LL DO!
I HATE THAT HEDGEHOG!
The End

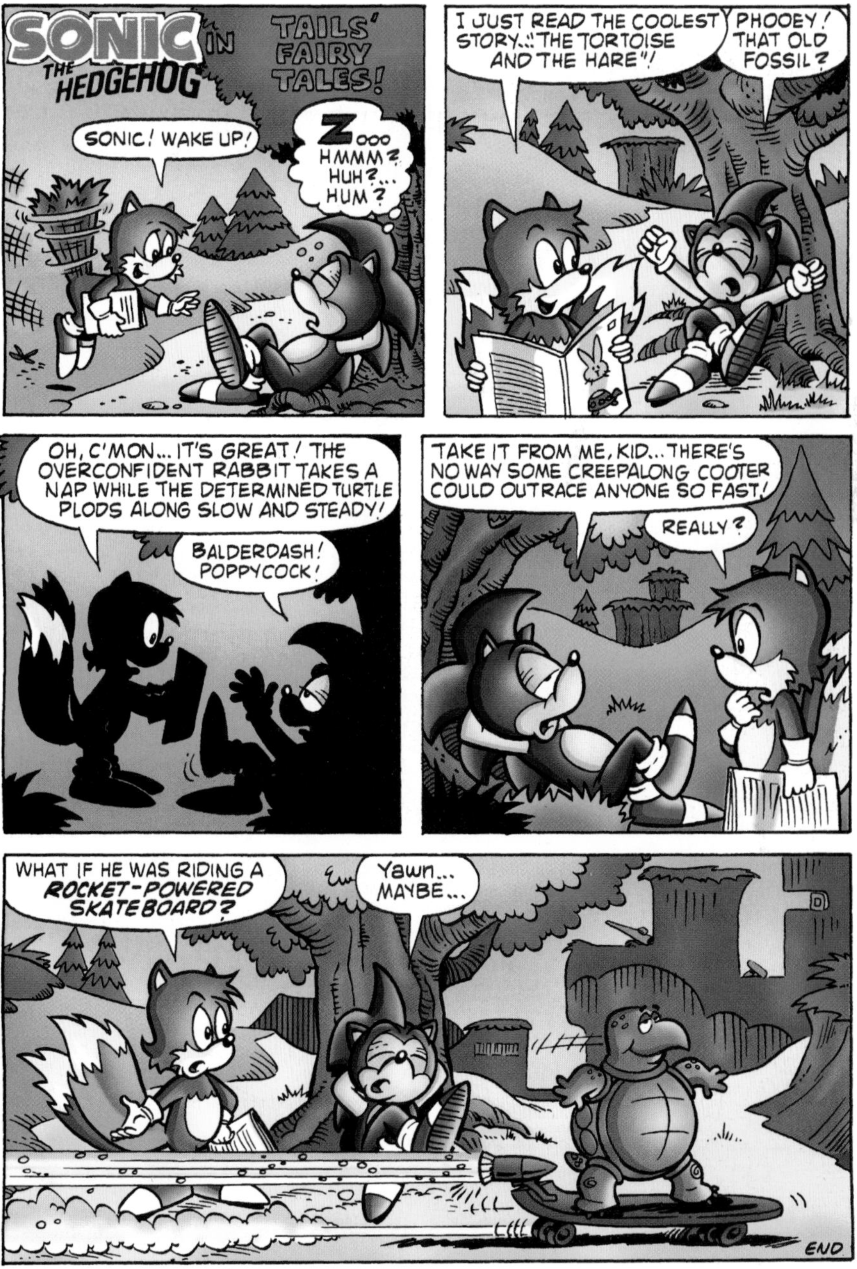

SONIC THE HEDGEHOG IN
TAILS' FAIRY TALES!
SONIC! WAKE UP!
Zooo HMMM? HUH?... HUM?
I JUST READ THE COOLEST STORY...: "THE TORTOISE AND THE HARE"!
PHOOEY! THAT OLD FOSSIL?
OH, C'MON... IT'S GREAT! THE OVERCONFIDENT RABBIT TAKES A NAP WHILE THE DETERMINED TURTLE PLODS ALONG SLOW AND STEADY!
BALDERDASH! POPPYCOCK!
TAKE IT FROM ME, KID... THERE'S NO WAY SOME CREEPALONG COOTER COULD OUTRACE ANYONE SO FAST!
REALLY?
WHAT IF HE WAS RIDING A ROCKET-POWERED SKATEBOARD?
Yawn... MAYBE...
END

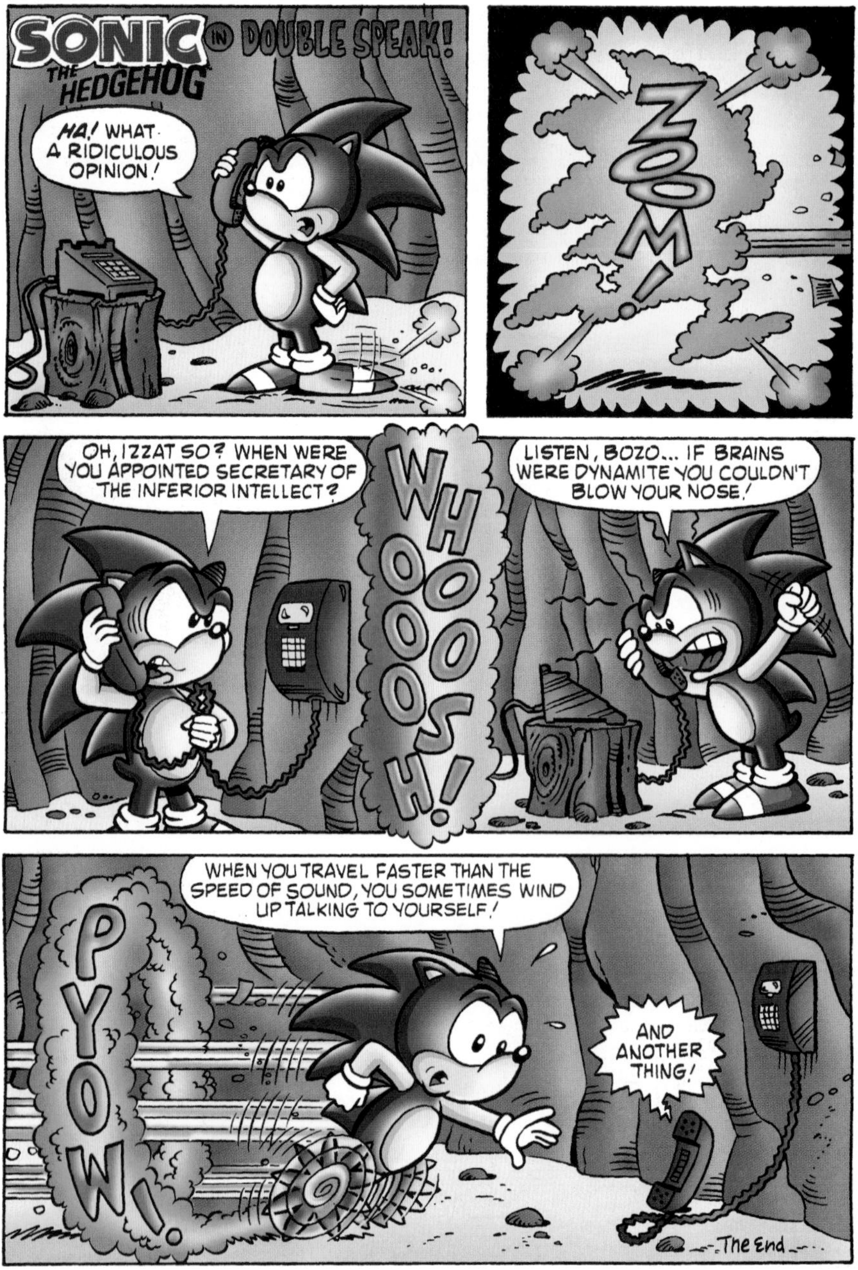
SONIC THE HEDGEHOG IN DOUBLE SPEAK!
HA! WHAT A RIDICULOUS OPINION!
ZOOM!
OH, IZZAT SO? WHEN WERE YOU APPOINTED SECRETARY OF THE INFERIOR INTELLECT?
WHOOOOOOSH!
LISTEN, BOZO... IF BRAINS WERE DYNAMITE YOU COULDN'T BLOW YOUR NOSE!
PYOW!
WHEN YOU TRAVEL FASTER THAN THE SPEED OF SOUND, YOU SOMETIMES WIND UP TALKING TO YOURSELF!
AND ANOTHER THING!
The End

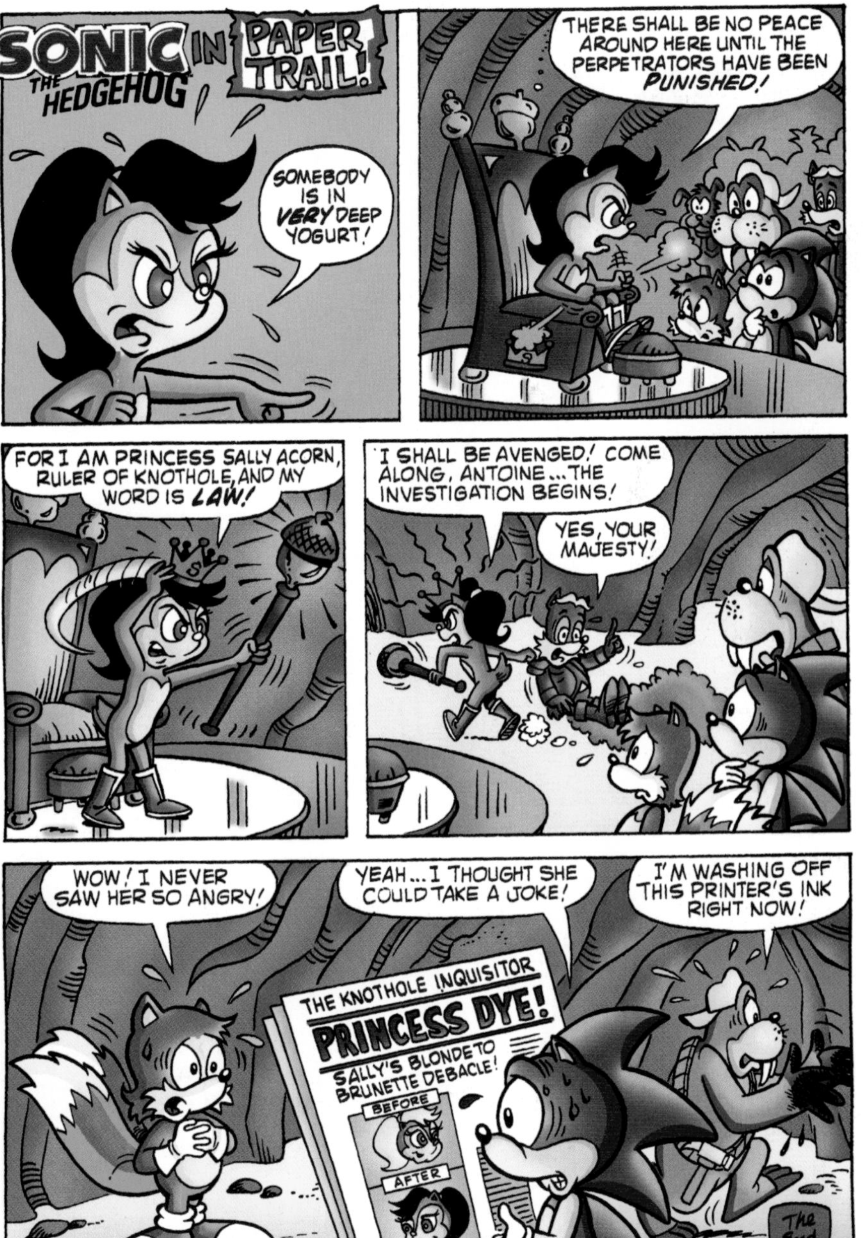
SONIC THE HEDGEHOG IN PAPER TRAIL!
SOMEBODY IS IN VERY DEEP YOGURT!
THERE SHALL BE NO PEACE AROUND HERE UNTIL THE PERPETRATORS HAVE BEEN PUNISHED!
FOR I AM PRINCESS SALLY ACORN, RULER OF KNOTHOLE, AND MY WORD IS LAW!
I SHALL BE AVENGED! COME ALONG, ANTOINE... THE INVESTIGATION BEGINS!
YES, YOUR MAJESTY!
WOW! I NEVER SAW HER SO ANGRY!
YEAH... I THOUGHT SHE COULD TAKE A JOKE!
I'M WASHING OFF THIS PRINTER'S INK RIGHT NOW!
THE KNOTHOLE INQUISITOR
PRINCESS DYE!
SALLY'S BLONDE TO BRUNETTE DEBACLE!
BEFORE
AFTER
The End

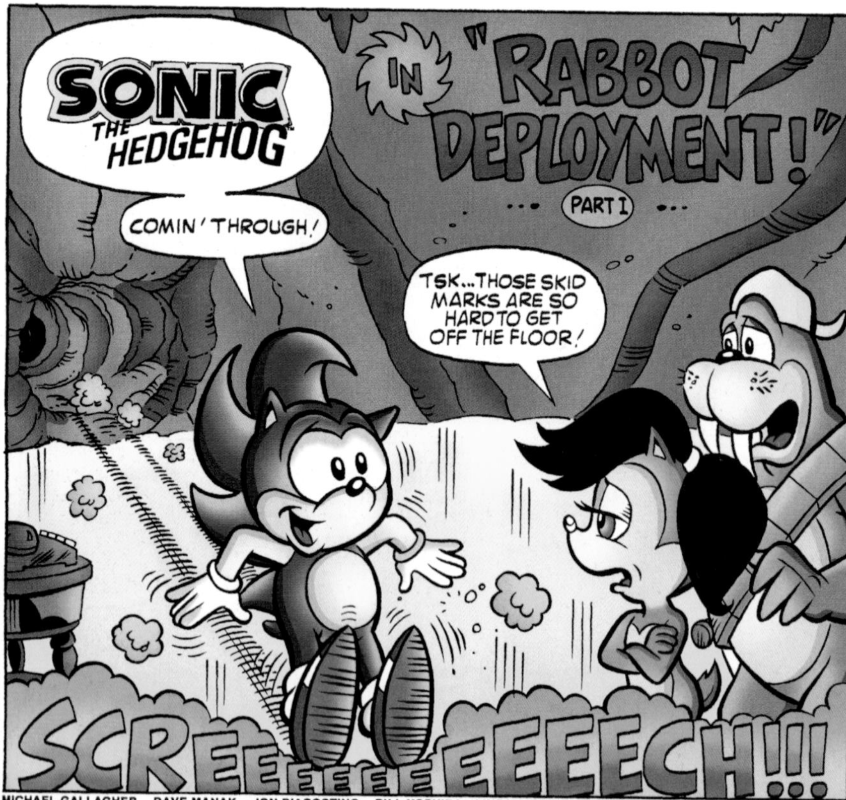
SONIC THE HEDGEHOG
IN "RABBOT DEPLOYMENT!"
... PART I ...
COMIN' THROUGH!
TSK...THOSE SKID MARKS ARE SO HARD TO GET OFF THE FLOOR!
SCREEEEEEEEEEEECH!!!

MICHAEL GALLAGHER *WRITER* · DAVE MANAK *PENCILER* · JON D'AGOSTINO *INKER* · BILL YOSHIDA *LETTERER* · LINDA & DARYL AMERICA *COLORISTS* · DARYL EDELMAN *EDITOR* · RICH AuH$_2$O *THE KING*

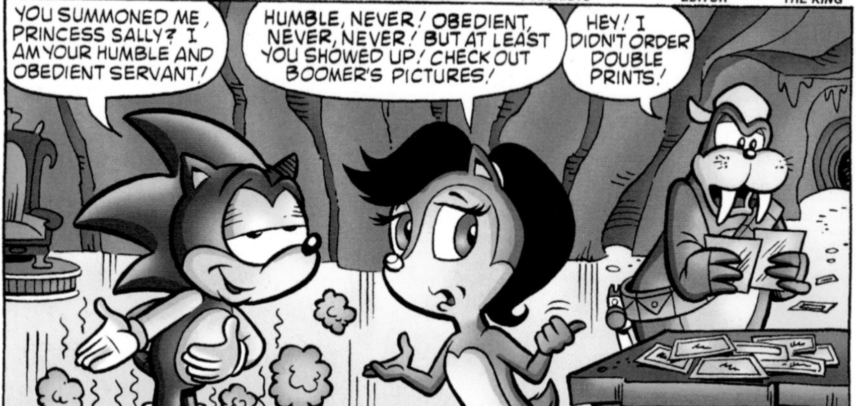
YOU SUMMONED ME, PRINCESS SALLY? I AM YOUR HUMBLE AND OBEDIENT SERVANT!
HUMBLE, NEVER! OBEDIENT, NEVER, NEVER! BUT AT LEAST YOU SHOWED UP! CHECK OUT BOOMER'S PICTURES!
HEY! I DIDN'T ORDER DOUBLE PRINTS!

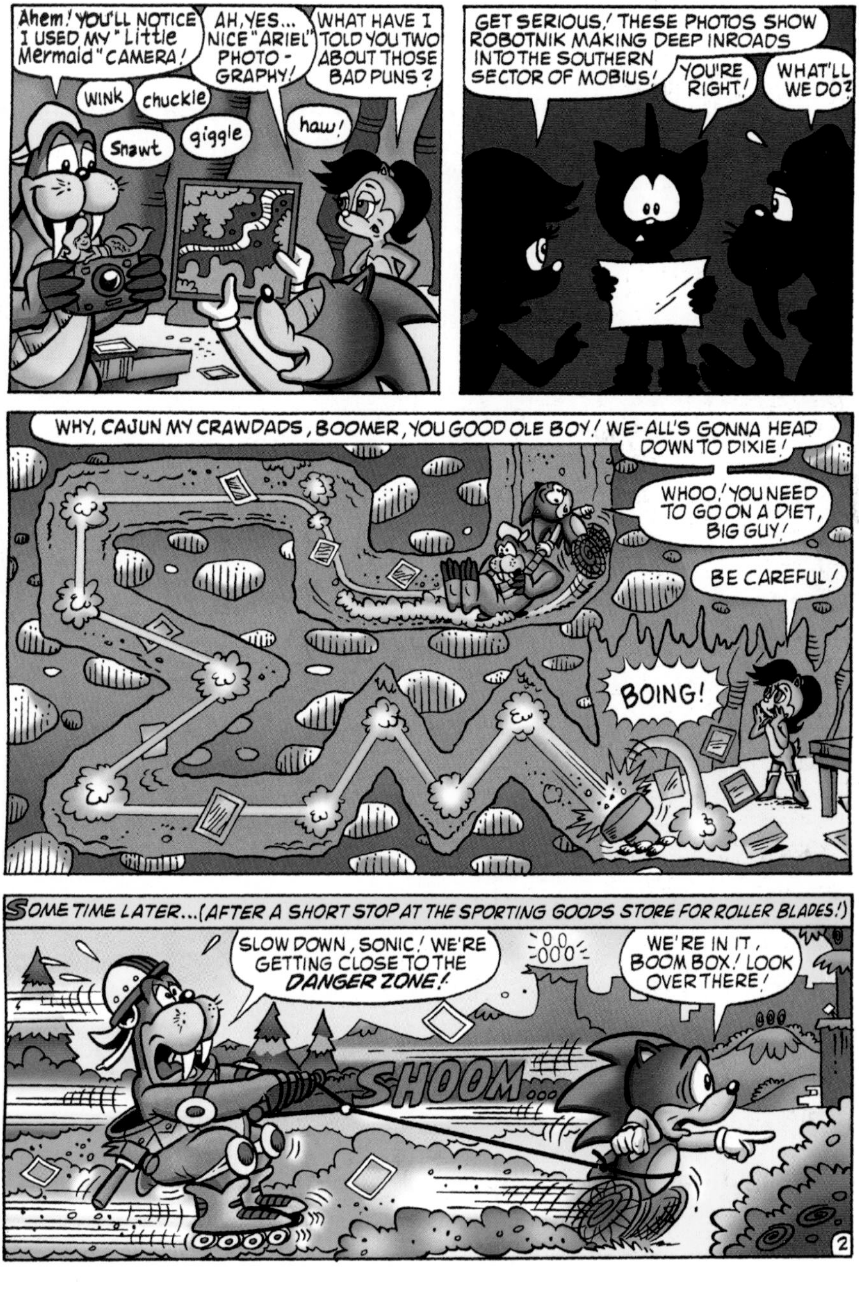
Ahem! YOU'LL NOTICE I USED MY "Little Mermaid" CAMERA!
AH, YES... NICE "ARIEL" PHOTO-GRAPHY!
WHAT HAVE I TOLD YOU TWO ABOUT THOSE BAD PUNS?
WINK
chuckle
Snawt
giggle
haw!
GET SERIOUS! THESE PHOTOS SHOW ROBOTNIK MAKING DEEP INROADS INTO THE SOUTHERN SECTOR OF MOBIUS!
YOU'RE RIGHT!
WHAT'LL WE DO?
WHY, CAJUN MY CRAWDADS, BOOMER, YOU GOOD OLE BOY! WE-ALL'S GONNA HEAD DOWN TO DIXIE!
WHOO! YOU NEED TO GO ON A DIET, BIG GUY!
BE CAREFUL!
BOING!
SOME TIME LATER...(AFTER A SHORT STOP AT THE SPORTING GOODS STORE FOR ROLLER BLADES!)
SLOW DOWN, SONIC! WE'RE GETTING CLOSE TO THE DANGER ZONE!
WE'RE IN IT, BOOM BOX! LOOK OVER THERE!
SHOOM...

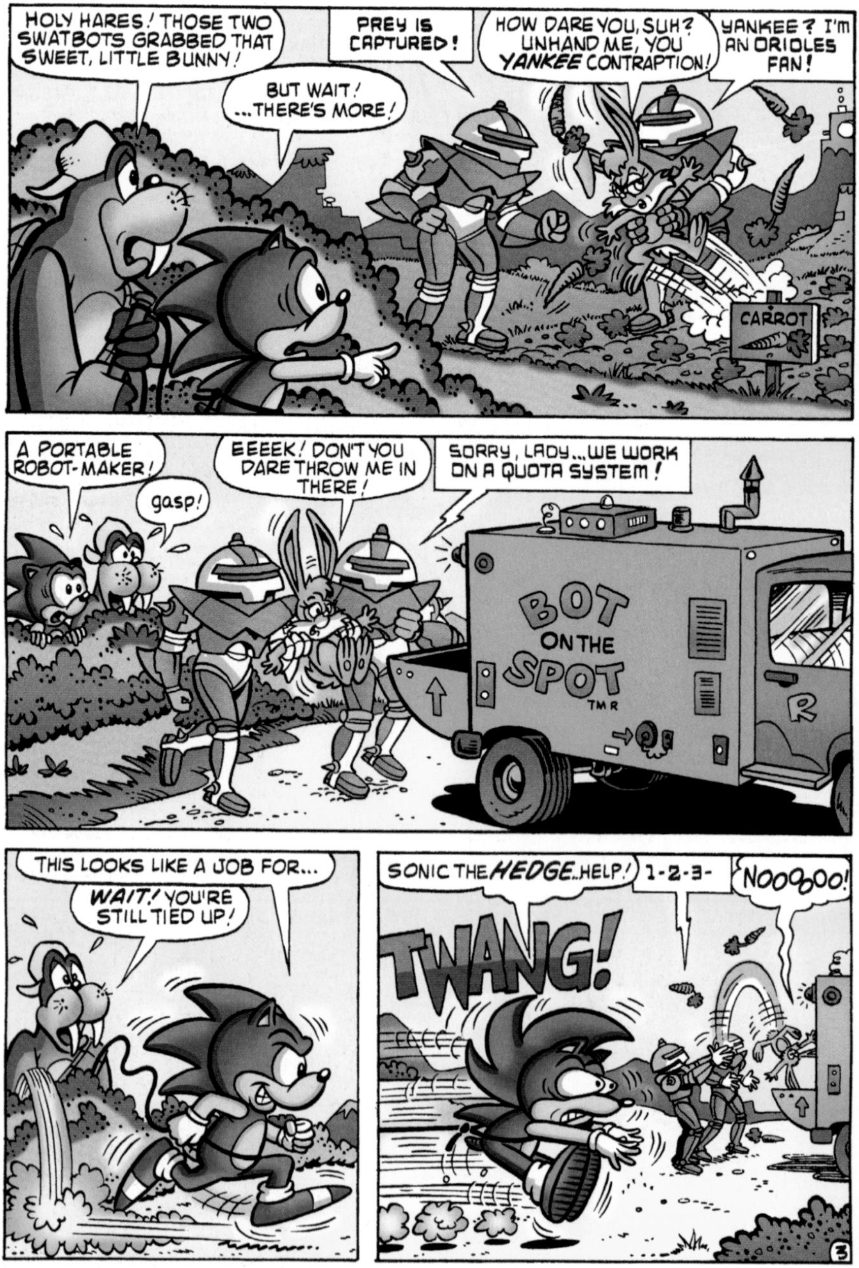
HOLY HARES! THOSE TWO SWATBOTS GRABBED THAT SWEET, LITTLE BUNNY!
BUT WAIT! ...THERE'S MORE!
PREY IS CAPTURED!
HOW DARE YOU, SUH? UNHAND ME, YOU YANKEE CONTRAPTION!
YANKEE? I'M AN ORIOLES FAN!
CARROT
A PORTABLE ROBOT-MAKER!
gasp!
EEEEK! DON'T YOU DARE THROW ME IN THERE!
SORRY, LADY...WE WORK ON A QUOTA SYSTEM!
BOT ON THE SPOT TMR
THIS LOOKS LIKE A JOB FOR...
WAIT! YOU'RE STILL TIED UP!
SONIC THE HEDGE..HELP!
1-2-3-
NOOOOOO!
TWANG!
3

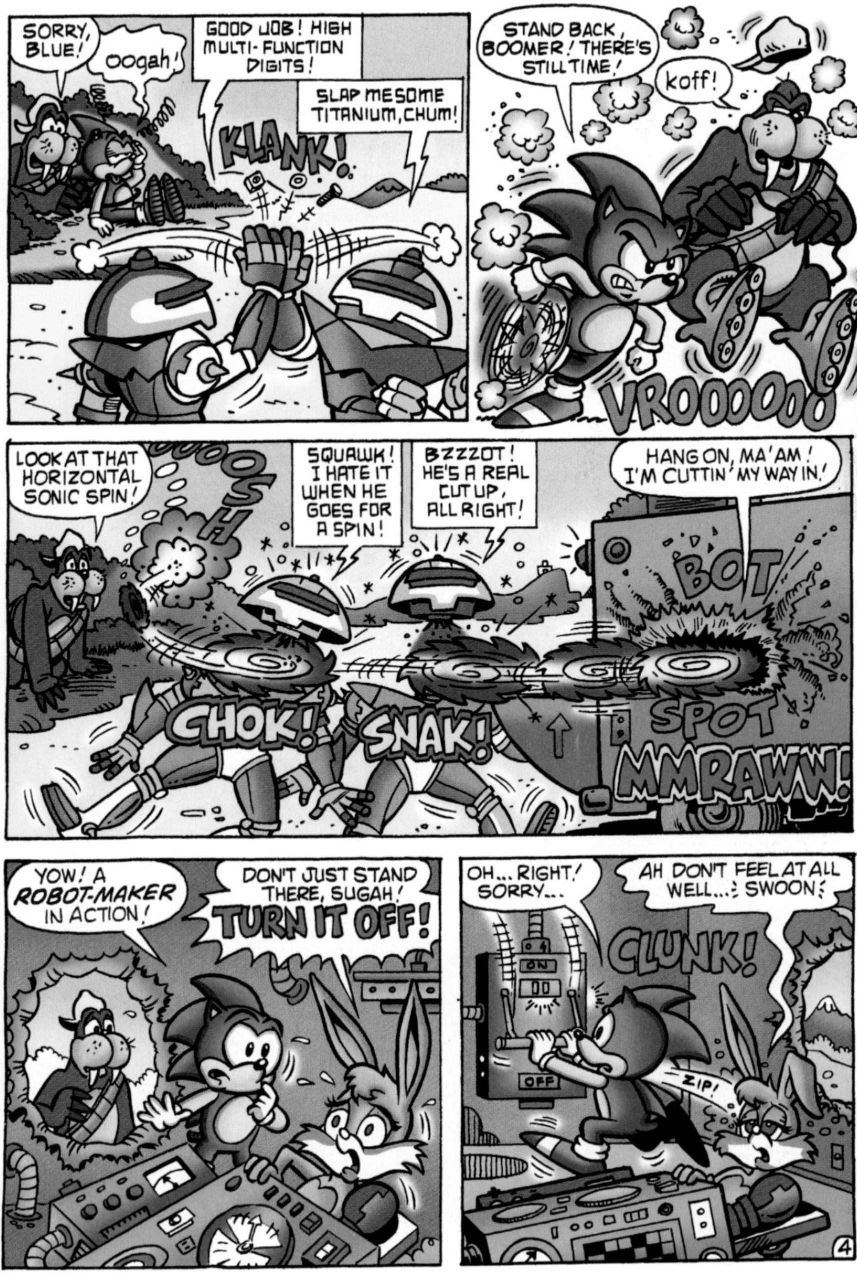
SORRY, BLUE!
Oogah!
GOOD JOB! HIGH MULTI-FUNCTION DIGITS!
SLAP ME SOME TITANIUM, CHUM!
KLANK!
STAND BACK, BOOMER! THERE'S STILL TIME!
koff!
VROOOOOO
LOOK AT THAT HORIZONTAL SONIC SPIN!
SQUAWK! I HATE IT WHEN HE GOES FOR A SPIN!
BZZZOT! HE'S A REAL CUT UP, ALL RIGHT!
HANG ON, MA'AM! I'M CUTTIN' MY WAY IN!
BOT
CHOK!
SNAK!
SPOT
MMRAWW!
YOW! A ROBOT-MAKER IN ACTION!
DON'T JUST STAND THERE, SUGAH! TURN IT OFF!
OH... RIGHT! SORRY...
AH DON'T FEEL AT ALL WELL... SWOON
CLUNK!
ON
OFF
ZIP!

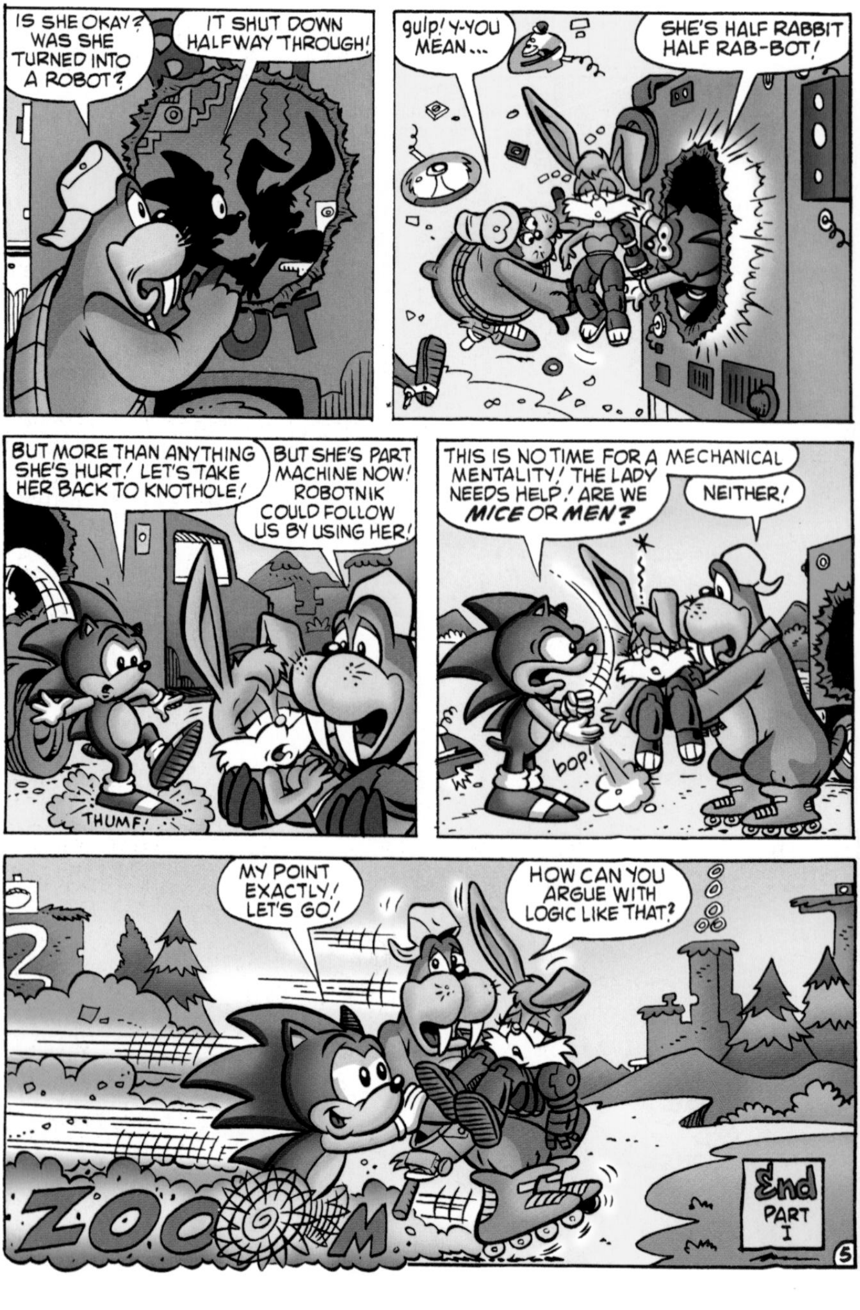

IS SHE OKAY? WAS SHE TURNED INTO A ROBOT?
IT SHUT DOWN HALFWAY THROUGH!
gulp! Y-YOU MEAN...
SHE'S HALF RABBIT HALF RAB-BOT!
BUT MORE THAN ANYTHING SHE'S HURT! LET'S TAKE HER BACK TO KNOTHOLE!
BUT SHE'S PART MACHINE NOW! ROBOTNIK COULD FOLLOW US BY USING HER!
THUMF!
THIS IS NO TIME FOR A MECHANICAL MENTALITY! THE LADY NEEDS HELP! ARE WE MICE OR MEN?
NEITHER!
bop!
MY POINT EXACTLY! LET'S GO!
HOW CAN YOU ARGUE WITH LOGIC LIKE THAT?
ZOOOM
End PART I

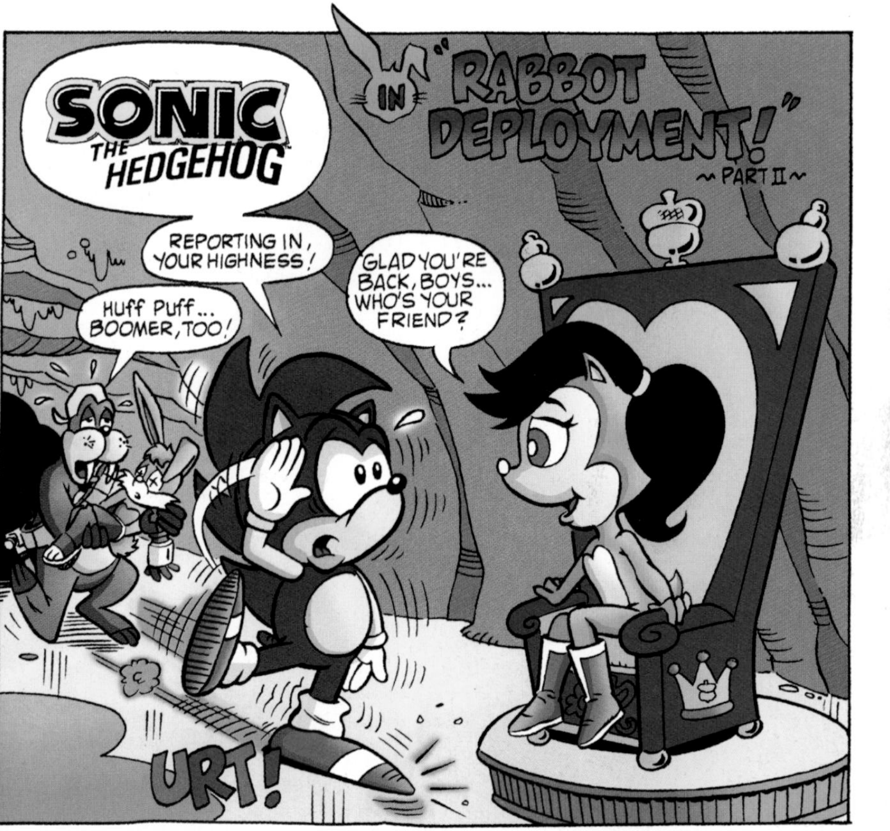
SONIC THE HEDGEHOG
IN "RABBOT DEPLOYMENT!"
~PART II~
REPORTING IN, YOUR HIGHNESS!
HUFF PUFF... BOOMER, TOO!
GLAD YOU'RE BACK, BOYS... WHO'S YOUR FRIEND?
URT!

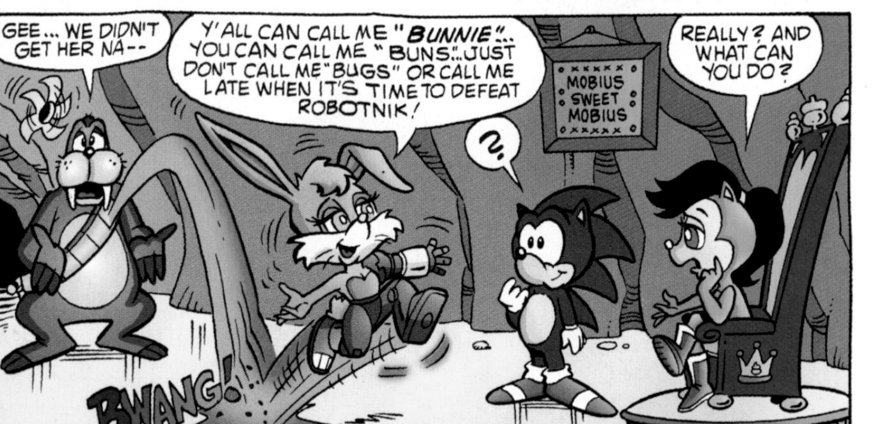
GEE... WE DIDN'T GET HER NA--
Y'ALL CAN CALL ME "BUNNIE"... YOU CAN CALL ME "BUNS"... JUST DON'T CALL ME "BUGS" OR CALL ME LATE WHEN IT'S TIME TO DEFEAT ROBOTNIK!
MOBIUS SWEET MOBIUS
?
REALLY? AND WHAT CAN YOU DO?
BWANG!

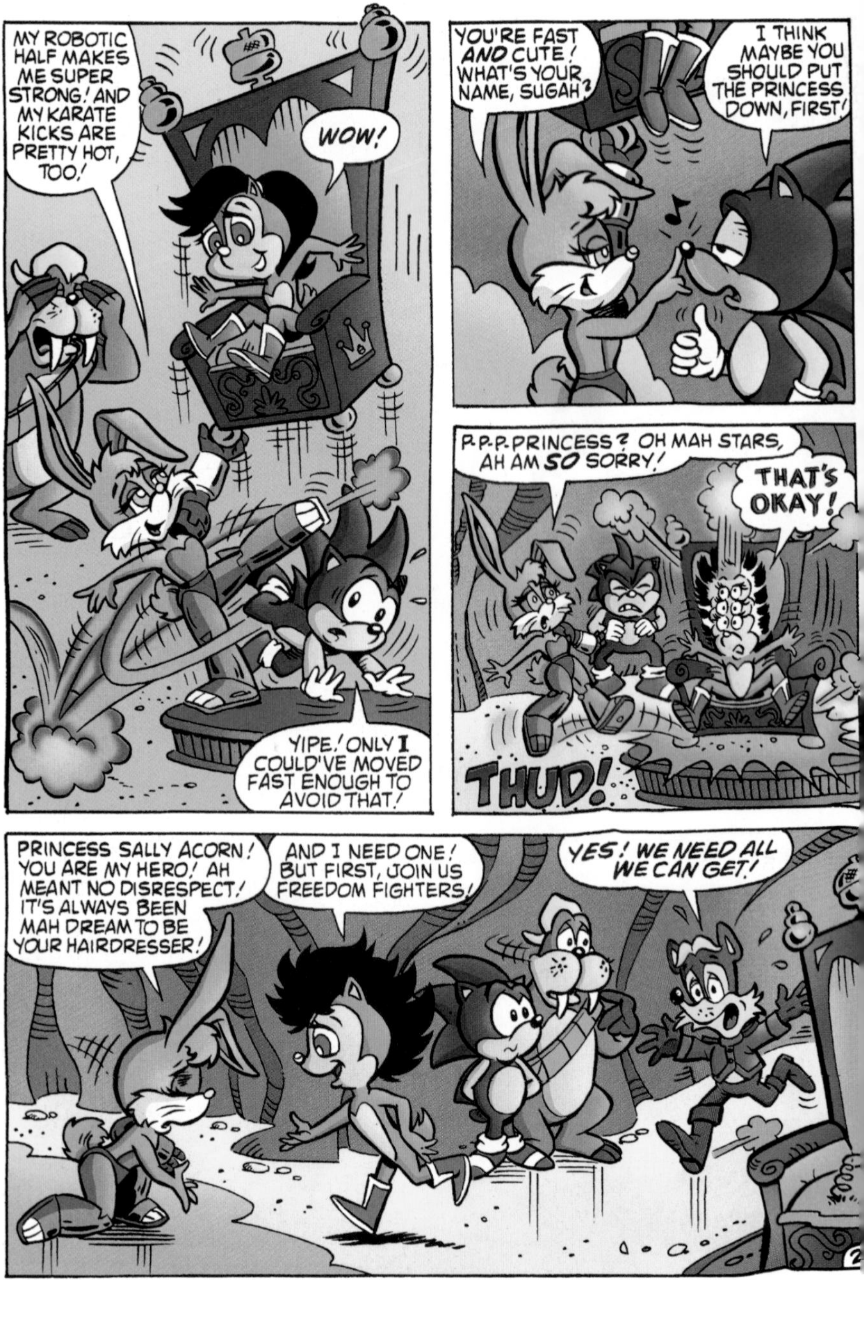
MY ROBOTIC HALF MAKES ME SUPER STRONG! AND MY KARATE KICKS ARE PRETTY HOT, TOO!
WOW!
YIPE! ONLY I COULD'VE MOVED FAST ENOUGH TO AVOID THAT!
YOU'RE FAST AND CUTE! WHAT'S YOUR NAME, SUGAH?
I THINK MAYBE YOU SHOULD PUT THE PRINCESS DOWN, FIRST!
P-P-P-PRINCESS? OH MAH STARS, AH AM SO SORRY!
THAT'S OKAY!
THUD!
PRINCESS SALLY ACORN! YOU ARE MY HERO! AH MEANT NO DISRESPECT! IT'S ALWAYS BEEN MAH DREAM TO BE YOUR HAIRDRESSER!
AND I NEED ONE! BUT FIRST, JOIN US FREEDOM FIGHTERS!
YES! WE NEED ALL WE CAN GET!

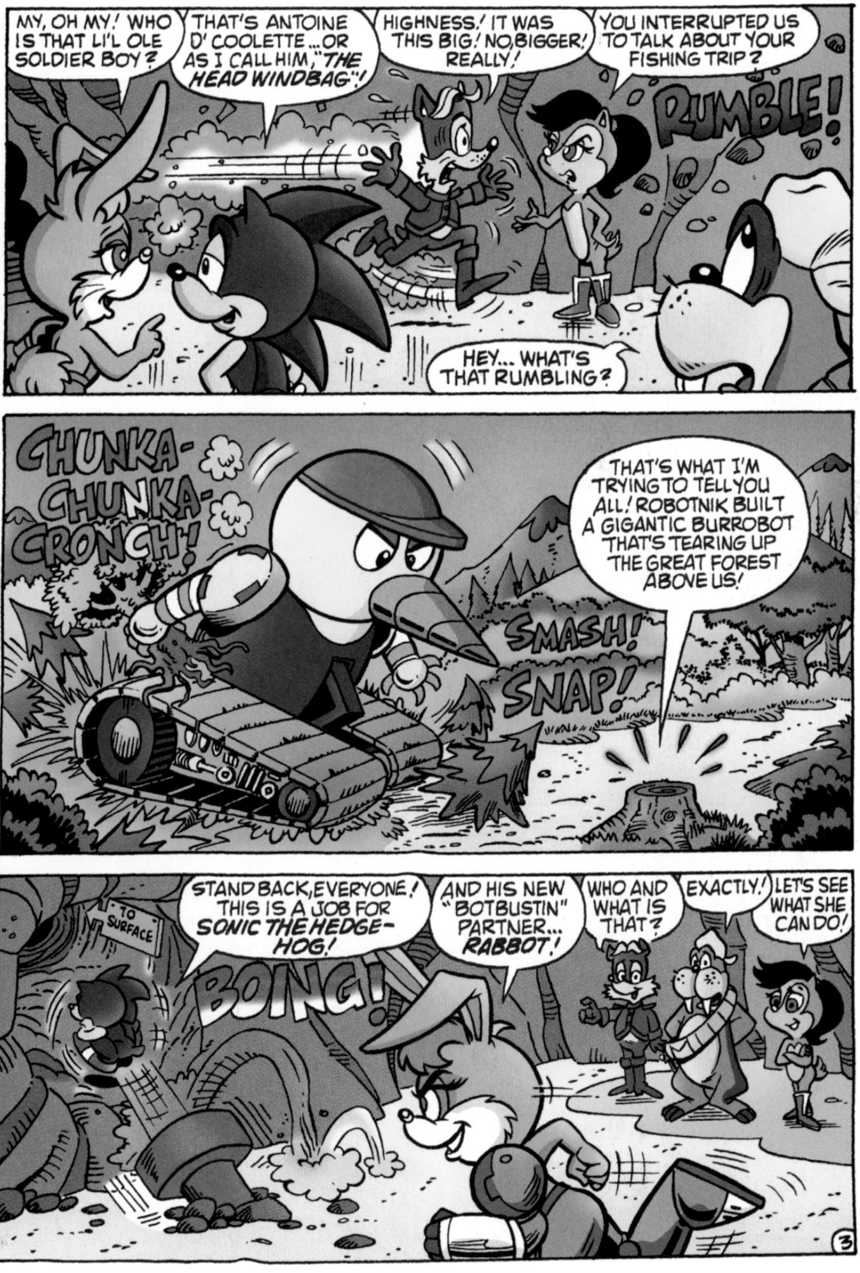
MY, OH MY! WHO IS THAT LI'L OLE SOLDIER BOY?
THAT'S ANTOINE D' COOLETTE ...OR AS I CALL HIM, "THE HEAD WINDBAG"!
HIGHNESS! IT WAS THIS BIG! NO, BIGGER! REALLY!
YOU INTERRUPTED US TO TALK ABOUT YOUR FISHING TRIP?
RUMBLE!
HEY... WHAT'S THAT RUMBLING?
CHUNKA-CHUNKA-CRONCH!
THAT'S WHAT I'M TRYING TO TELL YOU ALL! ROBOTNIK BUILT A GIGANTIC BURROBOT THAT'S TEARING UP THE GREAT FOREST ABOVE US!
SMASH!
SNAP!
TO SURFACE
STAND BACK, EVERYONE! THIS IS A JOB FOR SONIC THE HEDGE-HOG!
BOING!
AND HIS NEW "BOTBUSTIN" PARTNER... RABBOT!
WHO AND WHAT IS THAT?
EXACTLY!
LET'S SEE WHAT SHE CAN DO!

OKAY...WHERE IS THAT FLEA-BITTEN BUCKET OF BOLTS AT?

GET BACK DOWN HEAH, SUGAH!

CHUNKA-CHUNKA-CHUNK

ZIP!

CHUNKA...

CHUNKITA-CHOK!

WHOO! THANKS, BUNNIE! I WAS ALMOST A *SONIC* PANCAKE!

DON'T MENTION IT! ALTHOUGH I MAY USE YOU FOR A REFERENCE WHEN I APPLY TO HAIR-DRESSING SCHOOL!

MEANWHILE, LET'S DISPENSE WITH THIS ILL-MANNERED MACHINE!...YA'LL GOT A PLAN?

I SURE DO, BUNNIE...WATCH MY SMOKE!

BROWWW...

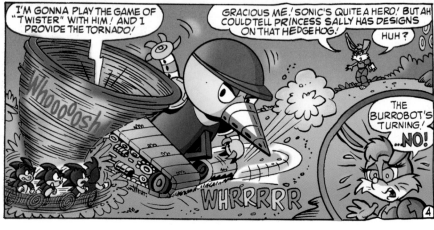

I'M GONNA PLAY THE GAME OF "TWISTER" WITH HIM! AND I PROVIDE THE TORNADO!

Whoooosh

GRACIOUS ME! SONIC'S QUITE A HERO! BUT AH COULD TELL *PRINCESS SALLY* HAS DESIGNS ON THAT HEDGEHOG!

HUH?

THE BURROBOT'S TURNING! ...NO!

WHRRRRR

4

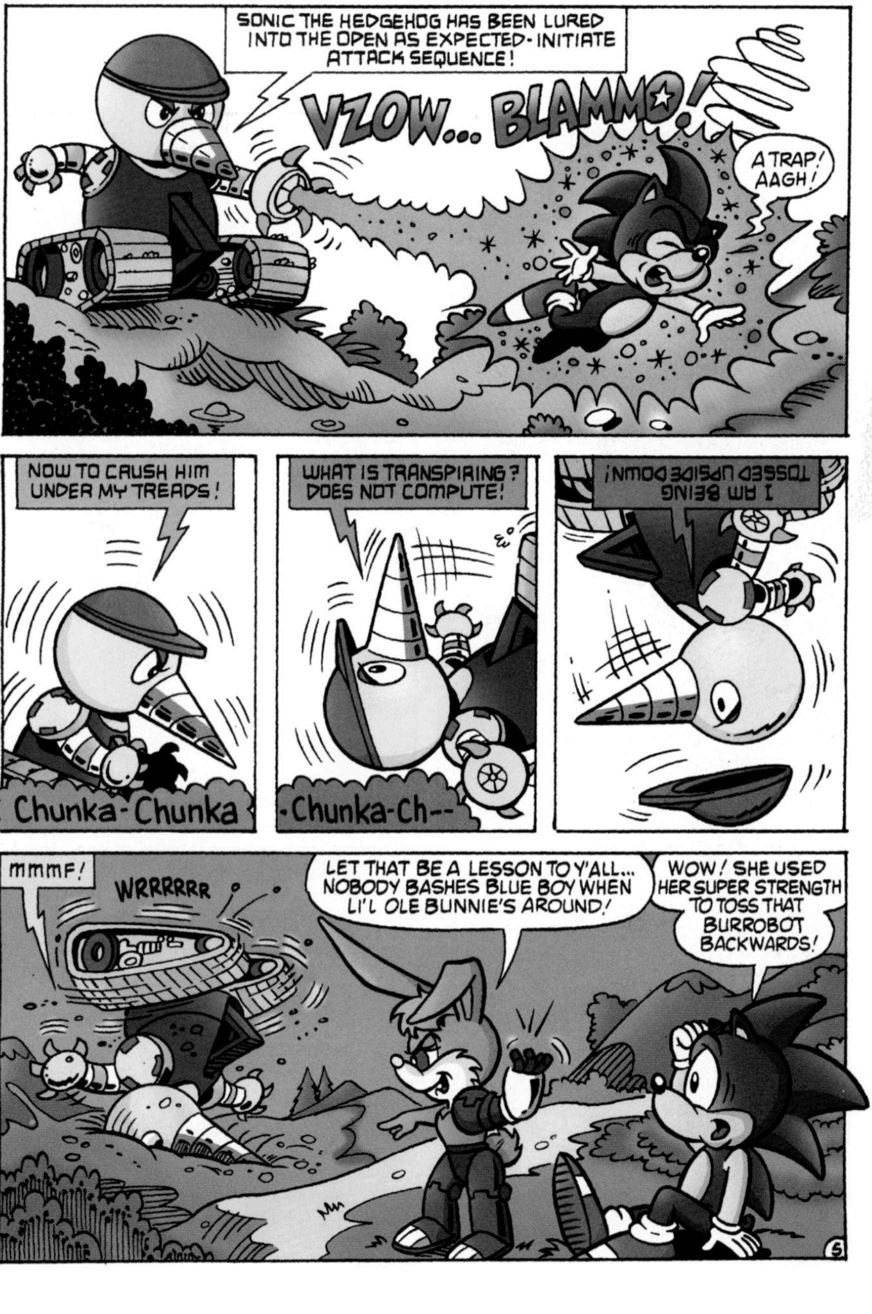
SONIC THE HEDGEHOG HAS BEEN LURED INTO THE OPEN AS EXPECTED- INITIATE ATTACK SEQUENCE!
VZOW... BLAMMO!
A TRAP! AAGH!
NOW TO CRUSH HIM UNDER MY TREADS!
Chunka-Chunka
WHAT IS TRANSPIRING? DOES NOT COMPUTE!
-Chunka-Ch--
I AM BEING TOSSED UPSIDE DOWN!
MMMF!
WRRRRRR
LET THAT BE A LESSON TO Y'ALL... NOBODY BASHES BLUE BOY WHEN LI'L OLE BUNNIE'S AROUND!
WOW! SHE USED HER SUPER STRENGTH TO TOSS THAT BURROBOT BACKWARDS!

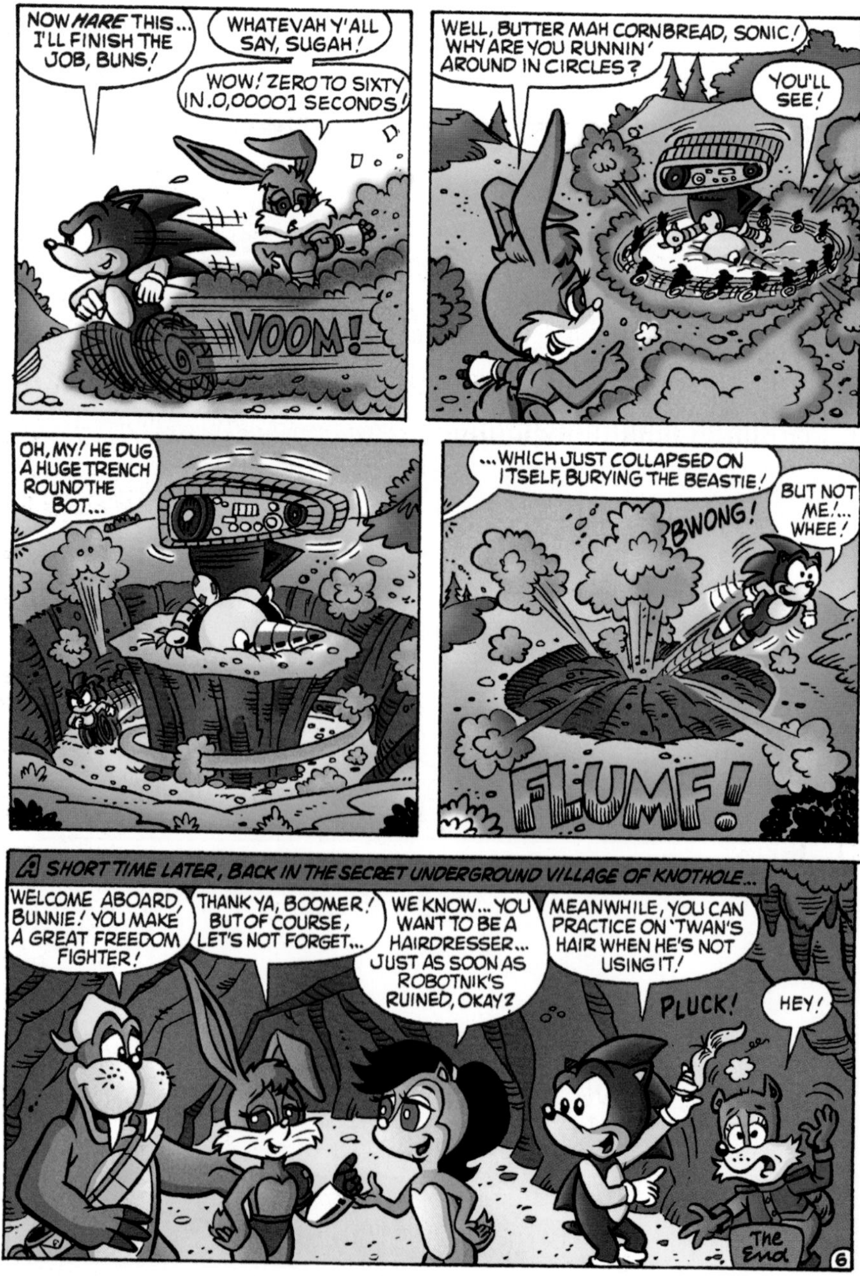
NOW *HARE* THIS... I'LL FINISH THE JOB, BUNS!
WHATEVAH Y'ALL SAY, SUGAH!
WOW! ZERO TO SIXTY IN .0,00001 SECONDS!
VOOM!
WELL, BUTTER MAH CORNBREAD, SONIC! WHY ARE YOU RUNNIN' AROUND IN CIRCLES?
YOU'LL SEE!
OH, MY! HE DUG A HUGE TRENCH ROUND THE BOT...
...WHICH JUST COLLAPSED ON ITSELF, BURYING THE BEASTIE!
BWONG!
BUT NOT ME!... WHEE!
FLUMF!
A SHORT TIME LATER, BACK IN THE SECRET UNDERGROUND VILLAGE OF KNOTHOLE...
WELCOME ABOARD, BUNNIE! YOU MAKE A GREAT FREEDOM FIGHTER!
THANK YA, BOOMER! BUT OF COURSE, LET'S NOT FORGET...
WE KNOW... YOU WANT TO BE A HAIRDRESSER... JUST AS SOON AS ROBOTNIK'S RUINED, OKAY?
MEANWHILE, YOU CAN PRACTICE ON 'TWAN'S HAIR WHEN HE'S NOT USING IT!
PLUCK!
HEY!
The End

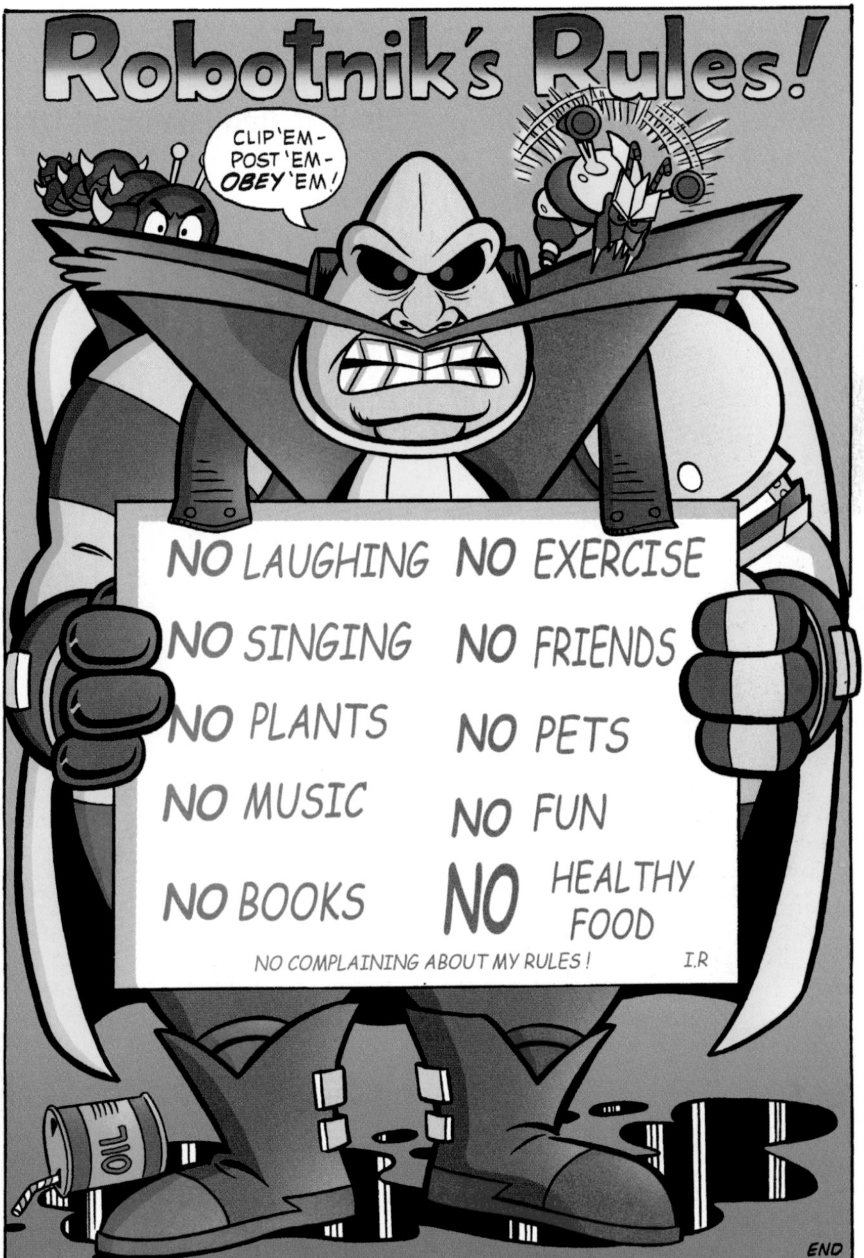

Robotnik's Rules!
CLIP 'EM - POST 'EM - OBEY 'EM!
NO LAUGHING
NO EXERCISE
NO SINGING
NO FRIENDS
NO PLANTS
NO PETS
NO MUSIC
NO FUN
NO BOOKS
NO HEALTHY FOOD
NO COMPLAINING ABOUT MY RULES!
I.R
OIL
END

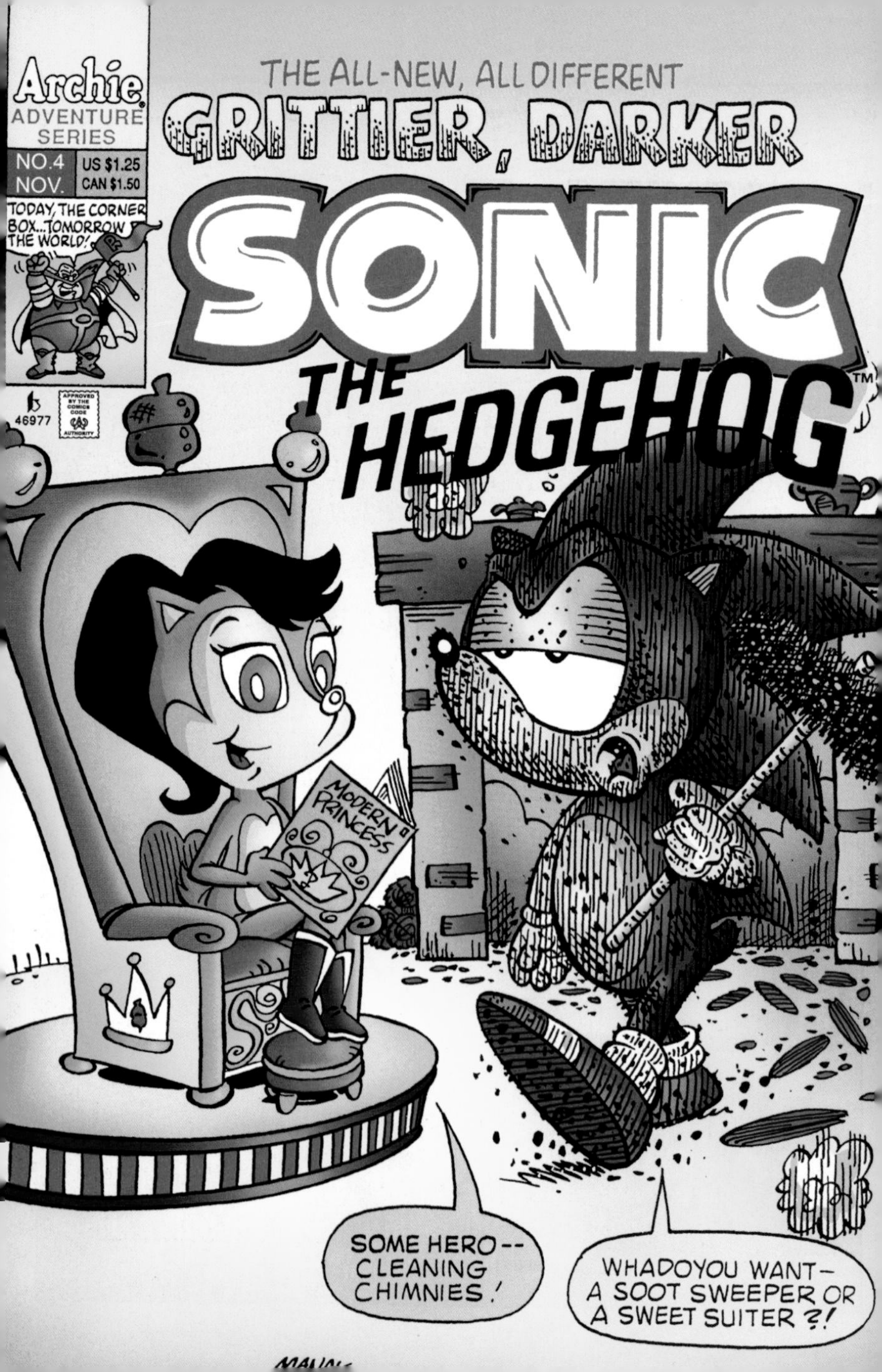
Archie
ADVENTURE SERIES
NO.4
NOV.
US $1.25
CAN $1.50
TODAY, THE CORNER BOX...TOMORROW THE WORLD!
46977
APPROVED BY THE COMICS CODE AUTHORITY
THE ALL-NEW, ALL DIFFERENT
GRITTIER, DARKER
SONIC THE HEDGEHOG™
MODERN PRINCESS
SOME HERO-- CLEANING CHIMNIES!
WHADOYOU WANT- A SOOT SWEEPER OR A SWEET SUITER?!

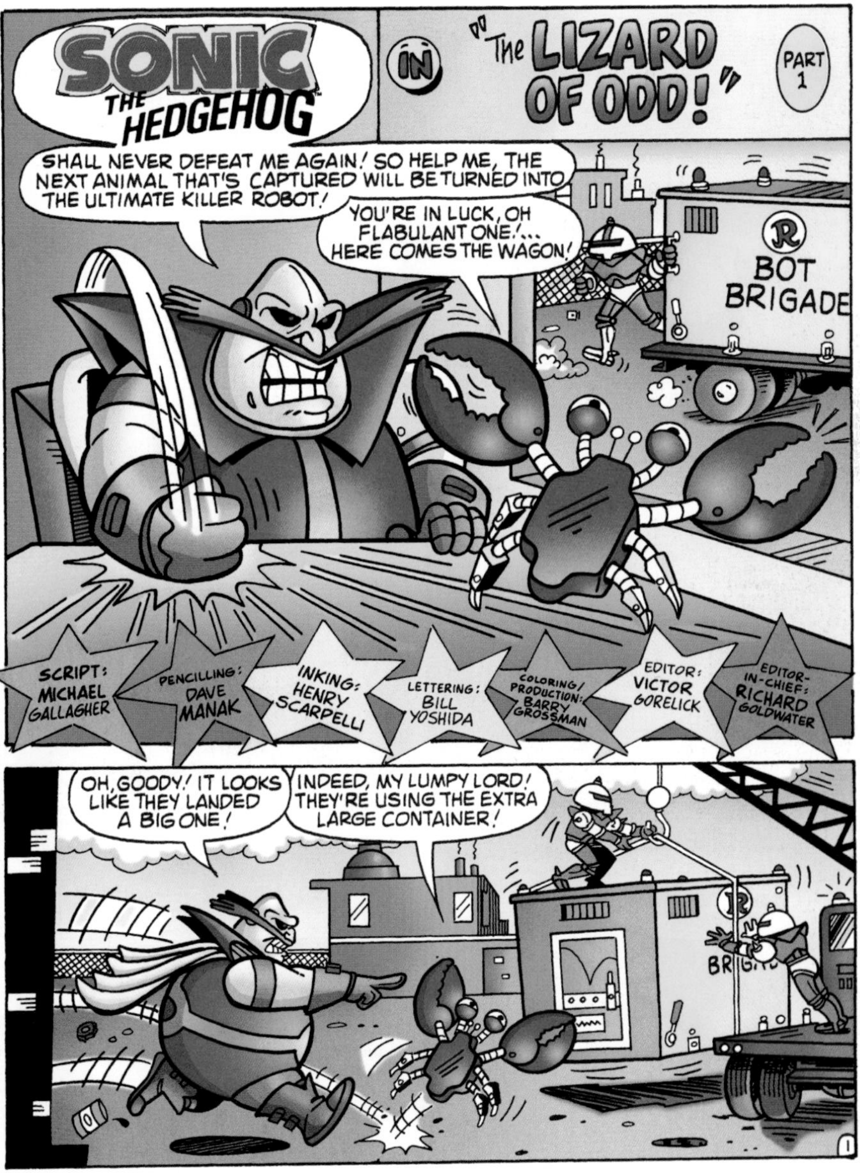
SONIC THE HEDGEHOG
IN
"The LIZARD OF ODD!"
PART 1
SHALL NEVER DEFEAT ME AGAIN! SO HELP ME, THE NEXT ANIMAL THAT'S CAPTURED WILL BE TURNED INTO THE ULTIMATE KILLER ROBOT!
YOU'RE IN LUCK, OH FLABULANT ONE!... HERE COMES THE WAGON!
R
BOT BRIGADE
SCRIPT: MICHAEL GALLAGHER
PENCILLING: DAVE MANAK
INKING: HENRY SCARPELLI
LETTERING: BILL YOSHIDA
COLORING/ PRODUCTION: BARRY GROSSMAN
EDITOR: VICTOR GORELICK
EDITOR-IN-CHIEF: RICHARD GOLDWATER
OH, GOODY! IT LOOKS LIKE THEY LANDED A BIG ONE!
INDEED, MY LUMPY LORD! THEY'RE USING THE EXTRA LARGE CONTAINER!
R
BR

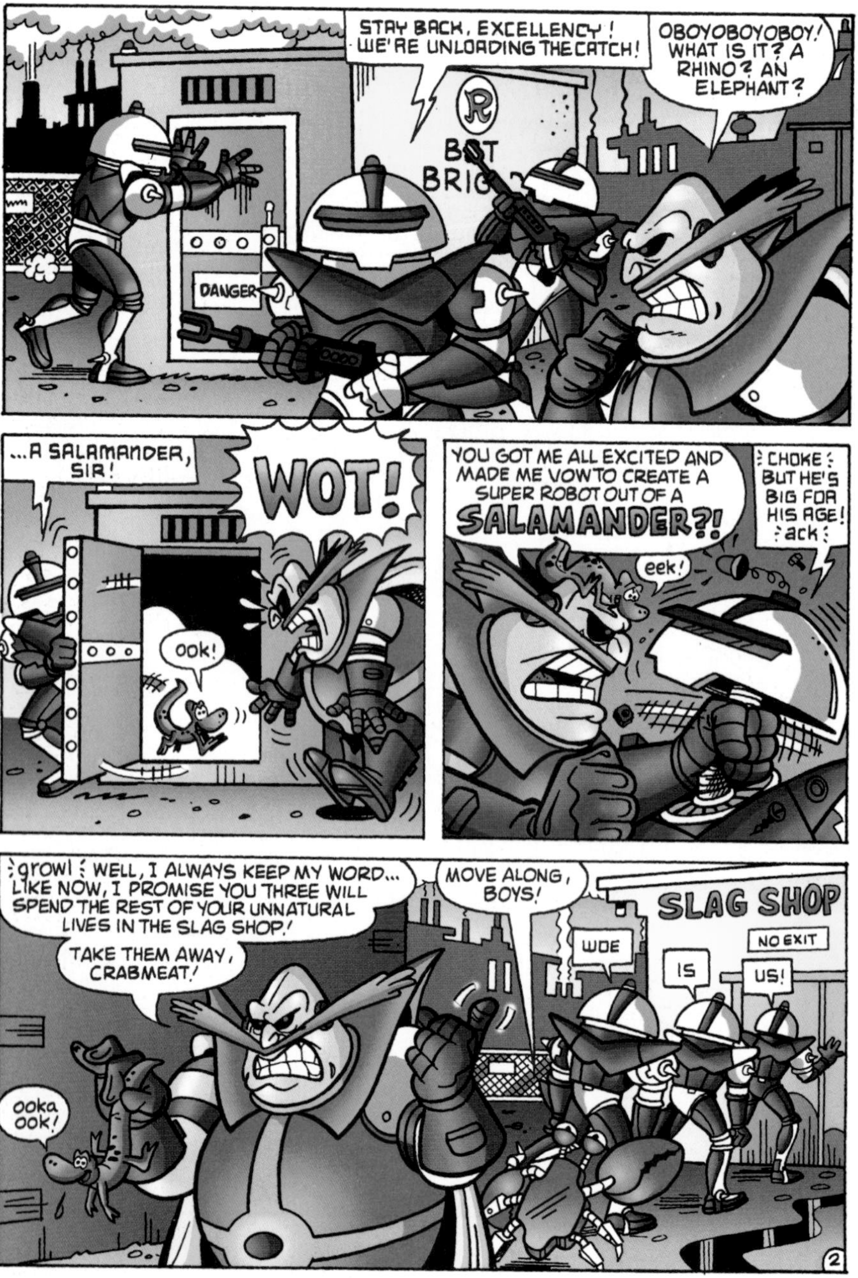
STAY BACK, EXCELLENCY! WE'RE UNLOADING THE CATCH!
OBOYOBOYOBOY! WHAT IS IT? A RHINO? AN ELEPHANT?
BOT BRIG
DANGER
...A SALAMANDER, SIR!
WOT!
OOK!
YOU GOT ME ALL EXCITED AND MADE ME VOW TO CREATE A SUPER ROBOT OUT OF A SALAMANDER?!
CHOKE BUT HE'S BIG FOR HIS AGE! ack
eek!
growl WELL, I ALWAYS KEEP MY WORD... LIKE NOW, I PROMISE YOU THREE WILL SPEND THE REST OF YOUR UNNATURAL LIVES IN THE SLAG SHOP!
TAKE THEM AWAY, CRABMEAT!
MOVE ALONG, BOYS!
SLAG SHOP
NO EXIT
WOE
IS
US!
ooka ook!

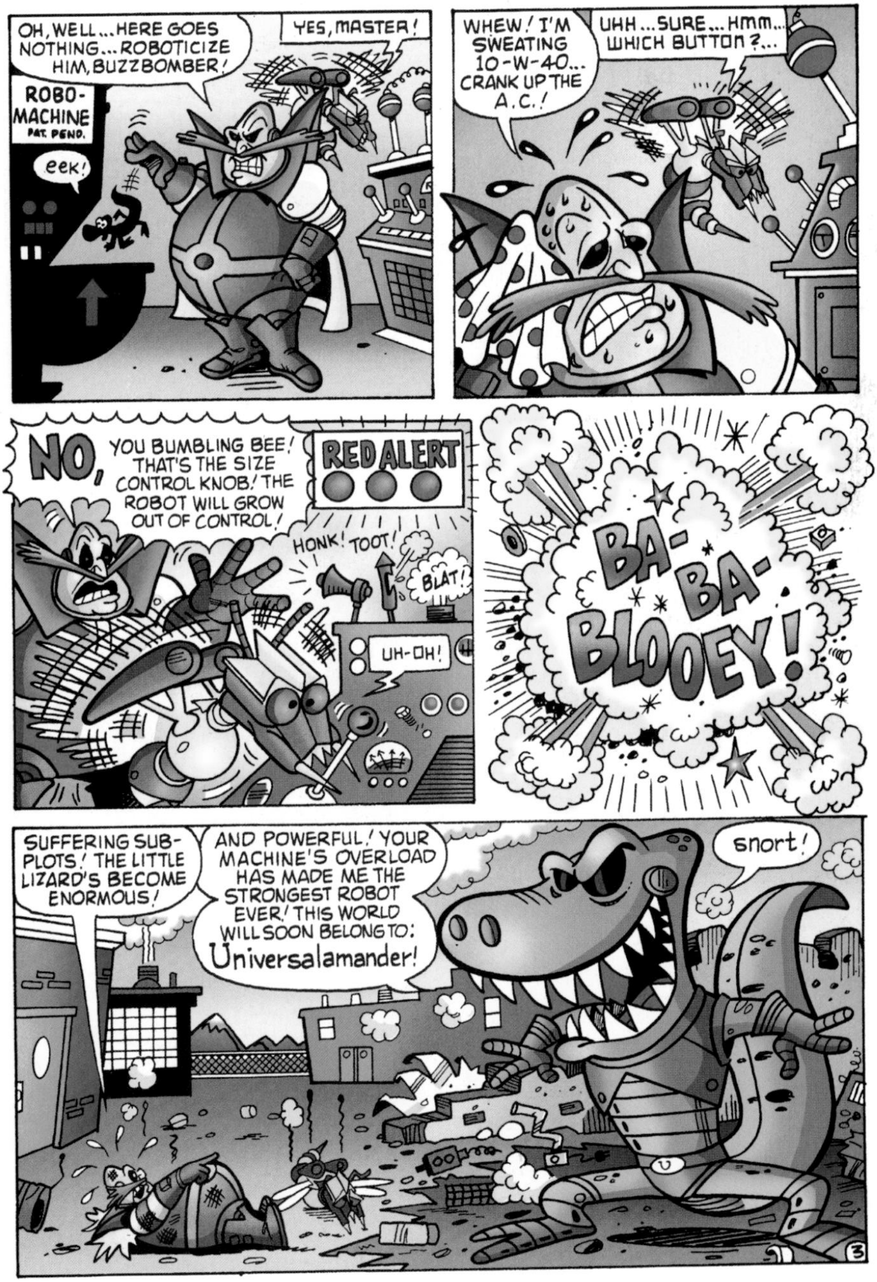
OH, WELL... HERE GOES NOTHING... ROBOTICIZE HIM, BUZZBOMBER!
YES, MASTER!
ROBO-MACHINE PAT. PEND.
eek!
WHEW! I'M SWEATING 10-W-40... CRANK UP THE A.C.!
UHH... SURE... HMM... WHICH BUTTON?...
NO, YOU BUMBLING BEE! THAT'S THE SIZE CONTROL KNOB! THE ROBOT WILL GROW OUT OF CONTROL!
RED ALERT
HONK! TOOT!
BLAT!
UH-OH!
BA-BA-BLOOEY!
SUFFERING SUB-PLOTS! THE LITTLE LIZARD'S BECOME ENORMOUS!
AND POWERFUL! YOUR MACHINE'S OVERLOAD HAS MADE ME THE STRONGEST ROBOT EVER! THIS WORLD WILL SOON BELONG TO: Universalamander!
snort!
3

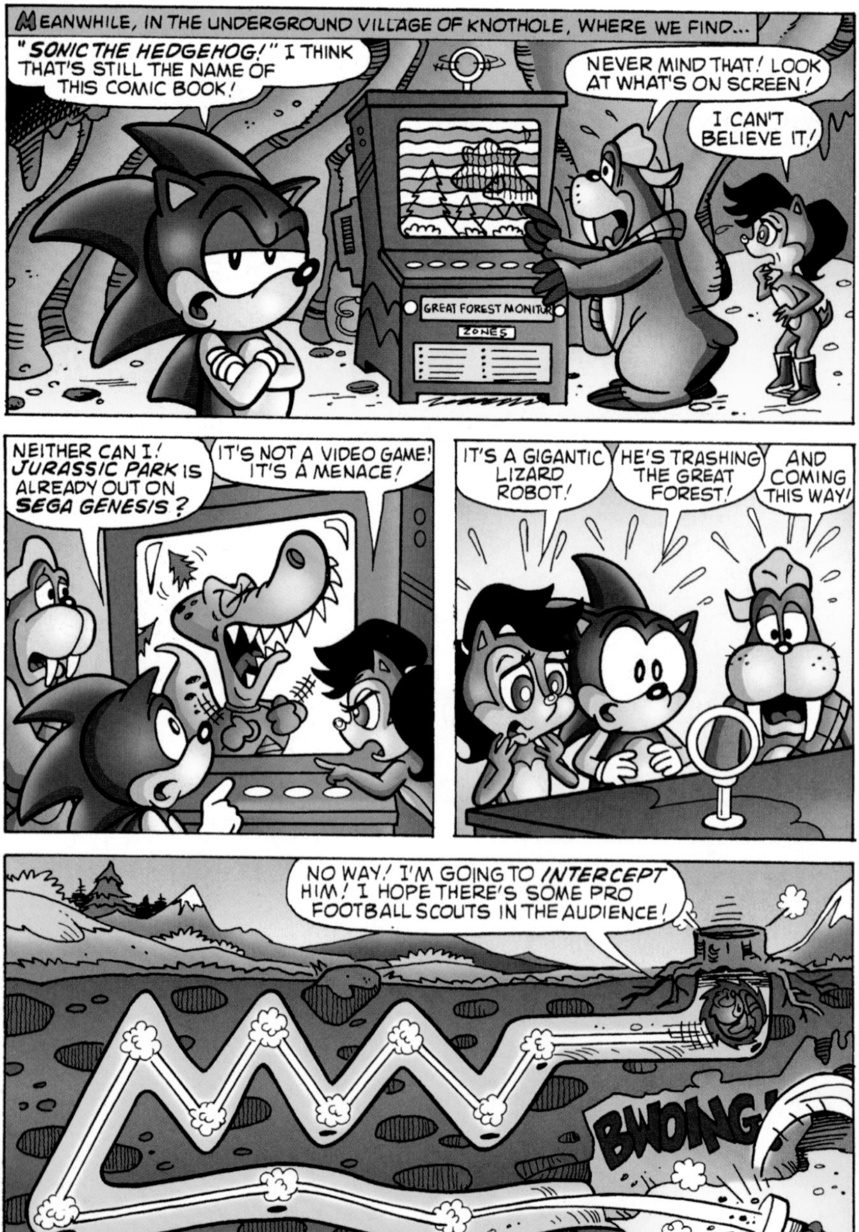
MEANWHILE, IN THE UNDERGROUND VILLAGE OF KNOTHOLE, WHERE WE FIND...
"SONIC THE HEDGEHOG!" I THINK THAT'S STILL THE NAME OF THIS COMIC BOOK!
NEVER MIND THAT! LOOK AT WHAT'S ON SCREEN!
I CAN'T BELIEVE IT!
GREAT FOREST MONITOR
ZONES
NEITHER CAN I! JURASSIC PARK IS ALREADY OUT ON SEGA GENESIS?
IT'S NOT A VIDEO GAME! IT'S A MENACE!
IT'S A GIGANTIC LIZARD ROBOT!
HE'S TRASHING THE GREAT FOREST!
AND COMING THIS WAY!
NO WAY! I'M GOING TO INTERCEPT HIM! I HOPE THERE'S SOME PRO FOOTBALL SCOUTS IN THE AUDIENCE!
BWOING!
4

WHAT THE--?! IT'S ROBOTNIK... TAKING OFF IN HIS EGG-O-MATIC!

UNIVERSALAMANDER IS TOO POWERFUL! I'M GETTING OFF MOBIUS BEFORE HE DESTROYS IT... AND ME!

WHAT'S HE SO AFRAID OF?...

YIPE! THINGS ON TV ALWAYS LOOK BIGGER IN REAL LIFE!

ROWR!

BOOM!

THUMP!

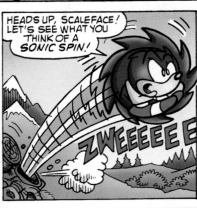

HEADS UP, SCALEFACE! LET'S SEE WHAT YOU THINK OF A SONIC SPIN!

ZWEEEEE E

I THINK IT LOOKS DELICIOUS!

CHOMP!

HEY!

5

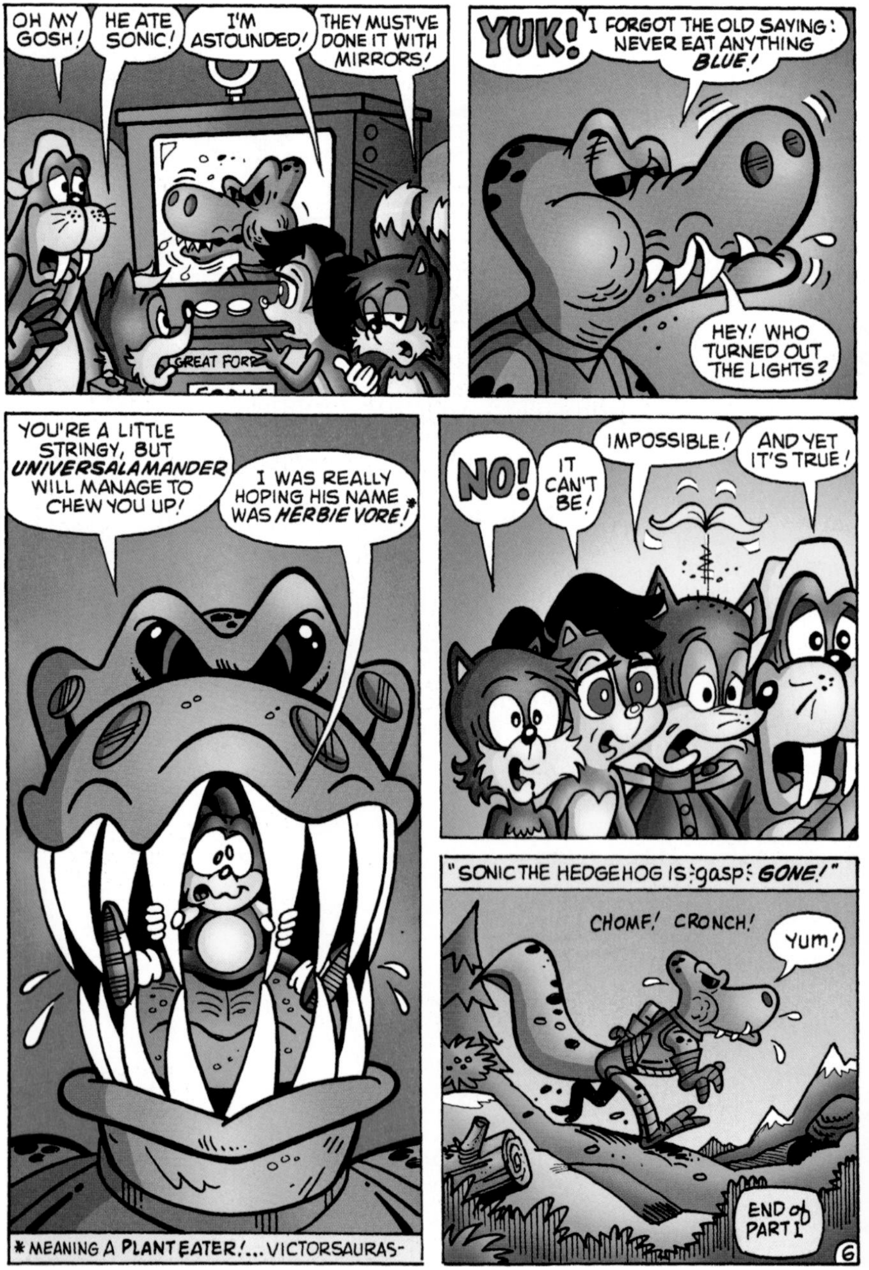
OH MY GOSH!
HE ATE SONIC!
I'M ASTOUNDED!
THEY MUST'VE DONE IT WITH MIRRORS!
GREAT FOR
YUK!
I FORGOT THE OLD SAYING: NEVER EAT ANYTHING BLUE!
HEY! WHO TURNED OUT THE LIGHTS?
YOU'RE A LITTLE STRINGY, BUT UNIVERSALAMANDER WILL MANAGE TO CHEW YOU UP!
I WAS REALLY HOPING HIS NAME WAS HERBIE VORE! *
* MEANING A PLANT EATER!... VICTORSAURAS-
NO!
IT CAN'T BE!
IMPOSSIBLE!
AND YET IT'S TRUE!
"SONIC THE HEDGEHOG IS :gasp: GONE!"
CHOMF! CRONCH!
Yum!
END of PART I
6

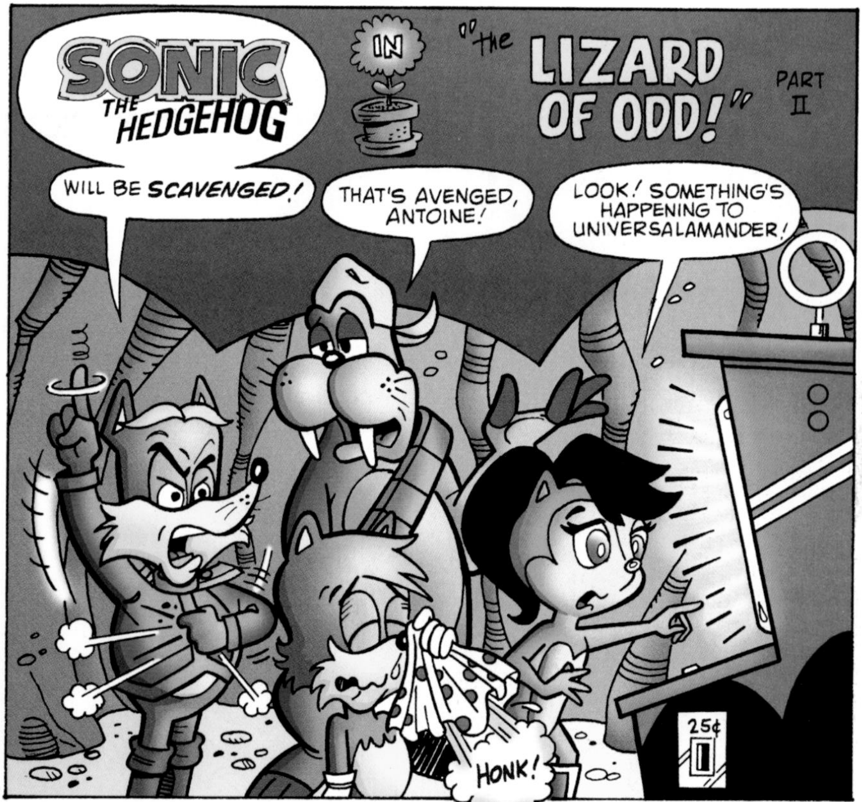
SONIC THE HEDGEHOG
IN
"the LIZARD OF ODD!"
PART II
WILL BE SCAVENGED!
THAT'S AVENGED, ANTOINE!
LOOK! SOMETHING'S HAPPENING TO UNIVERSALAMANDER!
25¢
HONK!

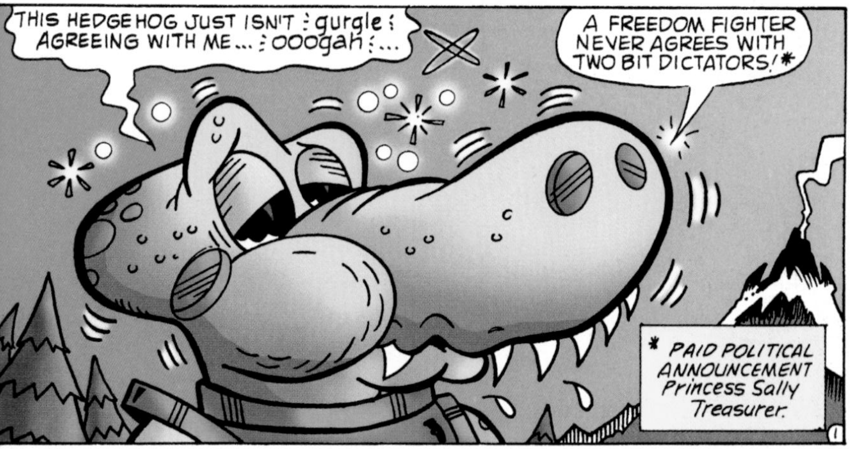
THIS HEDGEHOG JUST ISN'T ⁝gurgle⁝ AGREEING WITH ME... ⁝ooogah⁝...
A FREEDOM FIGHTER NEVER AGREES WITH TWO BIT DICTATORS!*
* PAID POLITICAL ANNOUNCEMENT Princess Sally Treasurer.
1

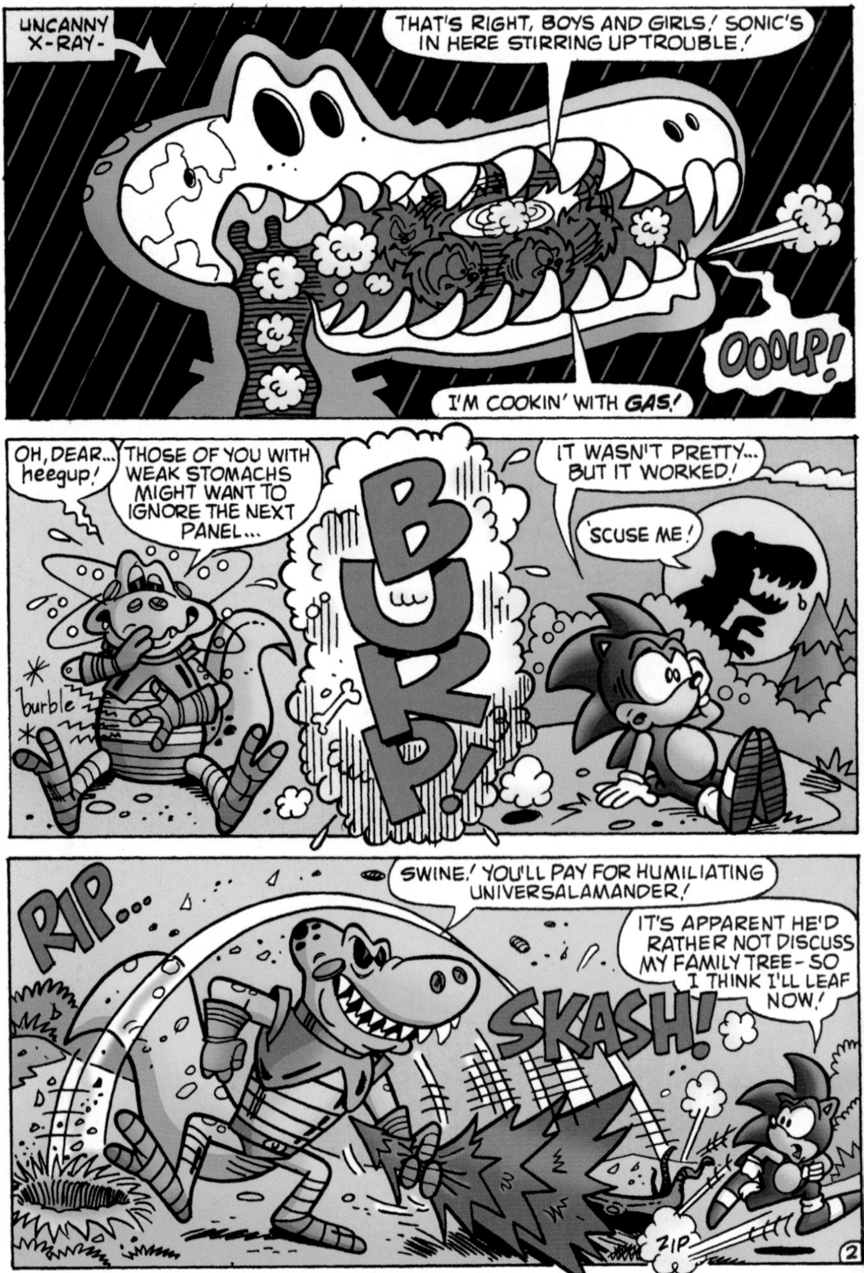
UNCANNY X-RAY-
THAT'S RIGHT, BOYS AND GIRLS! SONIC'S IN HERE STIRRING UP TROUBLE!
OOOLP!
I'M COOKIN' WITH GAS!
OH, DEAR... heegup!
THOSE OF YOU WITH WEAK STOMACHS MIGHT WANT TO IGNORE THE NEXT PANEL...
burble
BURP!
IT WASN'T PRETTY... BUT IT WORKED!
'SCUSE ME!
RIP...
SWINE! YOU'LL PAY FOR HUMILIATING UNIVERSALAMANDER!
IT'S APPARENT HE'D RATHER NOT DISCUSS MY FAMILY TREE- SO I THINK I'LL LEAF NOW!
SKASH!
ZIP

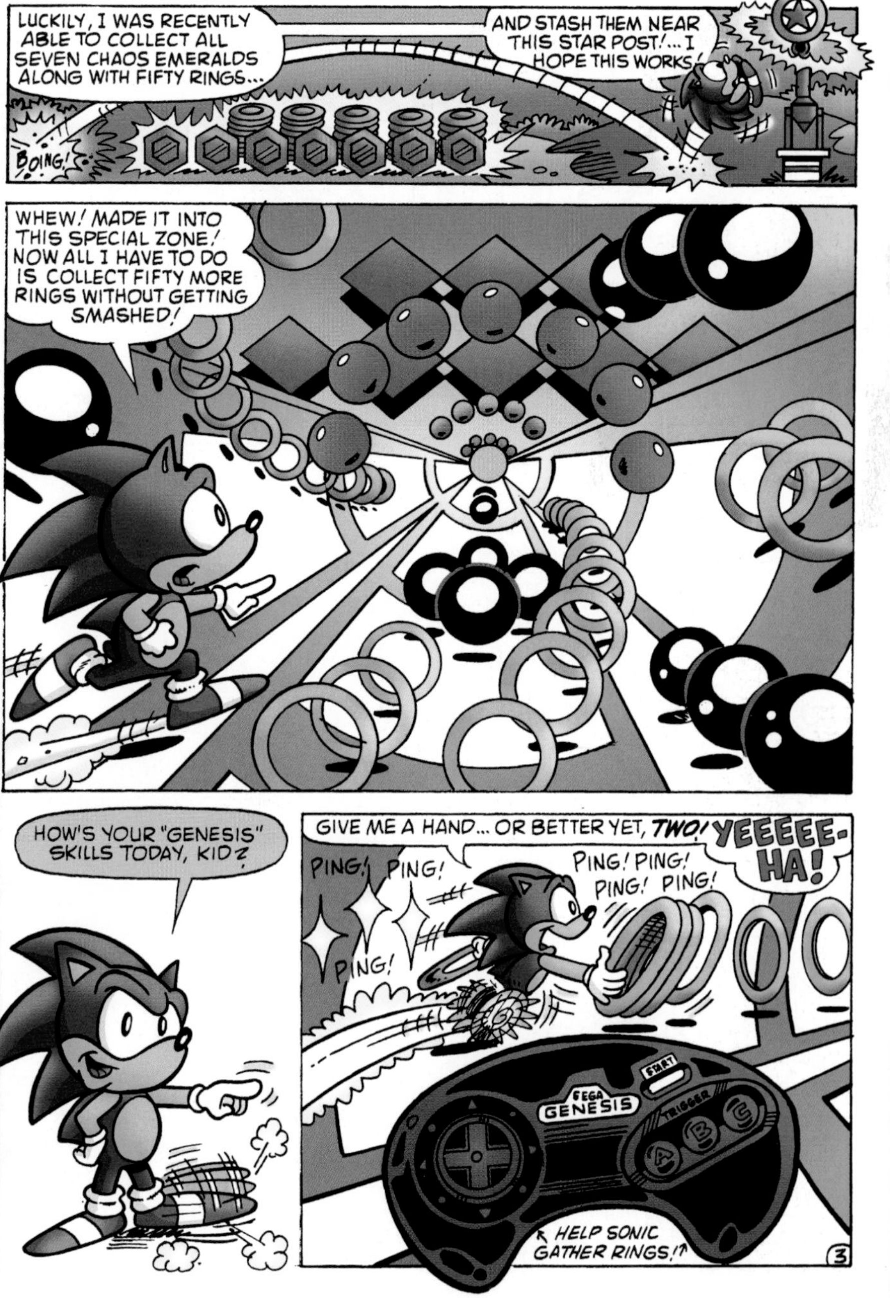

LUCKILY, I WAS RECENTLY ABLE TO COLLECT ALL SEVEN CHAOS EMERALDS ALONG WITH FIFTY RINGS...
AND STASH THEM NEAR THIS STAR POST!... I HOPE THIS WORKS!
BOING!
WHEW! MADE IT INTO THIS SPECIAL ZONE! NOW ALL I HAVE TO DO IS COLLECT FIFTY MORE RINGS WITHOUT GETTING SMASHED!
HOW'S YOUR "GENESIS" SKILLS TODAY, KID?
GIVE ME A HAND... OR BETTER YET, TWO!
YEEEEE-HA!
PING! PING!
PING! PING! PING! PING!
PING!
START
SEGA GENESIS
TRIGGER
A B C
HELP SONIC GATHER RINGS!
3

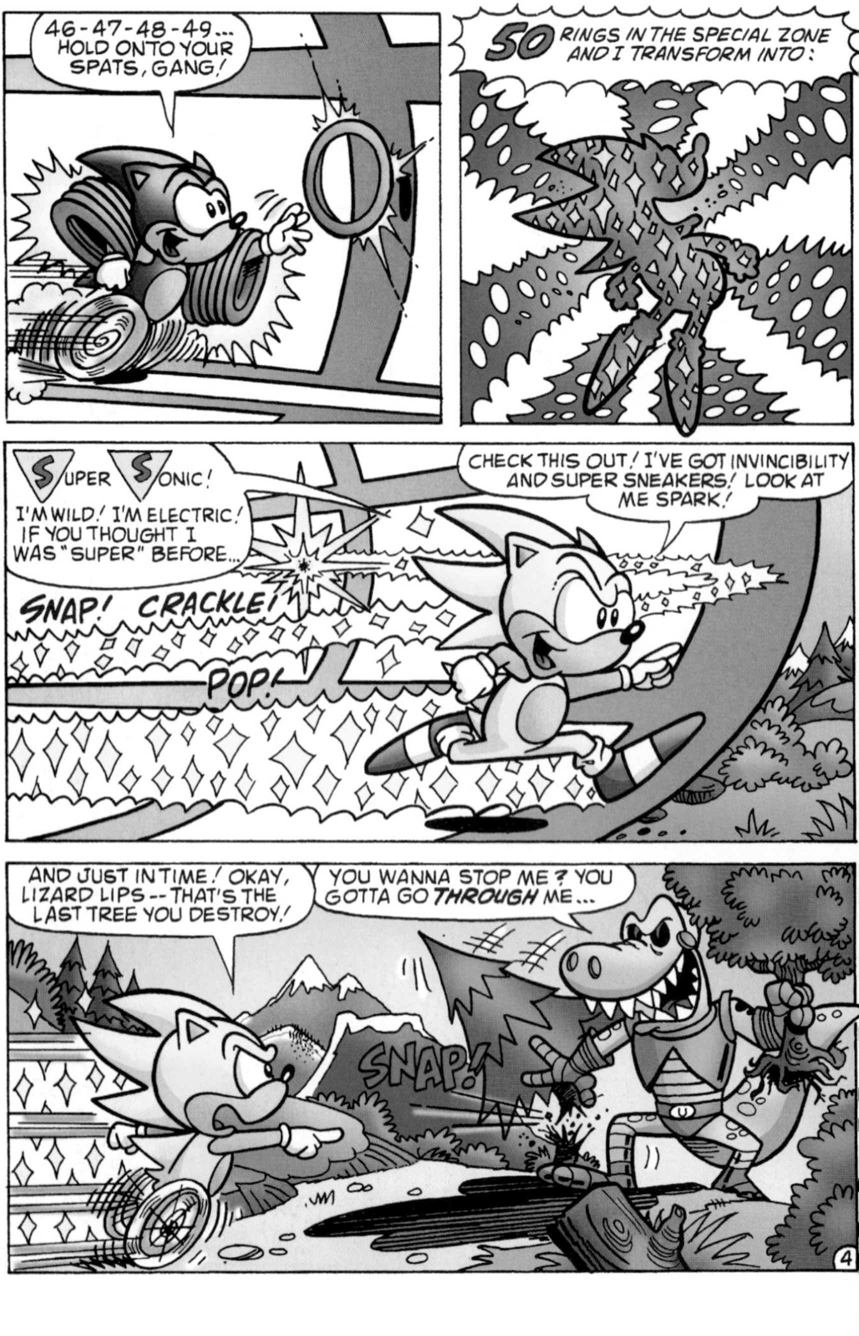

46-47-48-49... HOLD ONTO YOUR SPATS, GANG!
50 RINGS IN THE SPECIAL ZONE AND I TRANSFORM INTO:
SUPER SONIC! I'M WILD! I'M ELECTRIC! IF YOU THOUGHT I WAS "SUPER" BEFORE...
CHECK THIS OUT! I'VE GOT INVINCIBILITY AND SUPER SNEAKERS! LOOK AT ME SPARK!
SNAP! CRACKLE!
POP!
AND JUST IN TIME! OKAY, LIZARD LIPS -- THAT'S THE LAST TREE YOU DESTROY!
YOU WANNA STOP ME? YOU GOTTA GO THROUGH ME...
SNAP!
4

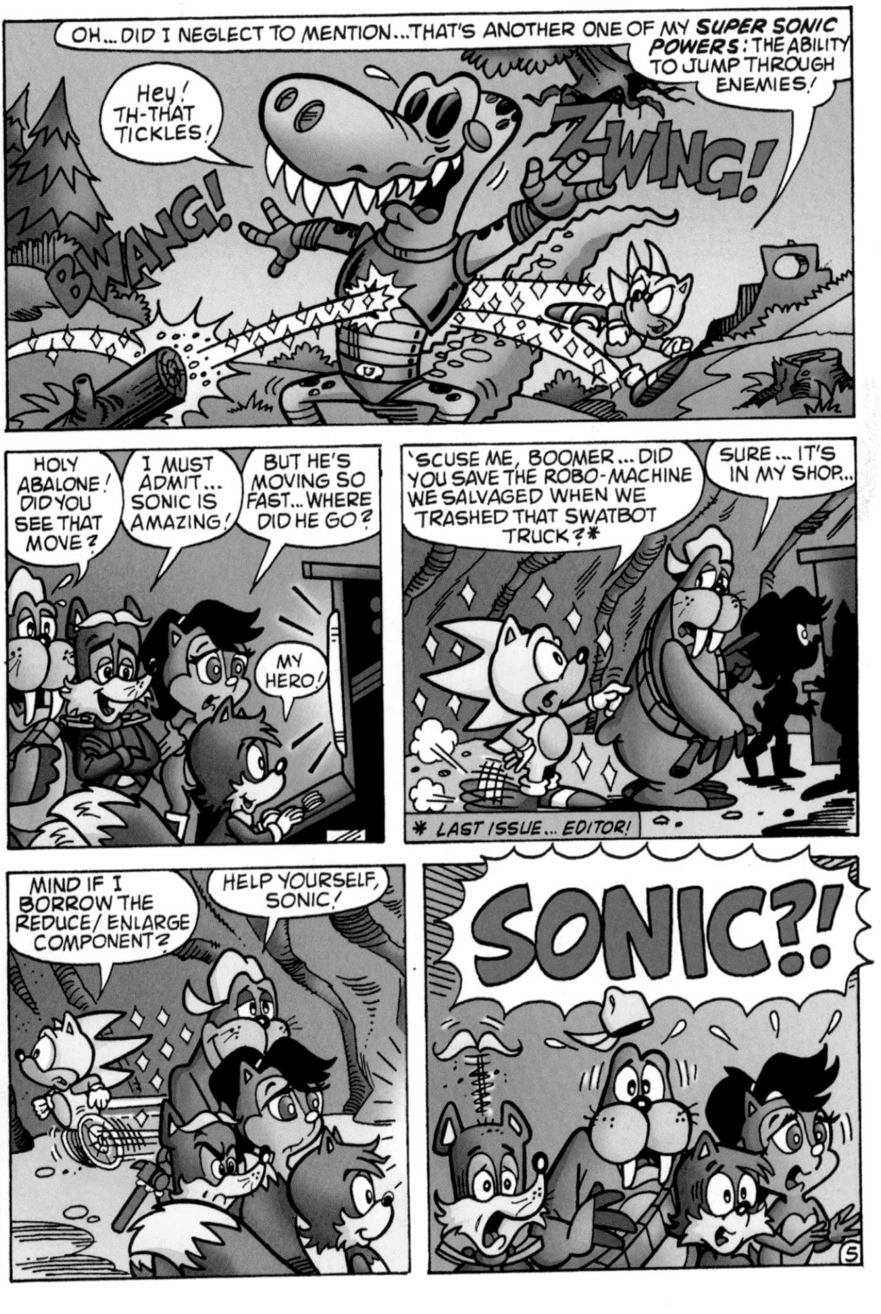
OH... DID I NEGLECT TO MENTION... THAT'S ANOTHER ONE OF MY SUPER SONIC POWERS: THE ABILITY TO JUMP THROUGH ENEMIES!
Hey! TH-THAT TICKLES!
Z-WING!
BWANG!
HOLY ABALONE! DID YOU SEE THAT MOVE?
I MUST ADMIT... SONIC IS AMAZING!
BUT HE'S MOVING SO FAST... WHERE DID HE GO?
MY HERO!
'SCUSE ME, BOOMER... DID YOU SAVE THE ROBO-MACHINE WE SALVAGED WHEN WE TRASHED THAT SWATBOT TRUCK?*
SURE... IT'S IN MY SHOP...
* LAST ISSUE... EDITOR!
MIND IF I BORROW THE REDUCE/ENLARGE COMPONENT?
HELP YOURSELF, SONIC!
SONIC?!
5

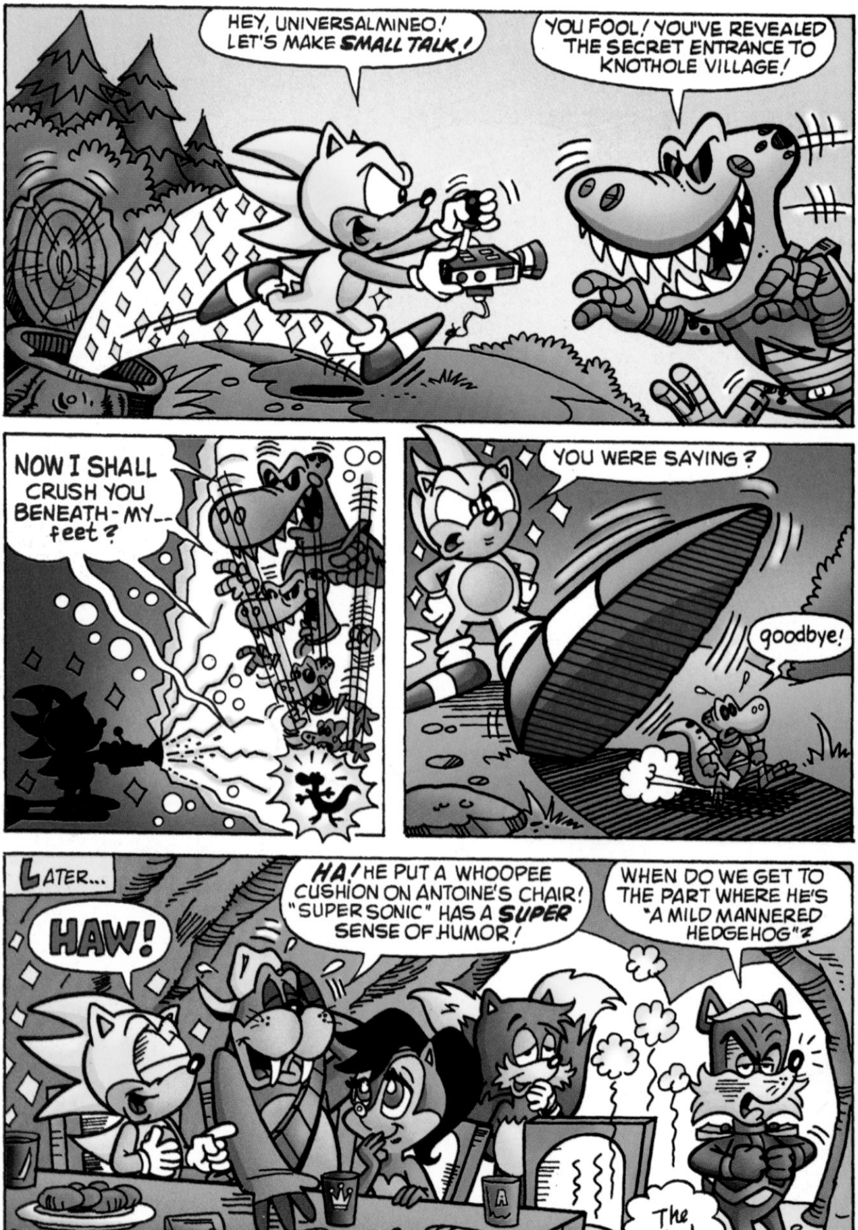
HEY, UNIVERSALMINEO! LET'S MAKE SMALL TALK!
YOU FOOL! YOU'VE REVEALED THE SECRET ENTRANCE TO KNOTHOLE VILLAGE!
NOW I SHALL CRUSH YOU BENEATH-MY... feet?
YOU WERE SAYING?
goodbye!
LATER...
HAW!
HA! HE PUT A WHOOPEE CUSHION ON ANTOINE'S CHAIR! "SUPER SONIC" HAS A SUPER SENSE OF HUMOR!
WHEN DO WE GET TO THE PART WHERE HE'S "A MILD MANNERED HEDGEHOG"?
The End

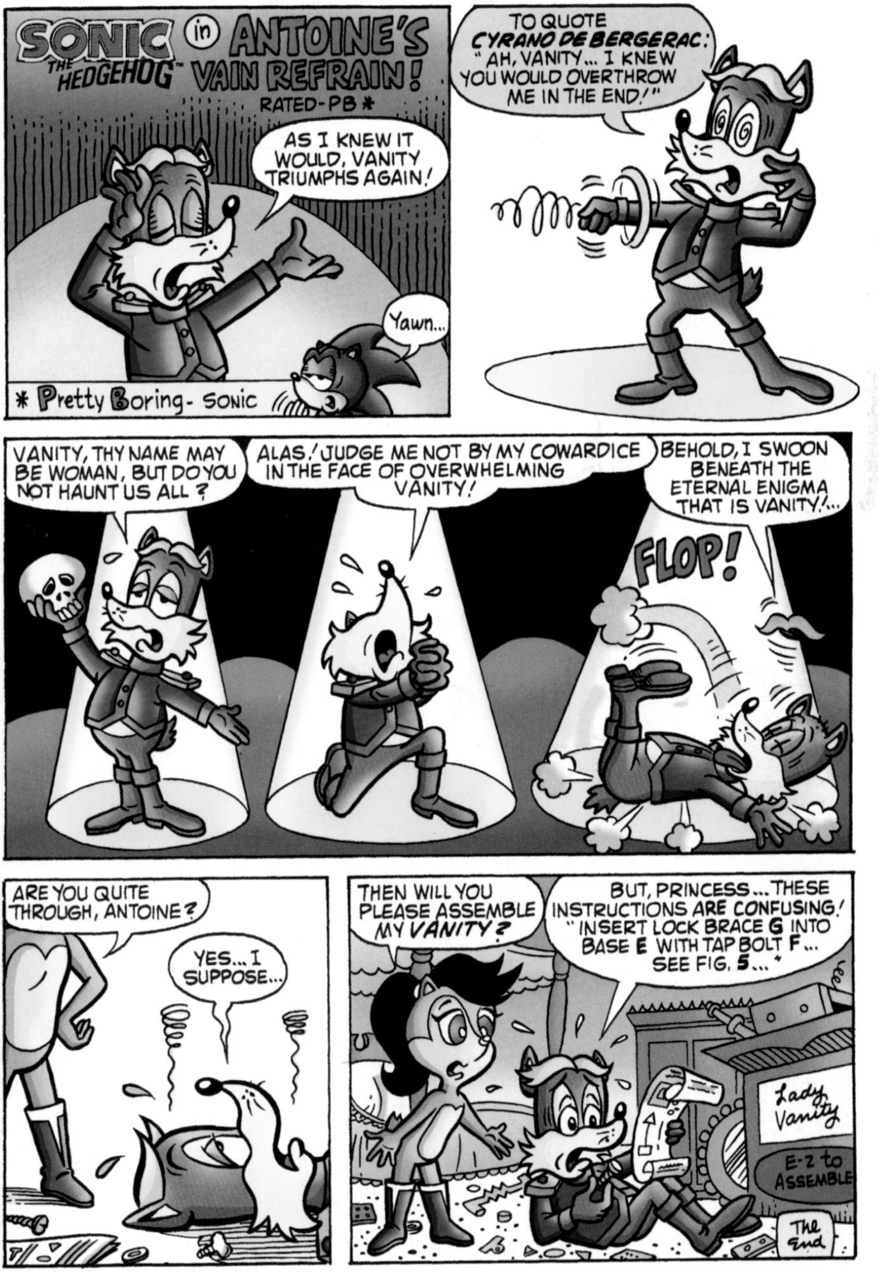
SONIC THE HEDGEHOG in ANTOINE'S VAIN REFRAIN!
RATED-PB*
AS I KNEW IT WOULD, VANITY TRIUMPHS AGAIN!
Yawn...
* Pretty Boring - SONIC
TO QUOTE CYRANO DE BERGERAC: "AH, VANITY... I KNEW YOU WOULD OVERTHROW ME IN THE END!"
VANITY, THY NAME MAY BE WOMAN, BUT DO YOU NOT HAUNT US ALL?
ALAS! JUDGE ME NOT BY MY COWARDICE IN THE FACE OF OVERWHELMING VANITY!
BEHOLD, I SWOON BENEATH THE ETERNAL ENIGMA THAT IS VANITY!...
FLOP!
ARE YOU QUITE THROUGH, ANTOINE?
YES... I SUPPOSE...
THEN WILL YOU PLEASE ASSEMBLE MY VANITY?
BUT, PRINCESS... THESE INSTRUCTIONS ARE CONFUSING! "INSERT LOCK BRACE G INTO BASE E WITH TAP BOLT F... SEE FIG. 5..."
Lady Vanity
E-Z to ASSEMBLE
The End

SONIC THE HEDGEHOG Presents "HorizontAL & VertiCAL"

HALOOO! HAVEN'T SEEN YOU SINCE OUR GRAND DEBUT!

AS YOU KNEW, IT WAS IN ISSUE TWO!*

*VERTIGO A GO GO! Ed.

THANKS FOR WRITING TO SONIC-GRAMS AND ASKING TO SEE MORE OF US!

IN CASE YOU DON'T KNOW ABOUT AL AND CAL, WE'LL EXPLAIN!

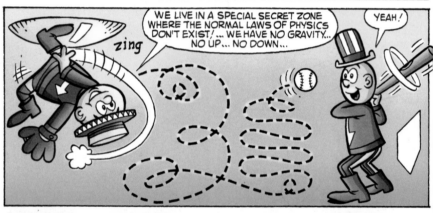

WE LIVE IN A SPECIAL SECRET ZONE WHERE THE NORMAL LAWS OF PHYSICS DON'T EXIST! ... WE HAVE NO GRAVITY... NO UP... NO DOWN...

zing

YEAH!

WHIFF!

BUT WE DO HAVE THE WICKEDEST CURVE BALL YOU EVER SAW!

STEE-RUH-HIKE ONE!

THE END

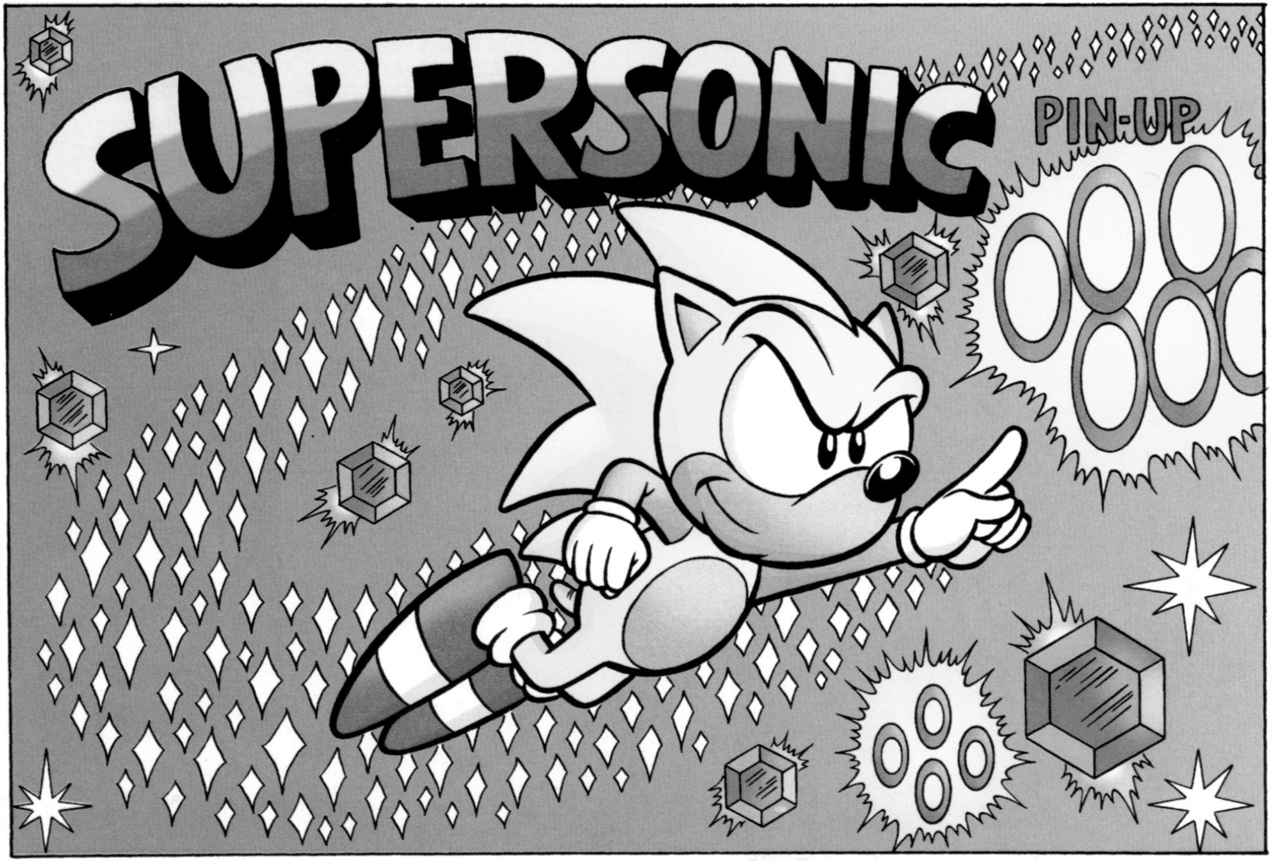
SUPERSONIC
PIN-UP

FREE!* Robotnik BIRTHDAY CARD!

(SOME ASSEMBLY REQUIRED)

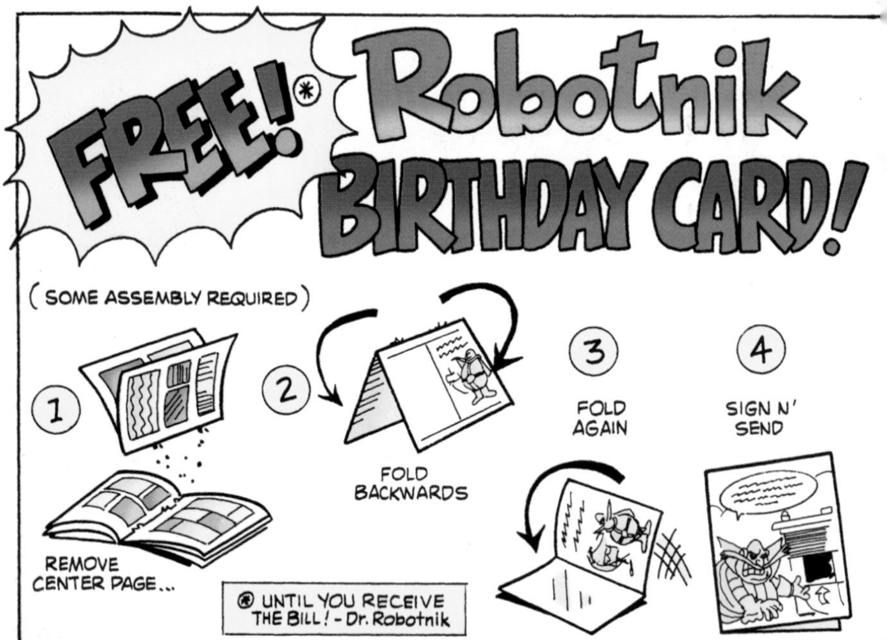

1
REMOVE CENTER PAGE...
2
FOLD BACKWARDS
3
FOLD AGAIN
4
SIGN N' SEND

* UNTIL YOU RECEIVE THE BILL! - Dr. Robotnik

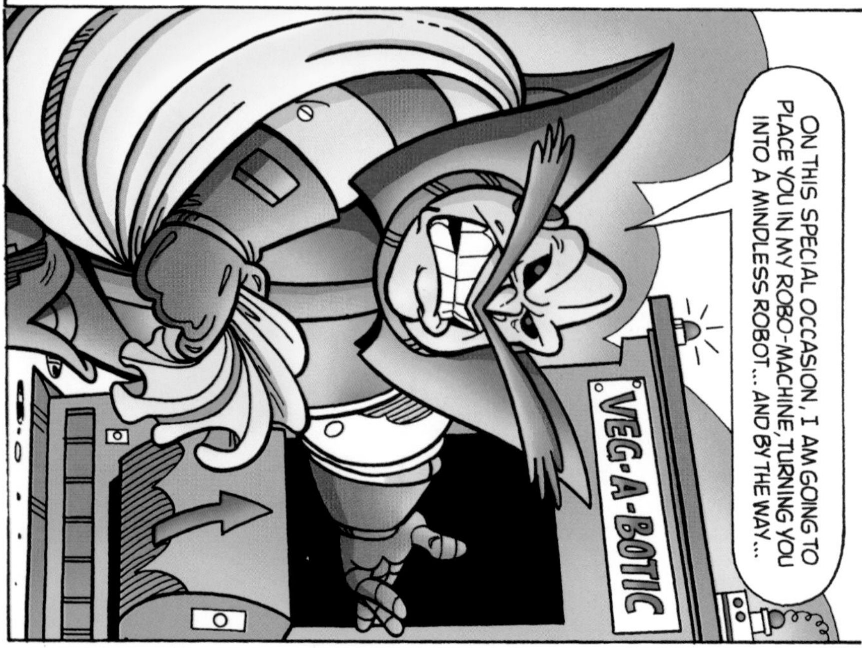

ON THIS SPECIAL OCCASION, I AM GOING TO PLACE YOU IN MY ROBO-MACHINE, TURNING YOU INTO A MINDLESS ROBOT... AND BY THE WAY...
VEG-A-BOTIC

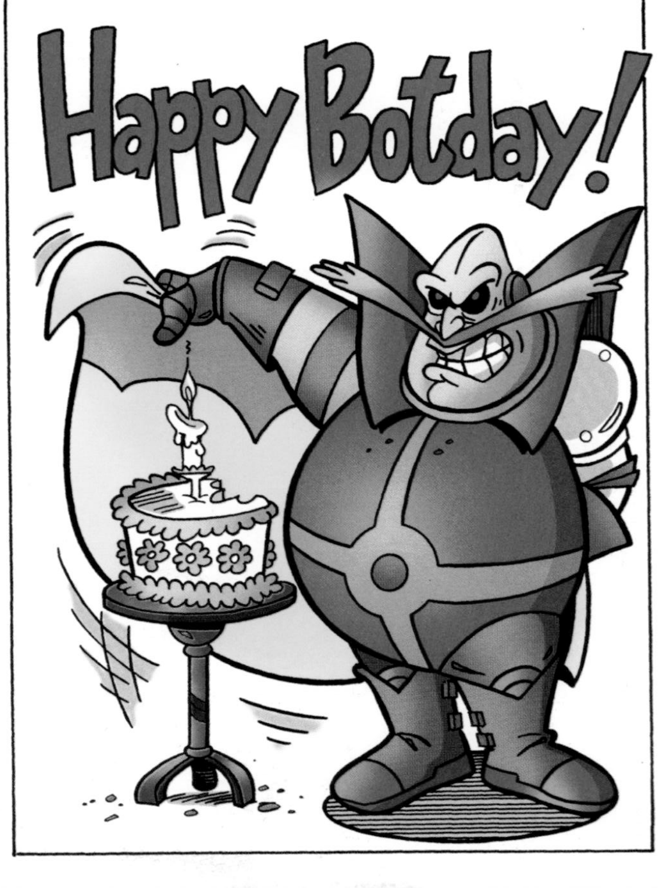
Happy Botday!

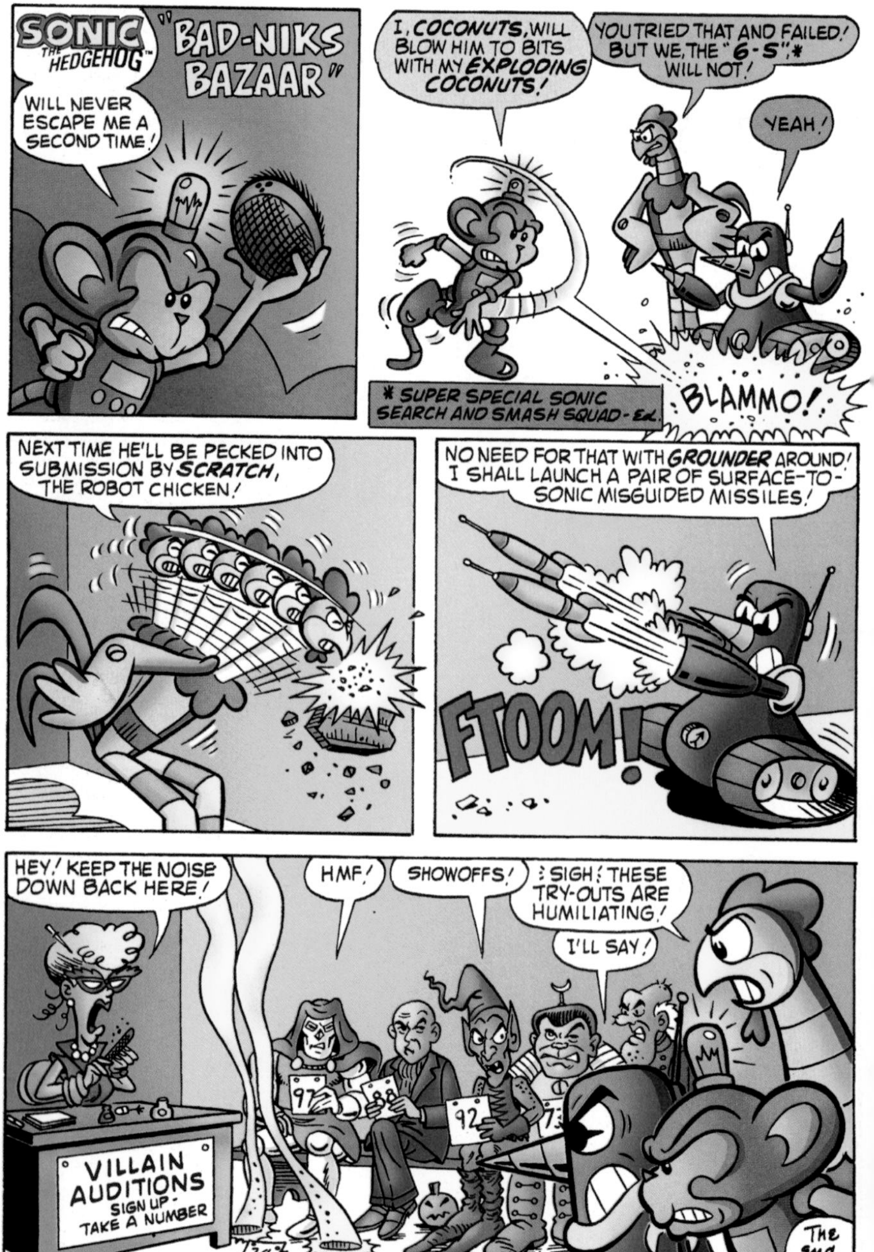
SONIC THE HEDGEHOG™
WILL NEVER ESCAPE ME A SECOND TIME!
"BAD-NIKS BAZAAR"
I, COCONUTS, WILL BLOW HIM TO BITS WITH MY EXPLODING COCONUTS!
YOU TRIED THAT AND FAILED! BUT WE, THE "6-S",* WILL NOT!
YEAH!
* SUPER SPECIAL SONIC SEARCH AND SMASH SQUAD - Ed.
BLAMMO!
NEXT TIME HE'LL BE PECKED INTO SUBMISSION BY SCRATCH, THE ROBOT CHICKEN!
NO NEED FOR THAT WITH GROUNDER AROUND! I SHALL LAUNCH A PAIR OF SURFACE-TO-SONIC MISGUIDED MISSILES!
FTOOM!
HEY! KEEP THE NOISE DOWN BACK HERE!
HMF!
SHOWOFFS!
:SIGH: THESE TRY-OUTS ARE HUMILIATING!
I'LL SAY!
97
88
92
73
VILLAIN AUDITIONS
SIGN UP - TAKE A NUMBER
24
The end

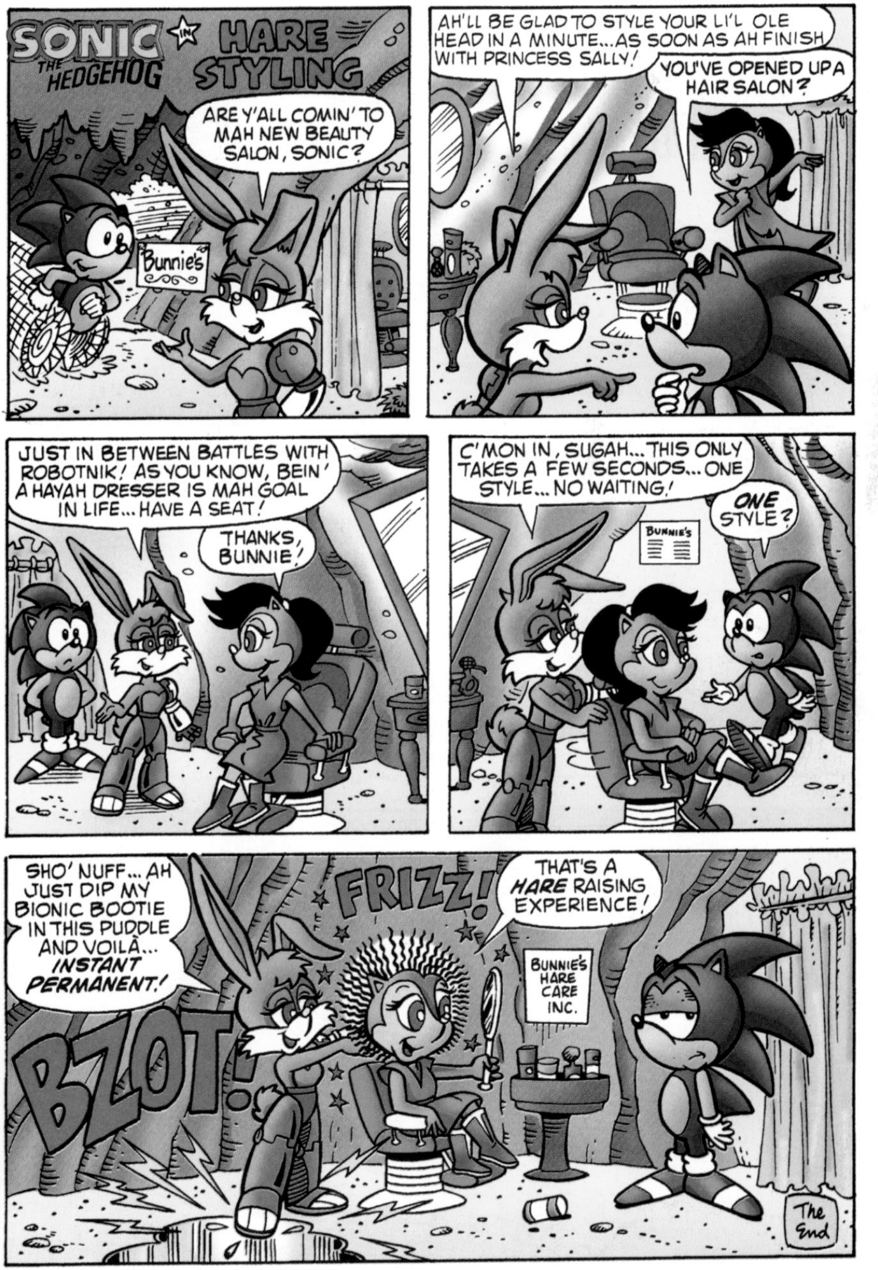
SONIC THE HEDGEHOG
IN
HARE STYLING
ARE Y'ALL COMIN' TO MAH NEW BEAUTY SALON, SONIC?
Bunnie's
AH'LL BE GLAD TO STYLE YOUR LI'L OLE HEAD IN A MINUTE...AS SOON AS AH FINISH WITH PRINCESS SALLY!
YOU'VE OPENED UP A HAIR SALON?
JUST IN BETWEEN BATTLES WITH ROBOTNIK! AS YOU KNOW, BEIN' A HAYAH DRESSER IS MAH GOAL IN LIFE... HAVE A SEAT!
THANKS, BUNNIE!
C'MON IN, SUGAH... THIS ONLY TAKES A FEW SECONDS... ONE STYLE... NO WAITING!
BUNNIE'S
ONE STYLE?
SHO' NUFF... AH JUST DIP MY BIONIC BOOTIE IN THIS PUDDLE AND VOILÀ... INSTANT PERMANENT!
FRIZZ!
THAT'S A HARE RAISING EXPERIENCE!
BUNNIE'S HARE CARE INC.
BZOT!
The End

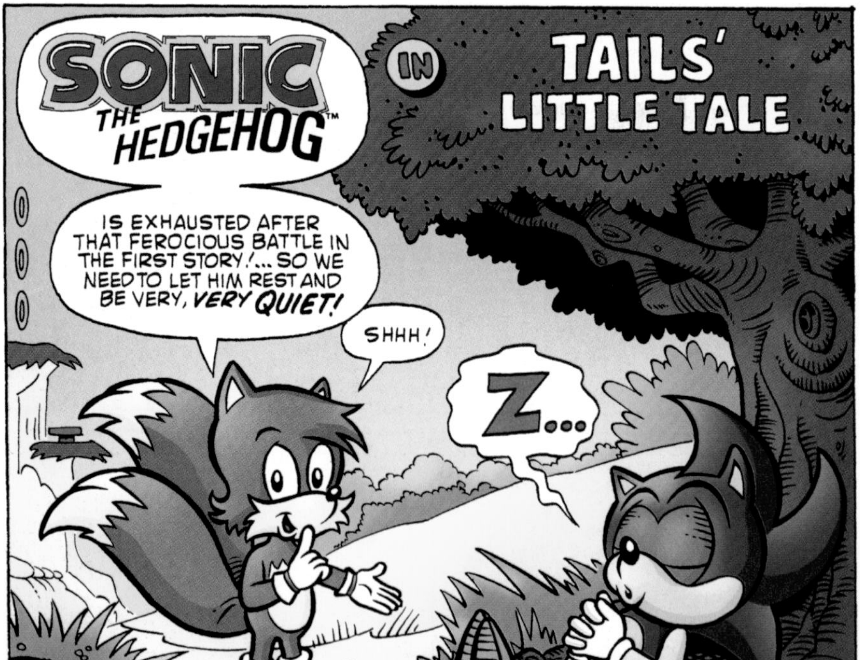
SONIC THE HEDGEHOG™
IN
TAILS' LITTLE TALE
IS EXHAUSTED AFTER THAT FEROCIOUS BATTLE IN THE FIRST STORY!... SO WE NEED TO LET HIM REST AND BE VERY, VERY QUIET!
SHHH!
Z...

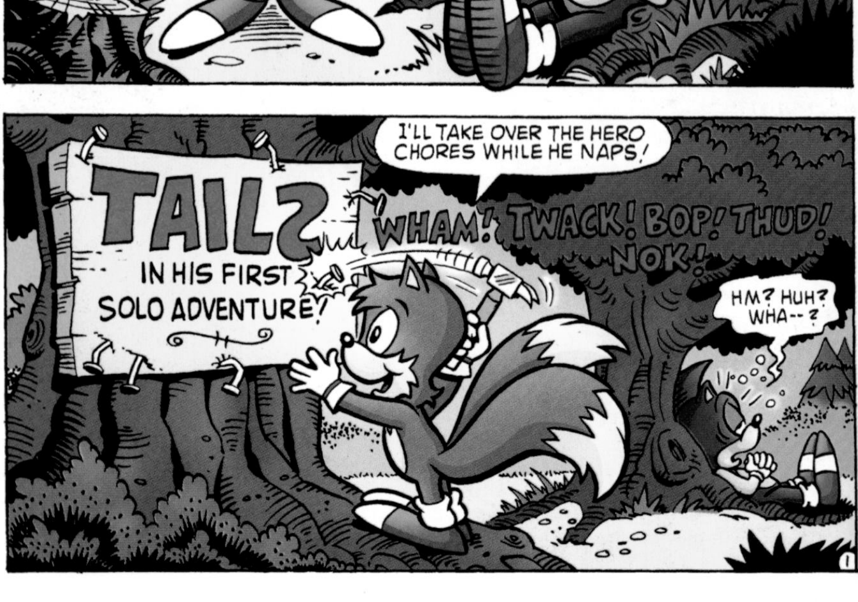
I'LL TAKE OVER THE HERO CHORES WHILE HE NAPS!
TAILS
IN HIS FIRST SOLO ADVENTURE!
WHAM! TWACK! BOP! THUD! NOK!
HM? HUH? WHA-- ?

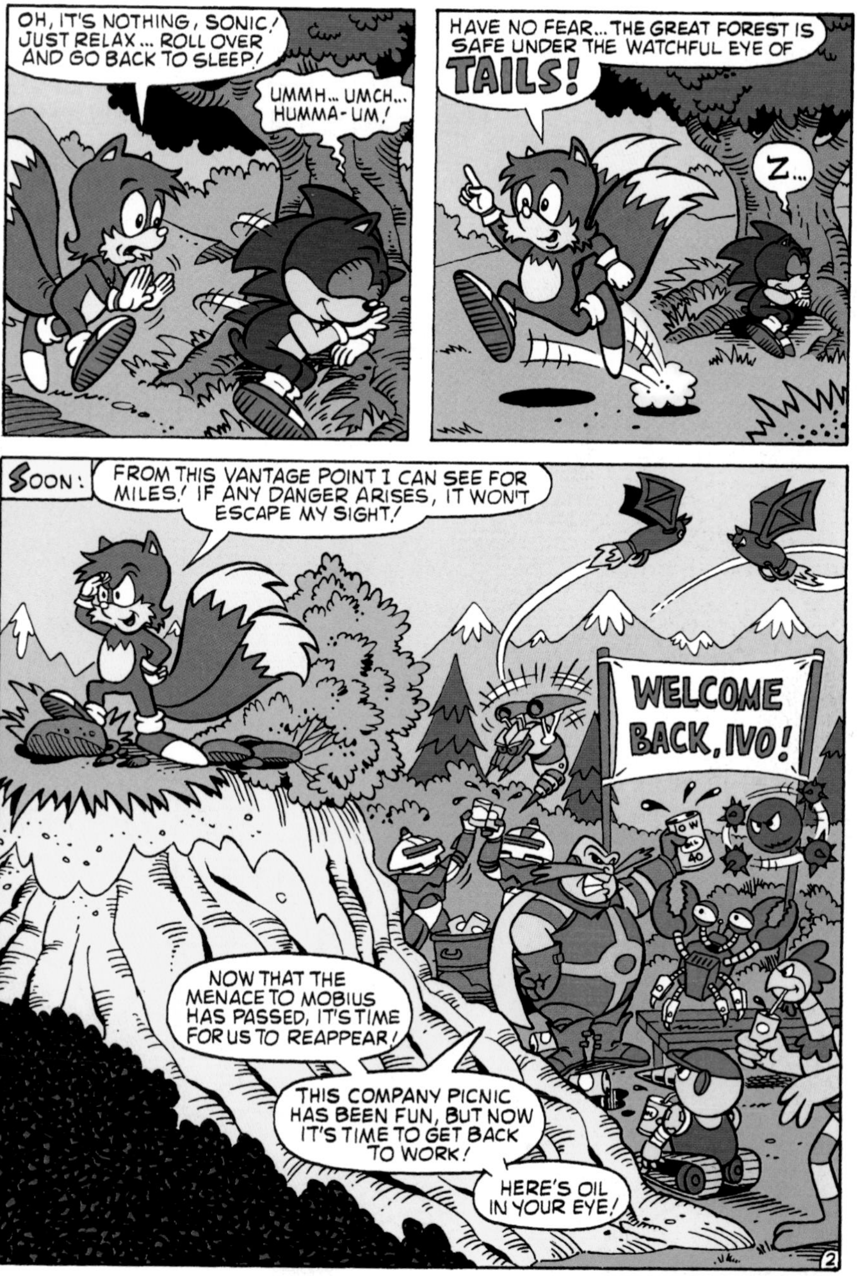
OH, IT'S NOTHING, SONIC! JUST RELAX... ROLL OVER AND GO BACK TO SLEEP!
UMMH... UMCH... HUMMA-UM!
HAVE NO FEAR... THE GREAT FOREST IS SAFE UNDER THE WATCHFUL EYE OF TAILS!
Z...
SOON:
FROM THIS VANTAGE POINT I CAN SEE FOR MILES! IF ANY DANGER ARISES, IT WON'T ESCAPE MY SIGHT!
WELCOME BACK, IVO!
NOW THAT THE MENACE TO MOBIUS HAS PASSED, IT'S TIME FOR US TO REAPPEAR!
THIS COMPANY PICNIC HAS BEEN FUN, BUT NOW IT'S TIME TO GET BACK TO WORK!
HERE'S OIL IN YOUR EYE!

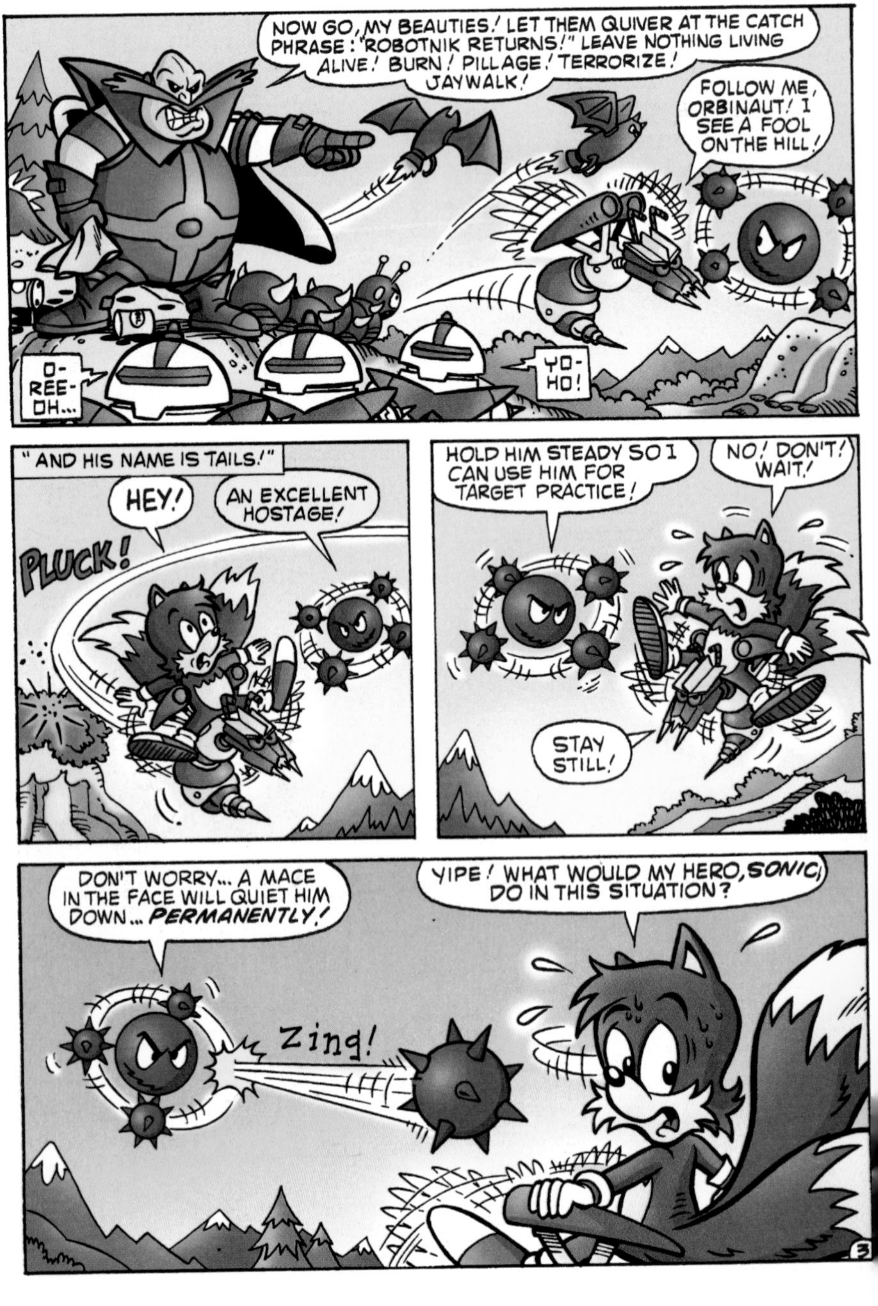
NOW GO, MY BEAUTIES! LET THEM QUIVER AT THE CATCH PHRASE: "ROBOTNIK RETURNS!" LEAVE NOTHING LIVING ALIVE! BURN! PILLAGE! TERRORIZE! JAYWALK!
FOLLOW ME, ORBINAUT! I SEE A FOOL ON THE HILL!
O-REE-OH...
YO-HO!
"AND HIS NAME IS TAILS!"
HEY!
AN EXCELLENT HOSTAGE!
PLUCK!
HOLD HIM STEADY SO I CAN USE HIM FOR TARGET PRACTICE!
NO! DON'T! WAIT!
STAY STILL!
DON'T WORRY... A MACE IN THE FACE WILL QUIET HIM DOWN... PERMANENTLY!
YIPE! WHAT WOULD MY HERO, SONIC, DO IN THIS SITUATION?
Zing!

FIRST OF ALL, HE'D MARK THIS THING *"RETURN TO SENDER"!*

TWACK!...

—WOKO!

UMF!

ugga!

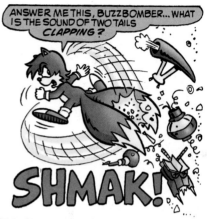

ANSWER ME THIS, BUZZBOMBER... WHAT IS THE SOUND OF TWO TAILS *CLAPPING?*

SHMAK!

MY PATENTED TAILSPIN WILL KEEP ME ALOFT WHILE THOSE TWO BADNIKS EAT TERRA FIRMA!

FUMF!

BLAP!

WHAT A GLORIOUS VICTORY! I'M UNDEFEATED!

I'M THE MICHAEL JORDAN OF FREEDOM FIGHTERS!

I'M GONNA TAKE OUT ROBOTNIK SINGLE-HANDED! OLD BLUBBER BOLTS DOESN'T STAND A CHANCE AGAINST *ME!* LUCKILY I'M NOT THE OVERCONFIDENT TYPE!

ROBOTNIK, INK.

BACK IN BUSINESS

KEEP OUT

4

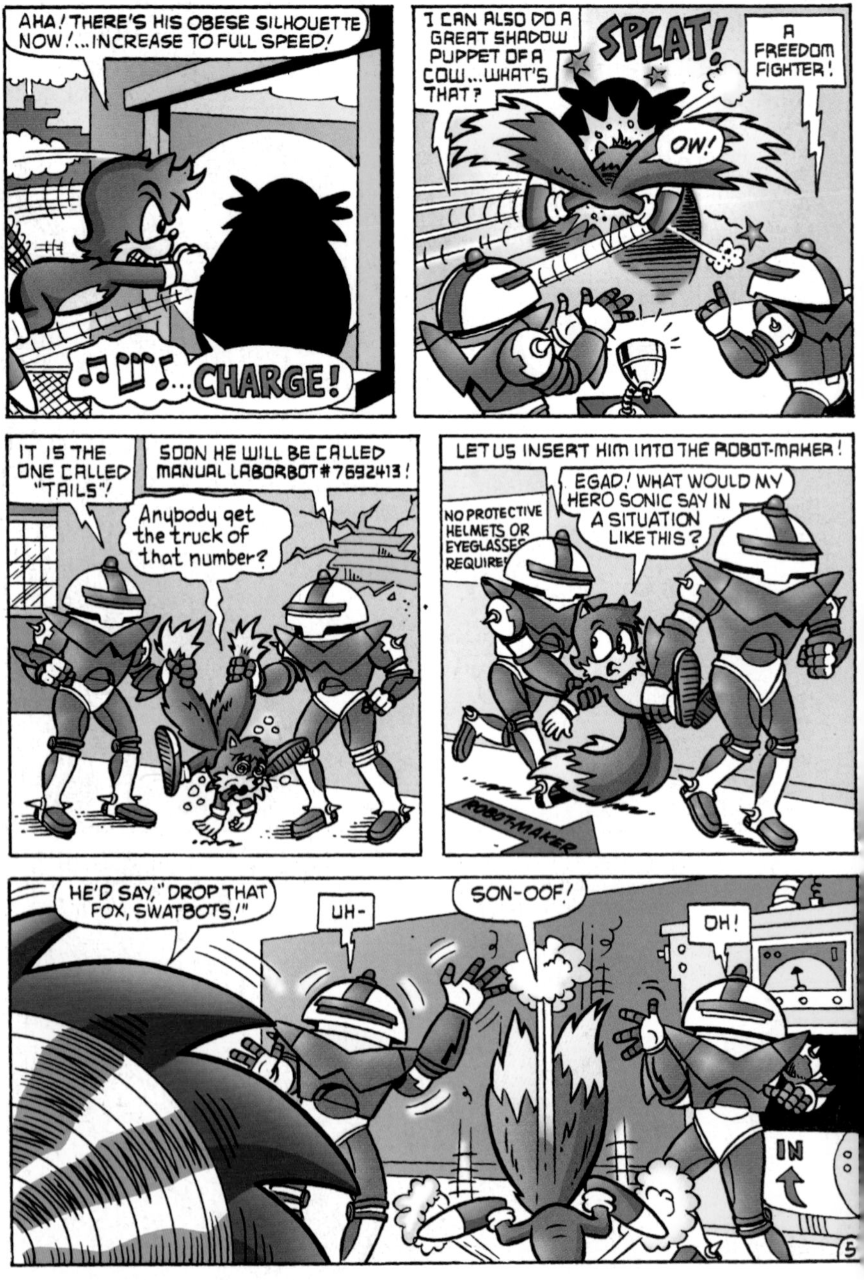
AHA! THERE'S HIS OBESE SILHOUETTE NOW!...INCREASE TO FULL SPEED!
♫♫♪...CHARGE!
I CAN ALSO DO A GREAT SHADOW PUPPET OF A COW...WHAT'S THAT?
SPLAT!
OW!
A FREEDOM FIGHTER!
IT IS THE ONE CALLED "TAILS"!
SOON HE WILL BE CALLED MANUAL LABORBOT #7692413!
Anybody get the truck of that number?
LET US INSERT HIM INTO THE ROBOT-MAKER!
NO PROTECTIVE HELMETS OR EYEGLASSES REQUIRED
EGAD! WHAT WOULD MY HERO SONIC SAY IN A SITUATION LIKE THIS?
ROBOT-MAKER
HE'D SAY, "DROP THAT FOX, SWATBOTS!"
UH-
SON-OOF!
OH!
IN

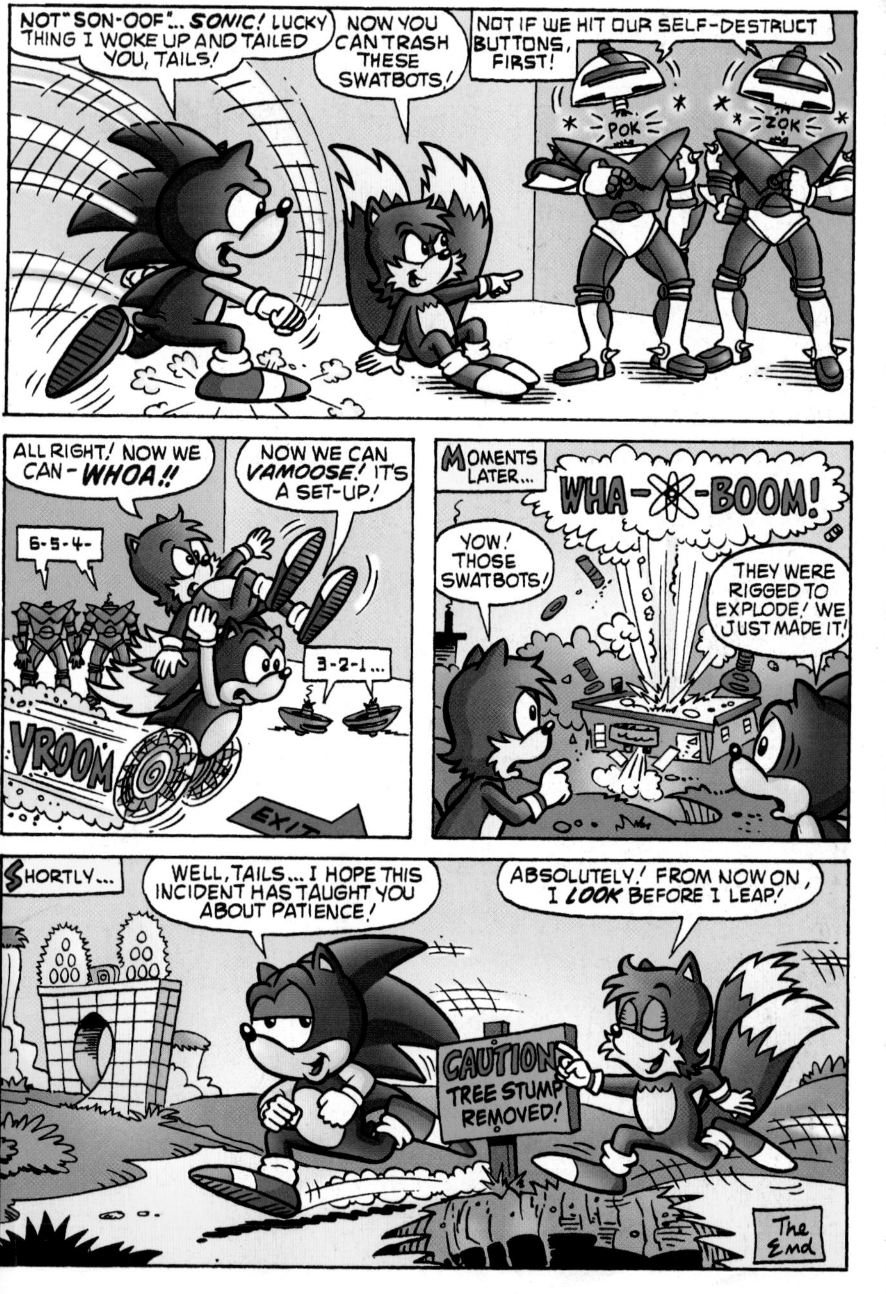
NOT "SON-OOF"... SONIC! LUCKY THING I WOKE UP AND TAILED YOU, TAILS!
NOW YOU CAN TRASH THESE SWATBOTS!
NOT IF WE HIT OUR SELF-DESTRUCT BUTTONS, FIRST!
POK
ZOK
ALL RIGHT! NOW WE CAN- WHOA!!
NOW WE CAN VAMOOSE! IT'S A SET-UP!
6-5-4-
3-2-1...
VROOM
EXIT
MOMENTS LATER...
WHA-BOOM!
YOW! THOSE SWATBOTS!
THEY WERE RIGGED TO EXPLODE! WE JUST MADE IT!
SHORTLY...
WELL, TAILS... I HOPE THIS INCIDENT HAS TAUGHT YOU ABOUT PATIENCE!
ABSOLUTELY! FROM NOW ON, I LOOK BEFORE I LEAP!
CAUTION
TREE STUMP REMOVED!
The End

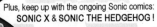